Catherine Texier was born and brought up in France. She now lives in New York where she co-edits, with Joel Rose, the literary magazine *Between C & D*. She has had a novel and a study of prostitution in Quebec published in French and is a prize-winning short story writer. This is her second novel to be published in England.

By the same author

Love Me Tender

CATHERINE TEXIER

Panic Blood

Paladin
An Imprint of HarperCollins*Publishers*

Paladin
GraftonBooks
A Division of HarperCollins*Publishers*
77–85 Fulham Palace Road,
Hammersmith, London W6 8JB

Published simultaneously in hardcover and
paperback in Paladin 1991

ISBN 0-586-09126-2 (paper covers)

Printed in Great Britain by
HarperCollinsManufacturing Glasgow

Set in Sabon

Grateful acknowledgment is made for permission to reprint excerpts from
the following copyrighted works:
"Leavin' On Your Mind" written by Wayne Walker and Webb Pierce.
Copyright © 1962 Cedarwood Publishing (3500 West Olive Avenue, Suite
200, Burbank, CA 91505). International copyright secured. All rights
reserved. Used by permission.
"I Fall to Pieces" by Hank Cochran and Harlan Howard. Copyright ©
1960 by Tree Publishing Co., Inc. Copyright renewed. All rights reserved.
International copyright secured. Used by permission of the publisher.
"I Love You Honey" written by Eddie Miller and W. S. Stevenson. ©
1982, 1988 Acuff-Rose Music, Inc. Used by permission. International
copyright secured. All rights secured.

To Céline

Acknowledgments

I would like to express my gratitude to the National Endowment for the Arts and the New York State Foundation for the Arts. This book could not have been completed without their generous assistance.

I would also like to thank my agent, Joy Harris, for her invaluable support and enthusiasm.

The first chapter of this book appeared, in a slightly different form, in *Between C&D* magazine.

Panic Blood

Panic blood

In the black of the night, three o'clock in the morning, the night from Saturday to Sunday (why does it always happen on Saturday night?), the cervix opens up, the cunt flushes out blood clots. It drips hot along the thighs. It makes a little warm puddle under the buttocks. It wakes you up from cozy co-

coon sleep. It wakes you up, this discharge, it makes your heart beat. It would have been the time for your period, as the midwife will later mention, bringing your attention to that fact. A memory of period. Except these clots, this discharge, it's life flowing running away from you trickling from inside. Life which did not hold up. Which did not take. The blood makes a big round brownish-red circle in the middle of the lavender sheet printed with pale blue flowers. A spic-and-span, country-house-style sheet, still fragrant with the fresh powdery scent of laundry flapping in the wind, but really straight out of the Forty-eighth and Ninth launderette double-loader.

The circle widens, thickens. Jump out of the bed. It's going to stain the mattress. Strange, these ideas one gets in such moments. Stain the mattress. Drip onto the floor. Make a mess. You think of that holding your crotch with both your hands to contain the blood. On the john it goes plop. You avoid looking. You hold your belly with both your hands. You tighten up your vagina you tighten your muscles to death.

Three o'clock in the morning. Is it the fetus that just dropped from the cunt, that goes splash in the reddened water? You notice it's thick, gooey. There's matter in there. Matter that spills. Womb things.

Heart beating you wonder if those are contractions that swing your belly.

The blood drips freely. Laps on the surface of the john water.

You count the minutes. The silence is black. The white bathroom bulb makes your skin green. The blood flows drop by drop like death. The womb that undoes itself. That opens up. That gives the death blow. No. That doesn't hold life. That shits it out.

Panic blood in emergency room. Now six o'clock big Manhattan hospital. Late Saturday night cases emerging into early dawn. Gray dirty predawn of nondescript October day. Overpowered by neon lights, more green on skin. Like decaying corpses. Life on hold in these plastic chairs.

The surgeon, the o.b., the anesthetist, the nurse, leaning above the wounded womb.

We've got to do a D&C. The fetus not viable anymore.

You mean, it's still in there, inside of me?

We don't know.

Pushing their clear-plastic-coated fingers up cunt up ass. Can't see with all that blood.

Here, Roger, give it a shot, your angle's better.

Open up hole some more with speculum, cold metal going dull then a sharp pain way in there. Legs spread out strapped into stirrups.

Can't see a thing, boss. Bloody dark in there.

Rummaging around deep trying to feel the uterus that tightens like a fist.

Risk of infection. Cervix open. Gotta clean that up. Clean you up. Don't want any rotten egg fermenting away in there now, do we?

Out out in the night. Put me out put me to sleep while they clean up. Scrub away. Make it all brand new.

That happens to women. These are things of women's lives, says Albertine. It happened to me six times. You know, abortion, miscarriages, births. The whole *tremblement*, how do they say in American, *megillah?*

Outside Albertine's window, she lives way west, as close to the Hudson as you can get, it smells of oil tankers when the summer air drifts in the opening, her starched muslin curtains billowing, sucked in and out, outside her window, now, which is not summer, but wet fall, the river flows gray and thick as lead. The wind blows in gusts rippling its surface. It's a day without reflection. Gray on gray. Washed out black and white without contrast. Shade running into light. There's a broken-down building on the pier. A huge abandoned construction settling down in its debris. Eva walked through it once, after dropping Mimi off at Albertine's. Layers of dust fallen on broken glass, old needles and drug vials, newspaper pages blown across from end to end, wind gushing in through the paneless windows. Construction like a warehouse, just outside walls still standing up metal rusting, peeling off, falling in eaten-up plaques, rotted metal going to dust. Sediments.

You just have to look at it and it disintegrates in front of your eyes. Pfff. Gone. In a flicker. Life flowing into death. Solid into liquid.

If you have leaving on your mind
Hurt me now
Get it over

The old record scratches. It's an original release that Eva unearthed on Albertine's shelf. The needle bounces off the same groove over and over again. *Hurt me now hurt me now hurt me now hurt me now.* Albertine pours hot water into the two mugs from a teakettle she handles with a crocheted pot holder, the color and shape of a pumpkin. The tea bags float for a moment on the surface of the water then sink in. Eva stirs some honey in hers. *Hurt me now hurt me now hurt me now* grinds Patsy Cline's voice. Eva gets up to move the needle to another groove. Albertine says, where did you find that record? I haven't listened to it in years. Did I slow-dance on that one. How you feeling, kid? Wanna lay down? I'll bring you a sandwich with your tea.

I open my mouth while eating and it's as if I could smell, taste my inside, the inside of my stomach. Sometimes I can taste the blood on my lips, you know, the taste of red iron, before it drips into my pants.

I fall to pieces . . .

You know, Albertine says, biting into her own sandwich, baloney and Swiss on white, what we liked the best about this country when we got here was the instant food. Now people say that's what's bad about America, one of the many things that's bad. All that junk food. But we loved it. Coffee-Mate, Nesquik, Jell-O, macaroni & cheese. We thought it was so easy, so convenient. So MODERN. We'd come back from work and dinner would be ready in minutes. No more cooking. I remember I had a fight once with my girlfriend. We squirted Reddi Wip at each other's face. It was better than tossing cream pies. You don't think it's funny, *bein*, oh well. Remember, we were still kids. Everything we found here was toys to play with.

How many children do you have back in France, Albertine? Eva asked her when they first met.

Two, my lovely. Albertine counted on her fingers, which are surprisingly white and soft, sort of anemic-looking. Twenty-eight and twenty-four, no, twenty-five by now. God. How time passes. They'd be women.

Where, Albertine, where would they be?

I haven't the faintest. The second one I never heard about. She was raised by a foster family and I didn't keep in touch. Last I heard of the elder one she had run away from home (she had been living with a cousin of mine, out on a farm) and she had been arrested for soliciting men in the street. She was not quite eighteen. Far as I know, she's still missing.

Didn't that upset you?

Upset? Look, I was way past being upset about them. Upset, in any case, wouldn't at all be the right word. Let's say I pushed my guilt feelings just a notch deeper in. Gave them a big kick in you know where for daring to surface and come bother me.

In the fall, between bouts of honey-like Indian summer, there are frequent cold spells and the leaves turn yellow or red, then brown, and eventually fall to their death, blown off their twigs by the north or the west wind.

Did you see that article in the *Times* this morning? Albertine says, banging some pots and pans for no apparent reason, except that her fingers tickle her for something to do.

I thought you only read the *Post*.

What, me? Nonsense.

Anyway. No, I didn't read it.

It was about this young guy who hired someone to kill his father. The guy tried to stab the father but he screwed up. Only wounded him. Then the guy's girlfriend offered to take over. She showed up at the father's hospital in a nurse uniform and gave him an injection of strychnine. The old man must have had a hide like an elephant's. He survived. You know why the kid did that?

What I'd like to know is how the kid found all these people willing to kill for him. The father must be pissed.

No kidding. You know what he did to the kid?

Can't imagine. Wait: beat him up, chain him behind locked doors, rape him. Made him swallow his cum to the last drop when the kid was still wearing diapers.

You read the article.

I swear to God.

So how did you guess?

Can't think of a better reason to want to kill your dad.

He also did it to the older sister. Then he tried to rent her to one of his neighbors for two grand a night.

Albertine's cat spends her days watching the birds eating at the bird feeder balanced on the windowsill, a wooden contraption weathered by rain and snow that Albertine fills to the brim with feed. The cat is a large female the color of dog piss on city snow, with hair five inches thick (Albertine insists it's quarter Persian). It looks like a Buddha, all hair and two little pale eyes staring at the window. She quivers and pulses, instinct aroused, adrenaline running wild, in anticipation of sinking her teeth in the quick flesh of a tender dove or a minuscule red-throat barn swallow jumping about on its frail skinny toes. Anticipation never satisfied of course. Except that one time.

Remember the time she caught a bird? Albertine asks.

Mmmm, Eva says, eyes closed, trying to doze on the couch.

It was a stifling summer day and Albertine had left the kitchen window open a couple of inches wide and the cat had been watching the birds, like today. She had extended a paw faster than lightning and she had come back running around the apartment with a robin, wings flailing, clamped between her jaws, blood dripping in tiny drops on the floor, and brought her prey with just pride in her pale eyes, attempting to deposit it at Albertine's feet as regal present, which would have been graciously accepted but for the fact that Albertine's neighbor, Louise, the violinist, a self-proclaimed animal lover, happened to be there. Screaming, Louise grabbed the bird and pressed it onto the hollow of her palm, smoothing its ruffled feathers, but when she realized that the bird was mortally wounded, she proceeded to run wildly all the way to the roof, from where she tried to make the bird take off—to no avail—then briefly considered calling a vet, until Albertine took charge and flushed the tiny spasmatic body down the toilet bowl (eyes askance to avoid witnessing the death by drowning) while the cat watched in disbelief and without a full grasp of the situation, looking for her prey behind the stove, at the window, sniffing around the toilet, going back to the place where she had first deposited it, where it smelled strongly of its odor, presumably trying to retrace its steps and inevitably ending up at the john.

I remember, Eva says. But she doesn't, because she wasn't there. Only heard the story fifteen times. Wrapped in a blanket on the couch, Eva craves banana mush, the mashed bananas she used to eat for snack after school, with a dash of sugar. It was all gooey, mucus-like. It was like predigested banana, as if already decomposing in saliva juices. But she loved it. It tasted a little like baby food, hot cereal, that sort of thing. Sometimes she'll make some for Mimi, but Mimi's not crazy about it. Another of her mother's weird ideas. Yucky. So Eva eats it herself. Makes her feel good like eating oatmeal. Cuddled, irresponsible. Soft texture flowing without effort down throat, esophagus, wherever it goes.

Flowing effortlessly like blood. Staining the sanitary napkin tucked between her legs. Fat diaper for grown-up women. The body that drips. Juices a-flowing.

But look, Albertine says. You were going to have an abortion, right?

Right, Albertine.

So?

So?

You were damn lucky, you know that. Nature did your job for you.

The way these anxiety attacks come to you at night. Yanking your eyes open. With the strength of gnawing nightmares. Worse. Because instead of drifting images they present themselves with the authority of a rational mind. Alternatives fight each other, and pure fear grips you naked as you toss and turn your pillow over to find a cooler side to rest your head on.

Anxiety is like a cancer, Albertine says, pouring more hot water over the old tired tea bags. A parasite. It attaches itself to your mind and feeds off it. You've got to flush it out. Meanwhile unplugging the sink and letting dirty water go down the drain with a sucking sound.

Cleaned and plugged back. Whole again. Vacuuming achieved. Drano-drained.

I think it's going to be time to pick up Mimi. Want me to go? Now Albertine clearing the kitchen table from remnants of fabrics and threads from her morning sewing, making a neat pile with them on top of the sewing machine. Rubbing her hands on her hips, on their way to untying the apron's strings at her back. Patting the two ascending wings of her hair with her cupped palms.

If you don't mind.

She didn't tell Johnny or anyone. Just got up and flagged a cab to the hospital. Just a casualty of woman's life. Just one more impromptu chore. She rang Albertine's bell in the morning, her legs shivering.

You're not singing tonight? Why don't you stay here for dinner with Mimi.

Of course I'm singing. Who'd replace me? You said these are things of women's lives. Normal.

Still. You have to take it easy.

Go get Mimi. You'll be late.

It was Johnny's, of course. She was a one-man woman. Johnny's what? Johnny's sperm that did the damage. He wouldn't understand. Johnny's voice would turn to razors.

Mimi bursts in from the door, hair flying about, the wide circle of her skirt twirling high around her hips, wet kiss, hands dirty with marker stains, every color of the rainbow blurred and rubbed on the fingertips and following the bone fan on top, like a skeleton of a hand carefully redesigned line by line by shaky fingers.

Okay now, hands down, not on my blouse, Mimi, hands off.

The hug is like a puppy's. Wet smooch over the face, warm limbs kicking in, hurled across Eva's lap, hanging from her arms, fingernails digging like claws at the back of her neck.

Stop it now, Mimi. You're choking me.

Now leave your mom alone, says Albertine who's trailing behind, picking up Mimi's discarded coat, muffler and mittens that lie scattered in a crazy line on the floor and putting them away in the closet. Your *maman*'s not been feeling too well today.

Eva makes a face at Albertine, knitting her brow, shaking her head no, hard, but not so hard that Mimi would notice. Mimi's clinging to her, balanced on her lap, head down on one side, flailing her arms out and trying to grab the cat by the tail, legs kicking up on the armrest.

Oh, Mama's sick. Poor Mama's sick. What's the matter, Mama? Worming her way back to sitting position, flinging her arms around Eva's neck. Let me kiss my mama. Why you not nice to me, Mama? Why you not let me kiss you?

Eva laughs. Mimi knocks her down, hurling the full weight, full length of her body upon Eva who collapses under the shock. Mimi sends her little fists pounding like hail pellets on Eva's face and shoulders. I hate you, Mom, she says. You didn't even kiss me.

Can I do it now?

The pounding goes on.

Nope. Too late.

There is a velvet tapestry pinned to the wall in Albertine's living room. Golden sunset on plush indigo background framed in gold, and then hanging in the middle of it, a wooden cross with a carved Christ, his palms squirting blood-colored paint where the nails have been driven in. The face is twisted in agony under the crown of thorns. Pretty vivid, Eva said to Albertine when she first saw it. Isn't it beautiful? Albertine had said. I brought it with me from the other side. It was above my mother's bed. Used to stick a branch of holly behind it at Christmas time. Every evening I'd pray kneeling at the foot of the bed, looking at it. Did you notice the color of his skin? Isn't it realistic? I mean it seems to be just the right color for a man in his situation, wouldn't you think?

Back home, Eva thinks of the waxy face with the drops of blood falling like tears on his caved-in cheeks as she watches the city sky sway from her high window. She didn't even call Johnny. She didn't want to raise the issue with him, not tonight. Miscarriage, blood, her body doing its gig. There are men who can't deal with these things. They burden you with their fear, double your load. They make you feel guilty. It was her own business. Nurse her body back on her own. It gave her a strange sense of power.

The seasickness of early pregnancy is gone, now. She's back on land, where things are hard and steady. Lying flat on her back, she watches the top of the buildings fade away in the fog and feels the ache recede deeper and deeper until it's just a fist of black tightening in the dead center of her.

Johnny

This guy, Johnny, he is a sucker. All he wants to do is to suck you. He likes to suck women's twats.

Shut the fuck up.

He likes to look in the wet stinking cunt hair and sticks his nose in it. He likes that smell of oysters and urchins turning bad.

You're sick.

You're the one who's sick to hang around men like that. Real men go at it with their wang. Full gorged with blood, purple veins slithering and pulsing. With their quivering cocks. That's man's noble tool. No hands no mouth they know better than that. Look Ma no hands. Little boys need their hands to go at it. Men don't need crutches anymore. The hands are firmly planted on either side of the girl's body. For leverage. Perfect place (depending on man's size in ratio with girl's size) at about the vicinity of the breasts. The virile member finds its way by itself (provided the cunt is well lubricated, of course). A good girl is all dripping juices just from the sight of man's pulling out, being sucked right in, pubic hair to pubic hair. Mouth to mouth. Not mouth to ass.

You get it all mixed up. She crosses her legs with the soft swish of the nylons rubbing against one another and lights a cigarette. Ass, cunt, mouth. You just love to say these words. You want to spit these words out of your mouth. You want to spill them out into my ears. Mouth to ear. You want to create that link between us, that complicity.

Hey. Stop your bull.

Eva walks down the street in a black leather suit, the tight skirt slit up at back, showing the stretch of leg up the thigh, the underside of the knee, the place where men like to run their hands, where it makes a woman shudder, where a nerve connects straight to her clit. It's a tease, the slit that opens and falls with each step coming down with the high heel hitting the pavement. Eva has it down to an art. The tilt of the hip, the tightening of the calves, the line of the seam up from the heel, an arrow pointing up to her ass. While the cinched jacket points down to the waist, then curves round to the crotch.

There is something in her walk. A bounce, if you know what I mean, that attracts men. Not like an exaggerated hip swing that some women develop starting at age three and perfect later with the use of five-inch high heels.

Why do you women dress like that?

How can you ask such a dumb question?

Johnny's always asking questions like that, in earnest. He craves her like chocolate candy. You make my body fluids flow, he says.

Yeah, I activate your glands.

There is something about Eva. The way she moves. As if she could never be stopped.

Her bush is the same color as her hair. Ebony black. Which is to prove that her hair is not dyed. Her cunt lips maroon. Her skin, dead white of the night. Do you know she powders her thighs, her breasts? To give them this pearly effect?

She lives in an apartment at the top of a hotel on the West Side, Midtown. There are four rooms, a sitting room opening on a kitchenette, short hallway leading to a bedroom and bathroom. The rooms are dark, heavily curtained. Peeling paint at places. Yellowish, brownish paint. The furniture is provided by the hotel. Plush, forties furniture on the shabby side. Lots of maroons, dark reds, some green. Velvet couch and armchairs. Flowered curtains at the windows.

Hi, Eva. Raspy-voiced. Two o'clock in the morning. She knocks off a glass of water on the nightstand to pick up the phone. Stumbles in the dark to get hold of a towel to wipe the wetness off the mattress. Eva. Just his voice saying her name.

It's late, she says. I was asleep.

I'd thought you worked late, he says.

I didn't work tonight.

I have to talk to you. The urgency in his voice like a bullet knocking her under the belt.

He was just a gaunt figure in black dungarees and leather jacket, collar up, standing at the back, leaning against a pillar, smoking a cigarette. That first night. Watching her the whole set.

Eva. Full voice on the telephone. With vocal cords taut like a guitar's. He plays the guitar, actually, with some band downtown. Sings, too. Can't make up his mind whether he should do vocals or instrumentals. But you're not really serious about it, right?

Why do you say that?

I don't know. You have this hungry look on your face. Like you want instant gratification. Even music isn't fast enough.

Music is fast enough.

But not becoming a musician, Eva says.

She calls him Johnny Guitar.

Her name, Eva, on the telephone. She dreamed about his voice that night.

It was the voice. Wrapping itself around her like a finger tracing circles on her skin.

Johnny is lying on the bed. *A poil*, naked, penis soft wrinkled squeezed between thighs. When in this state, the penis can be sucked in, its roots buried in the reddish pubic hair, a woman's triangle, not a trace of any protuberance. So this is what you'd look like as a woman, Eva says, kneeling above him. Pretty convincing. A shy maiden with tight legs—okay, hairy legs.

He pulls his sex back out, angrily flipping himself on his side.

Men don't like it when you say things like that, Eva says. If there's something they can't stand, it's having their symbol of virility being made fun of. Men don't have a sense of humor below the belt.

The sense of humor is an organ that usually resides in the brain. Below the belt we're all animals. And animals don't laugh.

Albertine's cat does, she says. She even sneers. Did you ever look at her?

Yeah, when she sees a pigeon. She licks her chops.

Eva pulls up her stockings of sheer nylon, checks the back seam with one nail, making sure it rises straight like an arrow from the tender heel bone. Johnny bends, runs his own finger along the two little depressions on either side of the bone, says, nice ankles.

What makes an ankle beautiful?

I don't know, he says. The movement it evokes? The speed it's built for?

You mean like a plane, or a tiger?

Yeah, right. How much the form suggests, fits the function. Let me see your ass when you pull up your stockings.

Her fingers unroll the tight nylon hose up the top of her thigh. She tucks up her skirt to snap the suspender in place. He goes for her buttocks.

Hey! Hands down.

Aw, come on. You love it, don't you?

His hair tousled over his stubborn forehead, eyes limpid, generous mouth. They were walking side by side in the street. They were walking up Seventh Avenue, just getting to Times Square, they were going to see a movie in one of these theaters remnants of an older age, rampant with opera-red velvet and gilded scallops, but with 70mm screen and six-track Dolby sound systems, threading their way through the crowd, she was feeling that tautness of his at her side, when suddenly he turned toward her, put his arm around her shoulder, and kissed her, hard. She felt his warmth running through her, his urgency, she wanted it bad, there was no barrier between them, just pure energy circling freely, her lips met his halfway when he bent his face, hard and moist. Their bodies didn't touch, just his hand on her shoulder, and their mouths, wildly. They gasped, together. When they pulled back, their eyes stared into one another. There was panic there, and such a deep hunger Eva turned her head. It was a hunger as deep as hers she'd seen.

I can't wait to be in the dark with you, he said.

Movies are good for that. Hands everywhere, half-lit patches of skin. His Adam's apple jutting out and the youthfulness of the tendons and muscles under the chin. His breath reaching deep, that she wanted to swallow fast like hard liquor. They fumbled in the dark, gasping. His shirt was open two buttons down. The flesh in the opening was tantalizing. She pushed her hand in, front and back. The flesh gave in slightly. It was both taut and tender. The tension between the two was almost too much for her fingers to bear. They moved across his back, drunkenly.

So right now it's dark, night dark, except for the glow of nearby Times Square edging the shade. Eva is watching the night from her bed, in that moment before sleep presses down on your eyelids and blurs your mind. The bell rings a flat, low note. There is a stir of blankets and sheets on the bed, a scurrying of feet down the hallway. Struggling to get into her kimono, Eva goes to the door, opens it a crack, leaves the chain on.

Johnny's black eyes firing from behind the door.

What? What you want?

His foot in the door. His black cowboy boot with the sharp pointy toe pointing at her own feet, naked, vulnerable on the wood floor. The smell and creak of his leather jacket at nose level.

I am tired. What do you want?

Let me in.

Her black hair tangled falling over her eyes. She pulls it back. White night skin puffy from sleep. She wraps her robe tighter around her waist.

He doesn't push the door, doesn't kick it. He just looks at her. There's that urgency in his eyes. That's always there.

I gotta talk to you.

At this time?

She unlocks the chain, moves to the side to let him in, as he asked.

She has this little gig, sideline. She does phone fantasies. Great pay, very little pain, she'd thought when she started. Sounded like a good idea to get out of her financial hole. She talks sex a blue streak. It requires a perfect command of silences and breathing techniques. It has to happen between the lines, so to speak. Capture the electricity that runs between bodies. She says women who use graphic words and descriptions only work at the lowest level, the porn level. That you have to tap on the unspoken to really arouse. She says there's one man she can really do it to. She swears he keeps calling her, that he's hooked.

Maybe it's your voice.

Yeah, maybe it's my voice. But it's tricky. It's hard to control your voice. The voice carries the electricity like the eyes. Sometimes I think I give more of my voice than I would of my body. You can deaden your body. But not your voice.

So?

She's standing in the middle of her living room, the harsh ceiling lamp on. He's talking, helping himself to scotch in the kitchen, straight from the bottle that he swings between thumb and forefinger.

He looks mean, tough, a parody of a case of maleness, all leather, broad on top, narrow, pointy at bottom, hair flying about, crisp fast moves, a beat in the hips.

Johnny, Johnny fais-moi mal, she says between her teeth, leaning against the door frame, small soft wrapped in satin, her breath bittersweet, herself female to her toes spread out naked with their little delicate jewels lacquered carmine, watching him banging cabinet doors, opening and closing the fridge, shifting his weight from heel to heel.

J'aime l'amour qui fait boum!

What? Say what?

I want to know what you're here for?

His stretched arm moves the pint of scotch in a grand gesture, pointing to her breasts.

You. For you. What else?

He drapes his arm with the scotch around her shoulders, going for her crotch with the other hand, straight between the flaps of the robe, pushes his way between the moist flesh, rummages around in there.

For that, my dear.

Get off of me.

Oh, my. Do we speak firmly.

His middle finger goes right in, then pops out with a plop sound, sort of like a corkscrew pulling out a cork. He flourishes it in front of her nose, upright, all other fingers folded, sucks it, pretends to wipe his ass with it, and forces it into her mouth. She tightens her lips, mmmmm, moving her head quickly back and forth to resist him. He drops both arms. Takes a hit of whiskey. Licks his hair back. Nods. That's what's wrong with you, he says. Tight cunt tight ass tight lips.

Not for everyone.

Yeah. That's the other thing that's wrong with you. Don't think you can fool me.

She moves away from him. He grabs her arm.
Stay here.
You're drunk.

The men have their tongues sticking out. They want to lap. Saliva is drooling down their tongues into the corner of their mouths, dripping down their chins. They are looking for cunts. For moist pussies. With black hair glued with sperm, with thick period blood. Red/black pussies. Don't you see what they are doing to you, says Johnny. Don't you see?

They're doing it to themselves. They're hungry. We're all, permanently, forever, hungry.

Now it's not a dream. It is on television, a close-up of swollen tracks on legs and arms, on ulcerous bruises where the needle has struck. If decency permitted (God forbid), they would show tracks on genitals. That would really gross them out. Too bad they can't go that far. They are content repeating over and over the story of the kid who could slide a handkerchief from one nostril to the other because the inside cartilage of his nose had been burned by cocaine.

A certain flower can be the kiss of death after all. Deadly sweet. Deadly sweetness. Sweet rose.

Johnny's breath tastes dark and sour. Whiskey coming out of the depth of liver and stomach. Intimate. Sharing his insides with her. Accomplices of that crime: opening one body to the other.

She stiffens against his hand at the small of her back.

I can't stand it, he whispers hard in her ear, so close she jerks her head back, your talking sex with men.

She laughs. Aw, come on, it's a job. A weird job. I'd think

you'd be sensitive to the sociological angle. You know: man's never-ending search for arousal.

The smell of him, making love. The first smell. He was wearing a scarf, an old silk scarf in tatters, around his neck. It was musty and musky. He kept the scarf on and the jacket, and leaned against the pillows on his bed.

His body, rounding itself, cushioned against the wall, waiting. Offered. The head, slightly tilted. Something in his eyes, a black hole. She, at a distance. Maybe two feet. Both fully dressed. Not a fragment of their bodies touching. Their eyes tracing lines, arabesques, taking possession. His knees were slightly apart, one of his hands hanging near his crotch.

She fell into his eyes. Again and again.

You're my perfect American, she says.

Why?

You grunt. You don't talk. You emit sounds from your throat.

Mmmm.

Right. You see.

Huh huh.

What was that? A yes or a no?

——

What's that?

Clears throat.

It was a no.

Let's try something else. You want to go to the movies?

Huh huh.

See what I mean. I still don't know if it's a yes or a no. I have developed a theory about the American language. American, understand, not English. In my opinion, American is a lot closer to Chinese than one thinks. It's not just the sound, but the pitch of the sound.

And then, there is, of course, the circumcised prick.

Circumcised, and not even Jewish.

Hey, I'm half Jewish. Well, a quarter.

But that's not why you're circumcised. You guys think that's cleaner, right? No germ stuck between the folds of the skin. No fermenting sperm and old urine giving off foul odors. I'll grant you one thing, though: off-duty American pricks look like little pink-cheeked stubby carrots, which is a lot prettier than ours—I mean our men's, our French men's—which tend to droop like dried-up hot peppers on a string.

He had this hunger in him. She didn't know what it was. But it was imperious. Not like a child's tantrum, kicking and grabbing. It had grown and taken a form and darkened. And it wanted her. It wanted her to have him. She could never resist that.

The knees opened one notch. It made her heartbeat quicken. The bulge stiffened under the buttons of his jeans. The knees opened wide. She cupped the bulge with her hand and leaned toward his mouth.

His mouth: soft and melting. His breath, strong, tasting faintly of alcohol. His tongue, thrusting and giving in. She circled his lips with one finger.

Johnny is like quicksand. She's never sure of her footing with him. She has to dance around him. Or, as he says: I keep you on your toes. His moods baffle her. A Dr. Jekyll and Mr. Hyde.

His friends say he can be difficult. That he goes off like a tornado, like a hurricane, that he has a short fuse, whatever. But he goes off. Seemingly without control. And you never know what's going to trigger him. Neither does he, apparently. I can't spend my time with you wondering if I'm going to press the trapdoor button by accident, Eva says.

You shouldn't.

Now, for instance: she's leaning against the wall, her arms folded on top of her kimono. He takes a swig at the bottle, playing macho. She can't help laughing. I thought you'd be intrigued by that. You know, how decadent it is. Lola's Live Phone Fantasies. It has an interesting ring to it, no? I'm sorry I even mentioned it.

The rage mounts in him. She can feel the muscles tense up, his whole body gather around the hot rage burning through him, his arms looking for something to bang, something to ram through. They find it. The scotch bottle. It's not much of an arc, but it hits the side of the counter in full force. Shatters in nasty shards across the linoleum, the rest of the whiskey dripping along a cabinet, forming a small golden puddle at his feet. For a second, she has this image of him pushing the broken bottle into her neck, slashing her with its lethal edges. But he stands in the middle of the kitchen, smashing the broken glass to smithereens under his boots.

Then he walks out. In three strides he's out the door, bangs it so hard it rattles on its hinges.

Dressmaker

After the tragedy, Albertine says—Albertine is always talking tragedy, tragedies. She feeds on them, they make her feel like life is worthwhile, like a good show, but deep, intense—after the tragedy she turned to God. She was always mystical, mind you. She had that in her.

Who are you talking about, Eva asks, busy tightening a dart at her waist.

Albertine gives a sharp tap on Eva's hand. This is my job. What's a matter? Not tight enough for you? You're going to have to wear a corset otherwise the seams will burst open before you even get a chance to belt a *la*.

I am going to lose weight.

They always say that.

The dress Albertine is trying on Eva is iridescent green taffeta, strapless with a heart-shaped bustier and ballooning at the back under the waist, designed by Eva after a model found in a French fashion magazine. It makes me think of the bustles our grandmothers used to wear at the turn of the century, Albertine had snorted, pointing to the exaggerated backside. It's going to make you look like you have a big fat one. Sure that's what you want? Positive, Eva had said.

One thing I have to admit: the color becomes your hair and your skin.

Outside the window, a brick wall partially repointed with cement, flaking off like a skin disease. In the foreground, a tree grown in the well, now leafless, an ailanthus palm, one of those trees that grow like weeds anywhere, anyhow, even through the asphalt, dry branches, knotty, skeleton-like fingers.

Staring at the tree, Eva twitches under Albertine's expert fingers. She's nervous, *les nerfs à fleurs de peau*. On edge. The edge of what? Of the blade, of the razor. Her nerves have been cut with a razor blade. Which tickles their tips. In the silence, now that Albertine has stuffed her mouth with pins and breathes heavily as she dances around Eva's bust, modeling the fabric to her shape, Eva tries to hear herself think. The beat is too fast. Her thoughts get jumbled. She thinks of the set of prints for her portfolio that she picked up at the photographer's this morning. Black-and-white prints, eight by eleven, close-ups of her head against a cracked wall a bit like the one she sees from Albertine's window. You can see the grain of the skin. You could almost stretch a finger and touch it, the fine lines at the edge of the eyes in the sunlit face. On the photos, the wall, behind her head, has a grainier texture, brown spots, cracks, cement blotches. You could stretch an arm and touch it too. It is like a gross replica of the skin. Like an aged, crinkled hide. Late afternoon light grazes the wall, grazes her cheekbones, grazes her chin. They are more interesting photos than the classic studio portrait but something in them bothers her, something to do with the grain, with the light. Something too personal about them, that gives too much away.

You're too rigid, Albertine says. Look at these shoulders. Relax. Think of something pleasant. Let your body hang naturally, otherwise the dress is going to fall crooked. Want some music?

Okay. Put on your old Patsy Cline hits. A little heart-bleeding won't hurt.

If that's what it takes to relax you.

I know. You'd go for Frank Sinatra. Or Charles Treinet.

That makes me think, Albertine starts, having unloaded her mouth from its last pin and stabbing a waist dart with it, that makes me think—you know Louise, my neighbor, she died two days ago.

Eva was going to say, another one of your tragedies, but the name, Louise, stops her. Louise with her head of blond frizzy hair and her long sweeping dresses she wore with army boots and hand-knitted sweaters in earth colors. Louise, the one who tried to save the robin in Albertine's kitchen. But that was before, when she was still playing the violin, her long hand holding the instrument's neck, that graceful gesture, elbow up, patiently teaching how to move the bow to her students, who came up the five flights of stairs, that staircase which always smelled of potato soup, no matter the season or the time of day. Before the illness got her. Albertine's flow of words sweeps over

Eva with images of Louise's illness, of Louise's last days at the hospital.

A soft white/blond down on the head growing back the last weeks when they stopped the treatment. Body shrinking to the essence of itself. Flesh receding caving in upon itself. The mask of bones. Pure lines unadorned by prettiness of skin. Skin flesh organs attacked from the inside, by their inside. Waging their internal wars. Beautiful nose lately a fine beak, eyes deeper, their intense blue washed down, graying, a white film clouding the eyes like a fog, a mountain fog early in the morning floating over the pine trees, later to be dissolved by the sun. But this one didn't dissolve. Didn't ever. The eyes closed in the hospital forever when the brain shot itself, short-circuited itself. Shot itself boom-boom. Sizzled and fried. The hand light as a feather in the son's hand. Light, caramel-colored freckles on the hand resting finally relaxed between his palms. The body letting go. Almost—yes, absolutely—a sigh of relief.

Albertine falling back into silence, heavy breathing. Eva not feeling anything, just this all-purpose tightening in her throat. Louise's frail body in her long nightgown standing between them.

You know what I'm scared of?

No. So many things. You're scared of your own shadow.

Not worth a comment. I think it's not death I'm scared of, but of not knowing how to die.

Don't make me laugh. Death is about the only thing in life you don't need to know anything about to achieve. Can't miss it.

The pain. The pain must have been atrocious. How does one live through that pain. And the certitude that it's over. The knowledge.

The day before she died she said, tomorrow, I'll be somewhere else.

She knew it was coming.

She believed there was something else, somewhere else.

Do you think there is?

Walk around now, nice. You should see how it falls at back. Gorgeous. But the bustle!

Do you think there is?

What? A great beyond? Girl, I don't know. I am not asking myself the question anymore.

Ouch!

What? Sorry, did I prick you?

Right under the rib.

Careful, now. Don't move. Here. Look.

Eva takes a few steps sideways, rocking her hips in front of the mirror holding her elbows at her waist. She stands in profile, twisting her neck to see the line shoulder-back-ass-thigh-knee. She whistles. She says super. She says, Albertine, you're a genius, and plants a hard kiss on both her cheeks.

Albertine shrugs, not willing to admit her pleasure at her obvious success. If that's the dress you wanted, she says, you got it!

She turns Eva around holding her by the waist, until her back faces the mirror. Okay, don't move now, she says. I'm going to take the pins out back. Let you out of here.

The hotel night guard

She had men coming to her room. I don't mean several men the same evening. But different men, sometimes late at night. I don't know if they stayed the night or not. I have the night shift, eight to four. The morning shift would know. Of course we thought she was a hooker. A young

woman, an apartment in a hotel near Times Square. What else could she be? But classy. A call girl, as they say. Not one of these cheap girls caked with makeup and a foul mouth. Old-fashioned almost. Like a lady. A red mouth, glossy, and black-black eyes, and always showing her legs. Nice stockings, bags, shoes. You wonder, how do I know? Okay, me, a night guard in a run-down hotel? Not so run-down. There is worse around the Deuce, but still, not uppity. We keep it clean, safe, there are these nice furnished apartments on the top floors. Used to be a very nice hotel, classy. Look at the marble on the floor in the foyer, the brass and copper details around the doors, on the elevators. We wear a uniform. Not too many shady characters. Even so, we don't know what people do behind closed doors. We close our eyes.

Turns out she's a singer in a nightclub or something. Totally on the up-and-up. Has a little girl. Five, six years old. But no father. What a way to raise a child. But she doesn't ask my opinion. I tell you what. She doesn't talk to me a lot. Just good evening, Morris, or, has the rain stopped yet, or can you call me a cab, I'm late. But I get a sense that she doesn't ask anybody's opinion. Just does what she wants. Stubborn on her little smart shoes. They go pop-pop, pop-pop on the marble floor. The sound echoes down the hallway. Not good news for a man. No wonder she can't keep one. Even though there's been that fellow lately. Now, that one, I don't think I like. A thin fellow, something jerky about him. They came back fighting the other night. It was nasty. They didn't even make it to the elevator. It sounded like she was blaming him for something. They yelled at each other. But he turned against her, lashed at her. There was something like pure hate in his voice. He turned white. The way he grabbed her, I thought he had a knife, that he was going to kill her. I didn't know whether I should jump on him, separate them. But he just jerked away from her and stormed out of the door. She didn't turn around. From my desk I could see her back stiffen and her neck stretch up. She didn't move until the elevator door opened.

He's a new fellow. Keeps odd hours. Shows up late at night, way after she's come back from work. Moody. Sometimes polite, sometimes not. Can't place him. Stylish, in a way, not streetsy. But not a gentleman. Definitely not. Maybe an artist, or a druggie, one of these in-between types, neither here nor there. Hanging out. Handsome fellow, I'll grant him that. The kind of fellow women go for nowadays. Don't ask me why. On the skinny side, kind of delicate-looking and wild eyes. Underfed. Clothes hang well on him. Could be an actor, now that I think of it. Aspiring actor, that is. A three-time loser with a sweet tongue. I'll never understand why women fall for them.

To change the subject: did you hear about this young woman, married, two kids, somewhere around San Diego, who went and bought herself a gun, came back home, shot the two kids and herself? Kids aged three and eighteen months. They say the husband had no idea what happened, what made her do that. Maybe if he'd had a better idea . . .

Mimi

Eva picks Mimi up at school, which Albertine usually does. She arrives early, for fear of missing her. That Mimi, not finding her, would start crying in the middle of the huge hall, left all alone, the only kid parentless or babysitterless. Sobbing. The feeling of abandonment. The bitter, des-

perate feeling. End-of-the-world feeling. Eva remembers it well, like that time when she found herself alone in a crowded department store, no trace of her mother, just strange faces around, people going about their business, blank, towering over her, small bug having lost its link to the safe world, on the verge of being swept away in the jungle. Until her mother miraculously resurfaced behind a cosmetic stand. Well, maybe Mimi wouldn't feel that way, maybe Mimi had more confidence. But anyway, by now, the clock above the heavy wooden entrance door marks ten to three, dismissal time. Bodies suddenly surge forward, propelled out of doors, fired like bullets from the side, spinning around and around columns, short red hair rising above crown of head, ponytails whipping about skulls, shoulders inching forward, backpacks bobbing, whole classes marching in caterpillar-like, holding hands two by two, boy-girl, boy-girl, girl-girl, boy-boy, long braids, short curls, blond frizzy-fuzz, all the same height. Eva's panic coming, sweeping over her. Will she recognize Mimi in this crowd. Not Mimi's panic, Eva's panic, finding herself childless, erring forever in search of child.

Hi, Mom.

Black frizzy-fuzz, fuchsia tights, that blue dress she likes, her favorite, with pink piping, sparkling brown eyes. Open arms. Eva bends, almost kneels. Gets her own bullet shot against her chest. Panting. Soft nuzzle depositing one moist kiss on each cheek.

Did you think you wouldn't find me? Mimi asks with her small high-pitched voice. You were looking all over the place. You looked scared. But you know what, I was right there!

Pearls of laughter.

Eva squeezes the little hand.

Look what I got for you. She pulls something wrapped in Saran Wrap out of her purse.

What? Oh, my favorite, chocolate chip! Oh, two of them! Two cookies! Thank you, Eva.

They walk side by side. One long stride, two little strides, one even, one bouncy. That kid doesn't walk, she bounces, twirls, runs, spins, jumps, Albertine. I don't know how you can get her back home. With me, it's let's do this, let's do that, I'm tired, I'm thirsty, I'm hungry, I want to play, I can't wait to be home, when are we gonna be home, I want to wait for my friend, I don't want to walk, I want to take the bus, I want this, I want that. . . . It would take me two hours every afternoon to bring her back. How on earth do you manage that?

Just practice, says Albertine, who's already prepared the hot chocolate with the croissant she buys for Mimi every afternoon, just like when she was a kid in France. That was our daily snack, she says, croissant or pain au chocolat, we didn't think it was anything fancy, then.

Eva puts her hand through Mimi's curls, those tight corkscrew curls tumbling around her skull, above her forehead, over her shoulders. My little lion, she says, pushing her fingers deep in, rubbing the skull with the tips. You don't even need to wear a hat, with this fur growing on top of you. Mimi thrusts her head into the palms, a cat looking to be petted, then shakes it hard, growling, shaking, turning into a wild animal, finally knocking down her glass of milk which spills onto the bright enamel top of the kitchen table, white on yellow, a puddle stretching to the edge then going drip, drip. Hey, cool it, Mimi, Eva says, while Albertine picks up the sponge and kneels under the table to wipe up the mess. Mimi gets up, pissed, caught in the act of being only a child, out of control, walks out uppity, bangs the door, screaming, I didn't do it, I didn't do it. I hate you, Mom!

Oh, boy, Eva says, sighing, sitting back at the table, elbows down, her face between her hands. Oh, boy. *Jesus, Marie, Joseph.* Oh, boy.

It was snowing when the contractions started, the night before Mimi was born. Eva woke up with a start. Three o'clock in the morning, it should've been pitch-black but her window was a rectangle of translucent white. She felt the dull ache come and go, then come again, quite a bit later, then again, then again. It didn't really hurt. It was just a low-level cramp but it kept her awake, waiting for the next one, and the next one, and they kept coming back and she knew that was it. She got up to look at the window, feeling her belly with both her hands, the incredible tautness of it, the pure beauty of the line. A sculpture of human flesh growing out of her, made by her own body. The adjacent roof was thick with snow, big, fat snowflakes drifting down noiselessly. She pulled a chair by the window and stared at it, at how fast the white coating grew, rounding its edges as it rose on the window ledge, on the fire-escape steps, on the cornice of the federal building across the street, knowing she had nothing to do but to wait for nature to get on with its job.

Mimi's father was Frank Jackson, a drummer with a funkadelic band who wore his hair in dreadlocks and had a vicious smile that first made Eva weak in the knees, and later made her want to peel it off his face. They split up before Mimi was even born and it was okay. Eva knew all along she was doing it on her own. Staying pregnant was one of these nonacts that have as much to do with active rebellion and a sense of adventure as with a passive sense of fate. Besides, she thought it was sexy. She blossomed. Her skin turned a peachy glow, her hair thickened and her whole flesh seemed to tighten and get firmer. Frank Jackson himself was taken by it. He stroked her burgeoning belly and buried his face between her lavish breasts and muttered words of sexual arousal evoking the Great Goddess and the sexiness of fertility. All the time kidding her that he wasn't sure he was the father, that he'd wait to be sure it was a cappuccino-colored baby before admitting to anything, and even then. She didn't try to make him endorse his responsibility, the fatherhood. Frankly, she didn't think he would make a good father, would more than likely turn out to be more trouble than he was worth, yet they fought constantly about her pregnancy, him trying to pull out of any subsequent responsibility or entanglement or commitment and at the same time imagining wild schemes by which she could be taken care of by another, more responsible man, or even give away the baby to a rich family (he had a few lined up already). She'd look at him with a forlorn expression and quickly encase her rounder forms in a jumpsuit or an oversize sweater and storm out. He didn't get a chance to verify his fatherhood. He was long gone before Mimi was born. Gone on a tour with his band, never to return, never to be seen again. Can you believe the guilt feelings, Eva told Albertine. He had to exile himself. Even though she heard lately that he'd been seen, in fact, in a Jersey club or on the Island. If it was him. Hair cut two inches above the skull, black-painted fingernails and a cross hanging from his earlobe. Eva finds it hard to believe.

Where's my dad, Mimi asked once. She was about three and a half, four. Had finally caught on to the fact that all she had to pick her up at nursery school was aging Albertine or springy Eva, showing more leg than other mothers. Eva thought the hair on her back was going to stand on end just hearing the word "dad." You don't have a dad, she said, icy cold. No dad? No dad. Zap. Zap dad. Mimi repeated, zap-dad, zap-dad, a few times, enjoying the sound. But where is he? I just told you: you don't have one. But everybody's got one. No: what about Rebecca, and Melissa, and Josh, and Anna, they don't have a dad either. Yes they do, Mimi said emphatically, their dads just don't live with them. You *have* to have a dad. Eva thought kids knew too much already. All right, she said. You're right.

You need a man to make a baby. But it doesn't mean that it's a dad.

What's a dad, then?

Oh, I don't *know!*

So, where's my dad?

Eva broke down there and then. Okay, she said. And proceeded to tell Mimi about Frank Jackson. Which wasn't much, she realized. Particularly if you try to stick to the good stuff. But Mimi quickly discarded Frank Jackson out of her mind, after deciding that a gold tooth in the front of the mouth was yucky.

Mimi swings out of the bathroom, hips adorned by an array of rainbow-colored ribbons, mood changed. Eva once saw a sign on somebody's apartment door, saying: BEWARE, LUNATIC CAT (actually, it was written in French: ATTENTION, CHAT LUNATIQUE). She thinks she should have a sign on her door: BEWARE, LUNATIC CHILD. Mimi could be Johnny's child, no problem. Eva didn't remember Frank Jackson was moody, although to be honest he was one big fucking mood most of the time.

How do I look?

Very nice, Mimi. Where did you get these ribbons?

Mimi points to Albertine with her chin. She lets me play with them, she says.

Jesus, Albertine, Eva says, rubbing them between two fingers. These are real silk ribbons.

So, better a child play with them than letting them gather dust. Let her have fun.

So now Mimi lives with Albertine. Sort of. Eva and Albertine used to be neighbors. In this building. Eva had the apartment above Louise, the violinist who just died. Albertine took care of her like a child. Made sure she ate. Cooked for her. Sometimes did her laundry. She never said so, but Eva thought maybe she made up with her for what she'd never done for her own daughters. It suited Eva's temperament. She didn't want to worry about that, daily living, domestic arrangements. She was totally bored by that. She was a night person, thought life was one big adventure, and if the adventure turned sour she could always come back to Albertine and cuddle up on her Naugahyde couch eating *beignets aux pommes*, Albertine's specialty.

That was Albertine's idea, taking care of Mimi. She said to Eva, with the kind of lifestyle you have, what are you going to do? I'll give you a hand. Mimi as a baby ended up spending the nights at Albertine's when Eva worked. Albertine set up a room for her at the back and moved her sewing equipment to the living room. And when Eva moved next door to the hotel because it was cheaper and she liked the romance, the anonymity of the dark suite with its old-movie-star furniture, the arrangement became permanent. Of course Eva saw Mimi almost every day or every other day, and took her out to the park, the movies, read her books and put her to bed on her free evenings and gave money to Albertine to cover Mimi's room and board, but there was no getting around the fact that Mimi lived with Albertine and that Albertine was involved in her upbringing and Eva wasn't sure how she felt about that.

Eva forgets Mimi when she is with Johnny. An eradication. It is so brutal, so total, that it frightens her. It's as if the cord has been severed, temporarily. It's as if she had to forget she was a mother, in order to be the lover. But not only the mother, the daughter, the singer, and not only that, but even her language, her name. She feels in order to pass over to the other side, she has to strip herself of her self.

What of her language? Hasn't she already discarded it? Left it with her childhood memories, like a melody at the back of her head?

I am nobody, she says to Albertine. I come from nowhere. I am just Eva. And sometimes I even forget my name. I want to forget it. I am just these eyes, those lips, those hands, this mind.

Albertine says, there's nothing else. That's as close as being you as you will ever be.

But nothing stays attached to me. Things, people, memories, they slip off me.

Mimi calls her on the phone with her little voice, which sounds smaller and more high-pitched than face-to-face. Eva hasn't seen her in a couple of days. Mimi asks her, Mommy, where are you, I miss you. Why didn't you call me? And it's like being turned inside out. After Mimi was born, Eva wouldn't let any man come close. Even wearing lipstick and heels seemed like a betrayal, like she was openly going to court somebody else's favor instead of being a MOTHER. As if being attractive to men was a harsher, more strident mode of being that insulted her relationship to her daughter. With Mimi, she was supposed to be milk and satin, round and soft, available.

She stops by at Albertine's on her way to work. She's wearing her nylon stockings and a flaring skirt in black linen and a little linen jacket right on top of her bra and a pillbox hat with a *voilette* perched at a dangerous angle and her suede pumps and she hugs Mimi, she presses her cheek against her, not wanting to smear her fresh lipstick, she says good-bye to her on the sidewalk, while Mimi waves at her, her hand in Albertine's hand, and Eva walks a little way along the sidewalk and turns around and Mimi is still waving crying her name, and she starts walking more briskly till she reaches the corner and then she doesn't turn around anymore, she mixes with the crowd crossing the street. Mimi is in good hands, she says to herself. What kind of a life would she have with me?

Albertine

Now, Albertine, she's from Brittany, from a fishing village called S., in the vicinity of Brest. Family of seven kids, all boys, except her. Fishermen family. Mother's job was to mother, plus clean up the fish, take stock, operate the ice-boxes, sell at market, keep the books. According to

her daughter Mrs. Albertine senior was the brains in the family. All the boys at sea with the father. Dangerous life. Two of the brothers claimed by the enchanted mermaid. Albertine growing up, her hands deep in the fish guts, blood running up her forearms, had to wipe the snot off her nose with the back of her hand while fish entrails flowed from between her fingers. Albertine sick of the sea. The smell of fish won't go away. It won't leave the skin, it sinks deeper in as you rub away at it, your skin turns rough as scales, the rotten fish smell clings at clothes, at hair, at floorboards, just fades to an aftertaste. Imagine, the perpetual stink! Albertine laughs. Didn't laugh then. The garbage in back full of decomposing flesh. Graying pink flesh gone soft, falling off bones, swarms of flies buzzing out of fish eye sockets, trails of silver skins making paths around the can, left behind by the cats' forays, smell of fish in the cats' breath, fish heads still dangling from between their teeth as they run to hide behind a bush later to abandon them to the worms. Fresh fish flapping at the bottom of Father's dory, fish starting to go bad in two days. So fast from fresh to bad. Followed around by the odor of putrefaction.

It was my job to clean the fish, me, the only girl in the house. Left more time for my mother to box my little brothers' ears, straighten them out until they were ready to get on board. We sold at market three times a week. Up at four, five in the morning when the men came back. We loaded the truck and drove to town.

By that time the war had started. My elder brothers were recruited. My father kept fishing with the boys who were old enough to go to sea. Eventually, he, too, was recruited and we stopped fishing altogether. My mother got a job at the fishery. But that was later. By that time I had had it with fish in all forms. Maybe I was a snob. That's what they said about me. All I thought about was the city. I'd wear short skirts and cut my hair and go out with boys and have a job, like maid in a hotel or secretary. And when I thought of the city, I wasn't thinking of Brest, you better believe it, *non, ma chère*, I was thinking the capital. At least. And then one of my brothers died. My father lost a leg. It was getting to be too much. I finally made it to Paris at the liberation. The excitement, the freedom! It was incredible. I'll never forget it. People were drunk on it. We had taken such a beating in '39. The Americans drove down the Champs-Elysées like gods. They were our saviors. They were our new idols. I decided right then and there to see what it was like in the new world as soon as I would be old enough to leave.

You don't know what a trip it was. People don't know anymore what it means to cross the ocean. A plane is not the same. Goes too fast. It's the same whether you fly five hundred miles over land or halfway around the world and over three oceans. Now, a ship. An ocean liner. You really felt it in your bones. Your eyes took it all in. The water doesn't lie. The puking and the waves coming up to your throat, that doesn't lie. You go through hell and back. The word eternity takes on a new meaning.

There were so many people on that boat, you wouldn't believe. People sleeping six, seven to a cabin, two to a bunk, and not lovers, you bet you. The sexes were separated. Girls' cabins, boys' cabins. People everywhere on deck even though it was the dead of winter. Deck class, they called it. Some people had paid for a cabin and found themselves on the deck. Covered with blankets, and still they were freezing. I was smart. I had gotten a job in the kitchen through a manager of a fishery my uncle knew. Not cleaning fish, no sir, but peeling vegetables and doing odd jobs. I shared a cabin with three other girls at the bottom of the ship. It was dirty and as hot as a steaming caldron, but it was better than freezing on deck. There were rumors you could die of cold out in the open. Still, we'd go on up during the day of course. One day it started to snow. Have you ever seen snow on the ocean? The snow doesn't melt right away. The flakes cover the surface of the water like white dust.

I bundled up in blankets and watched the snow come down. The sky was like milk. I sat, a shawl over my head, not feeling wet or cold, thinking I would just flip through a curtain of snow all the way to America. I got to know some of the people on board. Some families, with five, six, seven kids. I thought you had to be mentally insane to take these little *gosses*, some were still sucking their mothers' tits, to start a new life over here.

When you got to the other side, it was a new life all right. You had shed skin and innards several times over, and only kept a dim memory of your past. You didn't think about going back. You had crossed the Rubicon and you'd take root on the new shore by hook or by crook. And remember: no more smell of fish. I'd smell my hair and under my armpits and it reeked gamy and of diesel and car exhaust and fried butter from the restaurant kitchens where I first worked, but guess what: not of rotten fish. It was delicious. On the ship the first evening I had trained my eyes on Le Havre lights. For hours I thought I could still see them. There was always a dot of light dancing at the edge of my vision and I thought if I looked sharply enough I'd see it all the way to the other side. I stayed up half the night on the upper deck where those who had no money were parked. I stared at the stars and I stared at the shoreline lights. I fell asleep in my cabin with the lights still in my eyes. And each day when I woke up I climbed back on deck and I imagined I could still see Le Havre at the edge of the horizon. But the last morning as we drew close to the American shore it was wiped clean. The line was razor sharp and round as a perfect ball.

Lola's fantasy line

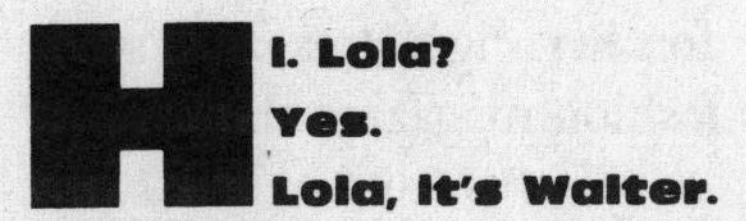

Hi. Lola?

Yes.

Lola, it's Walter.

Hi, Walter.

Lola, Lola, I want you so bad.

Credit card, credit card number, expiration date?

Lola. You're so cold. Can't you just be friendly with me?

Walter. You know we can't start before you've made your payment.

No credit, hey?

No, Walter, no credit.

Sigh. Okay. Let me get it. Here goes. MasterCard. . . . You probably know the number by heart by now.

Credit card number please.

4832 7064 6035 2339. Okay now?

Just a minute. Expiration date?

8–91.

Thank you.

Eva, in jeans and turtleneck sweater, is sitting on a high stool in front of the kitchen counter, holding the wall phone tucked between jaw and collarbone while she scribbles on the MasterCard form.

Are you naked? asks the voice on the phone.

No, she laughs, softly. I am the way you like me, you know, with the black corset laced in front with the see-through lace bra and my breasts are all pushed up and they almost come out of it, just showing the nipples?

And . . . and you're not wearing anything underneath?

Only the white anklets rolled down.

And the high heels?

Yes. And the high heels.

And you're not shaven.

No. Just natural. My black bush growing all the way between my thighs.

Eva bends backward, gropes for her cigarettes and some matches behind her and opens a fashion magazine that's lying on the counter.

Where are you, asks the voice.

Lying on the fur in the middle of my bedroom, at the foot of the bed.

She puts the cigarette in her mouth and lights up.

What did you just do?

I've opened my thighs. I am opening my cunt lips.

Are you wet?

(Exhaling the smoke through her nose and leafing through the magazine.) So wet, baby, so wet. It drips from my fingers.

Put them in your mouth.

She puts her cigarette in her mouth and exhales again.

What does it taste like?

It's sweet and thick. It smells like . . . oh God, I think I'm going to have my period.

(Groans.) Touch yourself, baby, put your fingers in there. Put them deep in there. Are you doing it?

Yes. (She shifts around uncomfortably on the stool, smokes some more, stabs the cigarette and leans over the magazine to study a close-up of a pair of earrings.)

Are you getting red and juicy?

Yes, oh yes, baby.

Touch your tits. Pull one out of your bra. Is it big?

Oh, yes.

Touch it with your fingers. I want to see it big, the nipple stiff.

She leans back against the counter, stretches her legs on it.

Is it?

Yeah. You're so big, baby, so big. Your nuts are hard. You're touching them right now. I am so juicy for you. Oh, you're so big. I love it.

You're so tight, you little bitch. You're scorching me.

It feels good, baby, oh, it feels so good.

Show me your ass. Let me put my fingers up your ass.

No, no, you're hurting me.

Oh, it's so good, good. Ohhhhhhhh!

She pants with him, her mouth wide open on the receiver, finishes with a moan.

She waits for a few seconds, listening carefully. She waits

to make sure the line has gone dead, then hangs up. Then she goes to the fridge and pours herself a glass of seltzer.

These sessions exhaust her. They're always short, but her concentration has to be intense, and her voice perfectly pitched in order to assure the smoothest flow of events. Her control has to be total. At first she had to restrain herself from giggling, then she gradually developed a firm grasp of her part and let the caller give her the cue. The job is to go along, play her part, but only so much. It's a fine line because past the giggles is the sudden tightness of the throat upon hearing that strange voice go blank with desire and she has to block that out. A job like that, you can't get turned on. She thought it would be a clean job, that she wouldn't have to dirty her hands, not unlike emergency psychological assistance. But curiously, these disembodied voices seem to have the power to reach her more intimately than, say, the naked body of a stranger grotesquely panting. She doesn't see them, she doesn't see their pot bellies, their bad skin, their dirty feet, their fat thighs, their ridiculous dicks, their flabby asses, their empty eyes. What the voice transmits is pure desire. The cliché is what saves her. The same repetitious litanies of baby and dick and suck and cunt and sighs and gradual panting, all so predictable that she could time every sequence and she could swear they would very nearly overlap. Their fantasies seem to turn around the same four or five classics with little or no embroideries. Sometimes she thinks she could give them a tip, embark them on a side trip, see how they would like it. But that's more than she would want to be involved in.

For three hours the phone doesn't stop ringing. She only opens the line for three hours, nine to midnight, the nights she doesn't sing. The rest of the time she has a taped message that says in a breathy voice, *you've reached Lola, the fantasy queen. Lola is unavailable right now but would love to hear from you on Monday*,

Wednesday, Friday from nine P.M. to midnight. Talk to you soon. She is not very good at keeping the hours straight. She comes back late and the answering machine is blinking feverishly. Or she doesn't come back at all and the endless string of messages sounds like reproaches from dissatisfied clients. It's like a store, she thinks. I've got to open at a certain time, close at a certain time. These people are expecting me to be there on schedule. Lola's fantasy store, she calls it. You name it, you got it. Her voice is like a mirror they hold to themselves. When she's had it, she unplugs the line. At first she was concerned that it would deter the callers, that it was bad business, but she gets enough calls to pay the rent and cover Mimi's needs, and she seems to get her regulars. She sometimes wonders if they get attached to her voice, or if their own schedule corresponds to hers.

She says, I am the real call girl.

Sometimes she thinks about Mimi walking into her apartment while she's on the phone and her whole body twists in horror.

After the calls, Eva takes a very hot shower and brushes her teeth for a long time. What she would really like to wash, though, is her ears. Wash out the voices that end up sounding all the same. A universal aroused male voice ringing in her ears. When she lies down, snippets of dialogue, isolated words float through her mind. To erase them, she watches the late night movie on TV and listens to the actors' voices until she falls asleep.

She dreams that Frank Jackson is back in New York. He is downstairs in the lobby, wresting her room number from Morris. He is standing in the hallway, knocking on her door. It's

3:33 A.M. on the digital clock. 3-3-3. Spooky. Frank is pounding at her door. He's yelling, open the door, open the door, the word "door" elongated in a triple diphthong, Brooklyn style. She doesn't recognize his voice.

She sits up in her bed, not moving, waiting for the pounding and the voice to go away. But it starts again. It's so close, a room away from her and the thickness of an old wooden door. She tiptoes to her closet, puts on a pair of pants and a sweat-shirt.

She's all dressed, now, waiting maybe a foot away from the door, not touching it. The voice seems to have dropped a few decibels. It's not Frank's voice. Or is it? There's an eerie silence surrounding the pounding. Who is it? she finally asks, feeling she's making a mistake just to acknowledge her presence. The voice drops to a forced whisper.

Open up!

She whispers back, Frank?

Linda there?

It's not Frank. Relief.

Linda? No. No. I don't know any Linda.

Open up. I want to know if Linda's here.

I told you there's no Linda. If you don't leave me alone, I'm calling the management.

Fuck, says another voice, of a man who seems out of breath. It's the fucking wrong floor. We're supposed to be on the tenth floor.

Sorry, ma'am.

One of the barmaids at the Follies told her it was not a good idea to have the line—Lola's fantasy line—installed in her apartment because someone can trace it back to her place. Even though it's an unlisted number? Even though it's an unlisted number. But, like who? I don't know, the cops, or somebody working for New York Telephone, or a nut.

Walk on all fours for me. Show me your ass. I'm so big, baby, so big. Hi, Lola, it's Rick. How do you like to be sucked on your little pussy? Lola, it's Max. Lola, it's Ron. Lola, it's Ricardo. May I speak to Miss Lola, good evening, Miss Lola, my name is Mr. Hikumi. Is your cunt red and hairy? Do you like men to go down on you?

She dreams of men's faces crowding her. Faces without eyes and enormous mouths like fish mouths that dance above her. She's spread flat on her back, pinned to her bed. The mouths open and close. But the voices she hears don't come out of the mouths. She hears them from inside her body. They are born of her bones and her nerves. They scream from inside her eardrums. They scream so loud they turn into a persistent ring.

It's Johnny calling. His lazy voice soothes her anxiety.

Why do you always call me so late?

I couldn't sleep. I kept thinking about you, about what we did together yesterday. I want more. I want you all the time. I want to touch your breasts, I want to feel them swell.

Johnny, she says. Not now.

Why?

I can't explain. Just talk to me.

I was talking to you.

Johnny, sorry. I'd better not talk right now.

You just said you wanted to talk. What's wrong?

Nothing. You caught me in the middle of a bad dream.

Are you all right.

Yes.

You want me to come over.

No. It's okay. 'Bye, Johnny.

'Bye.

The old lady takes a walk

In her big white house on the outskirts of Paris, Eva's grandmother is about to take her daily walk. She moves around in a wheelchair most of the time now, she only walks from her bed to her lounge chair, from the lounge chair to the wheelchair, but the doctor comes sometimes and makes her get

up, maybe he's not a doctor, but he's a young man and he is always very polite with her, he has a soft voice and sometimes she calls him Alain, the name of her favorite son, she thinks it's Alain who comes to visit her, Alain is so considerate with her, he takes her hand and tells her to stand up, he tells her she can do it, that she has to exercise these muscles, otherwise they're going to dry up, he says they will take a little walk across the drawing room together, and then, if she's up to it, down the hall to the dining room. His hand is warm and dry, very soft and he seems so tall next to her, taller than her son, she notices that he wears glasses, thick tortoiseshell glasses, and, well, of course it's not Alain at all, she chuckles a little bit, even though her hips hurt, every one of her joints feels like rusted metal, and she says, did I call you Alain? I am so sorry, doctor (but she's not sure he's a doctor, a doctor wouldn't just come to walk with her), my memory is leaving me, it's not much fun to be as old as I am, do you know, doctor, there's nothing left except these old bones, I should have been dead a long time ago, I think the good God forgot me down here. And meanwhile, they slowly make their way across the room, circling the Louis XV chairs and couch and the Napoleon III settee, all covered with white sheets like ghosts, the room is huge, they have to cross it from end to end as they are coming from the old library at the back where they have arranged a bedroom for her, and brought a new color television and a lounge chair stuffed with pillows to make her more comfortable, and where she spends her life, takes her meals, sleeps, receives the basin slipped under her by the nurse. The huge ghostly drawing room is bathed in gray light because some of the wooden shutters are shut tight, maybe they don't open anymore, it's a case of paralysis from lack of use, but some sun manages to work its way through the slats and you can see speckles of gold dust dancing in narrow stripes. They walk their way through the stripes, one by one, and it's as if the light was blinking with each of their steps. The old lady says to the young doctor, maybe we should open the shutters and let the sun in, it looks like a beautiful day today, I don't know why they keep them closed all the time, they must be afraid that I will run away. She chuckles again and the young man at her side smiles politely with a little throat noise simulating a laugh. How are we doing? he asks. But he doesn't wait for her answer. He says, we are doing very well today, very well. We walk like a young woman. Shall we go down the hall? And she presses her hand a little more firmly on his arm, she even lifts her cane in a jolly little flurry and says, let's go, after you, doctor, as they approach the door leading to the hallway, and, without letting go of her, he turns the brass handle and pushes the door open, it makes the creaking noise of old hinges badly lacking for oil and they slowly move down the hallway, the diminutive old lady dressed in black with a purple hand-crocheted shawl covering her stooped shoulders and the young man bending slightly toward her and as they make their way down the long corridor, she says, Alain, you should come and see me more often. Why don't you bring the baby next time? I'd like to hold him in my arms.

Mom, I don't want to die

Mom, I don't want to die by myself, Mimi says. Her eyes, dark brown, almost black, are so deep. Everything is there in those eyes. Eyes so knowing, the fear in them. As if we barely need to tell them, they know, about death. The unimaginable. Tears well in those eyes. She holds

Eva tight on her bed. I don't want you to die before me. I want to die with you. Eva looks in the eyes. Goes straight in, it's like with Johnny, in a way, but not the tumbling down of desire, it's the crystal-clear separateness that Mimi knows already. You gave me life, but you also gave me death, and I'll have to face death alone. Five years old and she knows it.

But Louise is not really dead? Mimi asks again, hoping against all hope. Right? She's in heaven. Eva looks straight in again in those eyes. It's not Mimi-the-child, but Mimi-the-woman, Mimi-the-person, whom she finds at the bottom of those eyes. Some people believe one goes to heaven after one's life, Eva says. But nobody knows what happens after death. Louise is really dead. You'll never see her again.

It's not the words, it's what the eyes know. Mimi puts her face on the pillow sideways, her little hands neatly resting on top of each other, palm to palm, near her cheek, the way Eva used to do every night to say her Hail Mary and Our Father in Heaven, but Mimi doesn't say her prayer, or maybe it is a kind of silent prayer, who knows, learning how to live with this black hole at the end of life, and she closes her eyes and falls asleep.

From the back, Eva's waist curves in, a soft S from shoulders to ass. Not a bone in sight. A thin waist but hips curving out. Eva feels Johnny's gaze on her back as she bends down to pick up her dress. His hands follow the curves. Eva feels the warmth of his fingers, the touch, light as air, electricity running between their skins. She moves her hips slightly to meet his touch.

If I told her, you'll never have to die, would she believe me? If I told her, we'll all meet in heaven and we'll be happy ever after, would she trust me, would she feel relieved? Would she feel the feeling of immortality? *Mon amour*, Eva said, whispering, touching the cheek, fine like the skin of a young fruit, with the back of her fingers, back and forth. I gave you life, the poisonous gift. Forgive me.

Mimi sleeps, mouth slightly open on pearly teeth. At rest her face looks like when she was a baby, only bigger. When Eva leans above Mimi, smells her bittersweet breath, the smell of her skin not washed, she has trouble remembering their fights, the deadly fights. The hands at each other's throats, the nails digging into delicate flesh inside the wrists. When she looks at Mimi, Eva, too, knows she will die alone.

Credit card. Credit card number. Name on the card. (Don't worry. It's confidential.) Expiration date. Excuse me, sir, ex-pi-ra-tion date.

Honey, I want to suck you, I want to suck you so bad.

Wait a minute, sir. Let me get it down.

What do they say to you, what do they say to you? Tell me. TELL ME. He grabs her by the shoulders, from the back, shakes her. TELL ME.

She pushes him back, half stands to slide into her dress, wiggles her ass into it. He forces her toward him. His face is livid with rage. TELL ME. She gets up quickly, looks for her balance on her shoes, pulls her dress down. All matter-of-fact, busy. Stop it, Johnny, she says. Let's not talk about it right now.

She dreams at night that her body swells with child. Her breasts are so tender, just the brushing of a shirt against the nipples arouses her. She dreams of water rushing, knocking down dams, of water lapping at her feet. She dreams of corridors in old houses, members of her family running through them, people she hasn't thought about for years, with whom she seems to be entangled in painful conflicts. She dreams her body expands, gets tight as a drum, the belly pushing forth, right out, she turns into an egg, and two chickens break through, big, giant chickens, lemon yellow, a weird color. She yells, I am giving birth to chickens, but nobody is here to listen to her, her room glows from the city lights, she turns over on her pillow toward the dark side, toward the wall and falls back to sleep.

Johnny puts his hand between her legs, tight, spread out across the crotch as if to close her up. She sighs in relief. You get juicy so fast, he whispers. You flow in my hand. (Run like an egg, she thinks.) He feels, fills her with his fingers. They toy with her, they get so intimate, she wants that intimacy, she wants to take him in, every one of her pores filling up with his sweat, the exchange of body fluids being the ultimate in love-making, not just through the prick hole and the cervix, but saliva and sweat mixing like exchange of blood from a cut, wrist to wrist, your body spilling over into the other's, she becoming male and him becoming female, him holding her breasts and feeling them grow into his hands, her fucking him sitting on him, impaling him with his own sex, which doesn't belong to him anymore but to both of them, he's lying down his legs wide open, his mouth open, his ass open, if she fills him up, he will spill out into her.

Her back is to him, her buttocks two semicircles with the beginning of the crack just showing. He can't resist pushing a finger in between. She slaps him on the hand. I gotta go. No you don't. Finger pushed deeper in. She turns around, teasing him with her breasts, dancing on his finger. Later. He falls back on the mattress, spread-eagle, watching her getting into her clothes, her little jacket with the shoulder pads and her pumps, her tight skirt, the buns moving loose under the fabric, the heels going down carefully around the islands of junk on the floor. She turns around, his hard-on is rising straight up from his flattened-out body. 'Bye. She waves at him. Fucking bitch, he says, to the closed door, going at his dick with a vengeance.

When she sings, Johnny sits at a table near the entrance, way back. He keeps his leather on, nurses a Jack Daniel's on the rocks, one arm draped around the empty chair next to him. He sits in the dark, where she can't see him. Sometimes he'll walk out before the end of the show and she won't even know he's been there. She comes on stage wearing a bustier dress of dark green taffeta with a bustle ballooning around her backside. Her face, her neck, her shoulders are powdered white, her eyes, charcoal and the cherry-red heart of her mouth. Her hands which clutch the mike have red fingernails too, cut short and blunt but gleaming, catching the light. She wears her female mask. Her hair waving away from her forehead and her temples like a black sun.

Johnny sips, watching her.

He knows her act by heart.

Her voice is raspy low, with jazzy undertones. It brings out a weird pathos. Johnny thinks if he closed his eyes it would make him think of Billie Holiday's. (Eva would say, you're flattering me, but I have a cheap cabaret voice.) But anyway Eva sings Patsy Cline's songs and fifties ballads, and then for the second part she pulls on long black satin gloves, with a rhinestone bracelet catching the light this time, and she sings her own songs, and now she's singing his favorite, he sets his glass down and she moves her knees to the mike stand, it's as if she needed the support, her fingers are crossed over the mike, before she starts she kicks her hair back, she always does that, maybe it's just to bring the voice out, fill in the lungs, and her knees now touch the (which he imagines) cold metal of the stand, he can just guess the tautness of the knees in the white pantyhose, under the hem, she starts with the throat digging deep in and then her voice goes up, with a halftone drop that's supposed to send shivers up and down your spine, and sure enough it gives him the chill, she balances herself on her black suede pumps, a slight swaying of the hips to keep the tempo, but basically she just stands there, stretching and rounding her red mouth and periodically kicking her hair back, and he stares at her, holding his cigarette between his cupped hands.

She is lying on top of him. His legs are smooth and slender. There's a slenderness about him. Even a roundness of the hips that often belongs to women. Her hands go down, open the legs. He sighs. His eyes are in shadow. They watch her. They have this naked look that runs through her. It's like the male mask has fallen off. Underneath it's raw and it runs and it spills out. He turns around and offers his backside, his crotch to her open hand, to her inquisitive fingers. Yeah, yeah, he says. Oh, yeah.

Johnny go lucky (if you dare)

Johnny's place is a dark loft with a mattress set on a platform in one corner and a tangle of sheets spilling on the floor, a fireplace roughly cut in the brick wall and his sound system spread all over the rest of the space. Wires running across the floor and forming thick nests near the electrical out-

lets, hundreds of tapes and albums struggling to remain on shelves.

At night they turn off the electric bulbs, light up the candles, and listen to the sound of New York. Distorted shadows stretch on the rough walls.

We are the last ones, Johnny says, the last generation. We live in the cracks like rats. Just one brick layer removed from the street.

You're lucky, Eva says. You can move out of New York.

And go where?

She points out the window in the direction of west.

To Jersey.

Never.

Oh, gimme a break.

I tell you. Never.

The nights are purple at Johnny's, not like in Times Square where they are red. The winter nights are crusty and silent, an icy vapor pressed against the windowpane. The open hands stick to the glass, on the patterns of frost. The nights are sharp like crystal.

They lie on the mattress with sweaters and socks and watch the last of the embers fade away.

One day, this building will go up in flames, Eva says. The way the Lower East Side burned down, the way Harlem burned down, the way the South Bronx burned down.

Johnny flips over to light a cigarette. The flame of the match lights up his eyes and draws deep furrows along his cheeks.

Nah, we're careful, he says, tossing the match across the room into the embers.

She hides in Johnny's place. Nobody on earth can reach her there. It's as far from New York as you can get and still be deep in the middle of the city. A no-man's land. A nomad's land. But Johnny is a nomad who won't leave Manhattan. He's a drifter with roots, a guy who watches the Yankees beat the Red Sox with a joint in his hand and a can of Bud at his feet propped against two pillows in the middle of the loose wires and dirty clothes just as he would do it in his Mom's Jersey den, while the city is raging its silent war around him.

Eva walks in, carrying a brown paper bag, steps over the wires from his sound system, kicks aside a heap of clothes in her path, pushes some dirty mugs and scattered magazines on the kitchen table and drops her bag of groceries next to the Mr. Coffee permanently on.

Johnny is sitting, his head in his hands, staring at the TV screen on which baseball players, tiny figures in white and blue, move across a great expanse of green. He doesn't move, doesn't lift his head. His body is pinched, folded upon itself in full hypnotic trance, maybe helped by a couple of joints, a sweet-acrid smell floats, traveling on the fanned air. He is bathing his blues in the TV milky light, flask of whiskey at his feet.

You drive me nuts. Stop moving around like this, he says, finally acknowledging her presence. The way you move your ass around.

You want it?

What?

My ass.

No. That's just it. I don't. You're throwing it in my face. Taunting me.

I am not. That's just my way of moving. You have a dirty mind.

Why did you come to New York, Johnny asked me once, when I told him I wasn't born here, that I came from France. You can tell at the end of my sentences sometimes, a softer attack on the consonant instead of the American-born smack, or click on the *t*, *d*, *m*, etc. Not the *r*, you can't tell from my *r*, which is rare, I know. The *r* is what betrays the French tongue. Maybe that's why Johnny didn't bring up the subject earlier. What brought me here was fate, I answered. I was thirteen, fourteen. I had budding breasts and wore Bermudas my first summer. I remember my breasts, they were so high up. Almost up to the shoulders. He asked if they became big very fast. They're not that big, I said. You know, full, he said. He likes that fullness when they hang above his mouth. He wants to gulp them, he wants to stuff himself with them. I said that no, they were tiny with hard little nipples. He laughed. We didn't talk anymore about my Frenchness. And what is there to say about it anyway? It's the past. It's like a secret self buried inside of me. Like a deep layer of me buried in Americanness. One day it will be like a fossilized stone. The pattern of my former self will emerge on my American surface.

Johnny takes a shot of bourbon and gestures toward the bag on the table. What's that stuff? Food? Did you buy any ice cream?

And cookies, she says.

What's the occasion?

I'm not working tonight. I thought we'd eat something here and . . . I brought stuff you like. A mango.

He lies down on the bed, legs wide open, stretches his arms above his head.

I kneel between his legs, open his leather belt, feeling the studs with my palms, unzip his jeans. Sometimes I wonder if what I like in American men is just the pair of jeans, the way it molds them. Fetishist.

So, it wasn't my dirty mind, he says, lifting his hips to let me slide his pants down, just keeping his T-shirt on. He is purplish-pink, large. He smells of piss and sweat, makes me think of a hot moist cavern. His hair, sticky, bushy, of the wet grass on the banks of a lake. I put my face in it. It's flesh in which I want to bury myself. It's primitive flesh, raw. It's like when Mimi came out of me, the blood sticky on my bush, the blood all over her, her skin moire blue like moonstone, color of rocks, of reptiles, smells of the earth in which decay slowly turns into stirring life. I bite his nuts with the tip of my teeth, I stuff one whole in my mouth. He moans. I want him to moan. I want him to lose it in my mouth. I want him to let his body arch under my hands, searching for it, that contact, searching for it like for water, like sweet fresh cream. I want him to undulate under me. I want him to turn to ribbons, to silk. I push my middle finger, the longest one, up his hole and I move it slightly. I wait until he stirs and whines. Then I pull it out. I want him to miss it. I want him to miss it so bad he'll scream. He rolls over on his belly and pushes his ass out in my face. I cup him with my hand. He fits snugly in one of my palms and the rolled fingers of my other hand. He fits in me no matter where I hold him. He would fit in my elbow, at the back of my knees, in my neck, under my arm. Wherever I can fold myself, wrap myself around him. I hold his toes in my hand, his tongue in my mouth, I roll his cock between the soles of my feet. He sighs. Then he takes me in his hands. He's got me tight at the crotch. I swell in his hand. I turn into curves, sinuous. We slither against each other. We turn into snakes. I dance on the tip of his tongue. He's got me there and he knows it. He makes me dance until I collapse.

I look into his eyes just before he comes and I can see the crack. I see his eyes naked. I see them pale, almost transparent. It's as if intense light washed their color, or maybe it turns them into mirrors and what I see is my desire.

When I stay with Johnny, the days drift in and out, day into night. We don't wash, we eat on the mattress, we stare at the fire in the makeshift fireplace. The blinds stay drawn. Our only witness, or mirror, is the TV set that he keeps on without sound in order not to miss a game or an afternoon show. There are images flickering at the corner of our eyes as if they were our shadows. Sometimes it seems that they mimic us behind our backs. I hate that constantly shifting screen. I fought a battle against it but I only won the sound. Johnny won the images. He says maybe he can do without the sound but what he needs is the low-frequency buzz that our ears pick up unconsciously even if we don't actually "hear" it. I am scared of the rays the TV emits. Sometimes I make a point of avoiding walking in front of it. I'll walk around it from the back or I just won't go at all in that corner of the room. It becomes like the body of a sick insect that can barely move. Why an insect, I wonder. It's so squat I can't imagine it getting up and leaving, but it doesn't look like a cat either, or a small bear. It's threatening in a more foreign way. It's the way it moves in front. This huge single eye staring at us and reflecting images, like irises in the sun.

I'll get two, three days in a row between singing gigs and I'll go to Johnny's and time will collapse upon itself and when I come out in the street the light and the sounds hit me as if I had emerged from an underworld. Even the hazy sunlight hurts my eyes.

I stop by at Albertine's on the way back, afraid to smell so funky that Mimi will ask me what it is. But she turns around from the kitchen table and she hands me a drawing. It's a princess drawing with a huge headdress, several layers of hair and ornaments including feathers and flowers and an elaborate hat looking vaguely medieval that sits as a three-tier crown on top of the precarious structure, long curly brown hair hanging past the elbows, and full skirts bellowing around her feet. What's peculiar about the drawing is that the princess sports a snake loosely wrapped around her neck and hanging down her chest and the front of her skirt. I know it's a snake because I asked, and Mimi said, it's a snake, of course, Mom, like it's so obvious, and it is, except I wonder where the image comes from, I hope she copied it from somewhere, or just saw images of snakes or a documentary about snakes, because otherwise it's kind of disconcerting to think of the snake symbol trailing Mimi's princess. It's her pet snake, Mimi explains, a boa, it goes with her wherever she goes. It even sleeps with her. No! Yes, Mom. It does. Now Mimi giggles like it's hilarious. Would you sleep with a snake? Me? Oh, no, yucky! I'd be too scared. And your princess is not too scared? She comes next to me, puts her mouth real close to my ear and blows more than whispers into it: Mommy, he's going to turn into a prince. I thought it was frogs usually that turned into princes, I say. Mommy! Mimi says. Not her, not my princess. She hates frogs.

So. She didn't notice how I smell. But sometimes she does, and I say, it's the smell of love, and it sounds so corny to me, I want to swallow it back, so to speak. But she takes it all in stride, like the fact that I disappear for three, four days in a row. But then when she hits me in the groin or tries to strangle me, I think she's got it all there and if she takes it in stride, the stride is building up and doesn't go down easy, but right now I breathe easy that life hasn't shattered during my absence and I even listen to the news while eating some beef stew left over on the stove and I watch the progress of AIDS and the arms race and I wonder which one is going to kill us first.

Angel's Follies

The Angel's Follies has been around for decades, Angelo, who manages it, told me. I asked him if the name had anything to do with his own name, and he laughed and he said, no way. *He* hasn't been around for decades. He thinks it's fate. Angelo believes in fate, like me. It's hard to imagine

Angelo having been an angel, even in a past life, with his belly round and hairy popping out of his waistband and his head of curls. More a monk, maybe, his shaven skull would probably be round as a billiard, you can imagine it shiny in the sun, a jovial monk belting down Budweiser by the quart. He does belt down the Bud, but he doesn't have to hide it under his robes, he just keeps a bottle next to him wherever he is. It gets warm, he doesn't care. It's like a pet. He extends the arm without looking, the familiar neck fits perfectly into his hand. Angelo is a great appreciator of my dresses. He says they are much too good for the Follies. He runs his fingers on the satin, he always says, you should go over on Broadway. You've got a good voice, why are you wasting your time here in this dump. You're too good for that joint. Even Angelo believes in careers. I ask him what about his own career. He shrugs. He says, I don't have an education. It's not a bad job. I say, well, same here.

He admires Albertine's new model, the one with the bustle at the back, green satin, and the bustier top. I hold myself upright in it, the laced-up bustier is tight like a glove. I fit so snugly in there, it's as if I was wearing a girdle. And I move like that, too, small tight steps. It's a part I play. Angelo makes appreciative motions with his hands, Latin style (I remember men doing that in France, too): following the curves in an exaggerated motion, in the air. I give him the finger and a swing of the hips to put him back in his place, and I go up on stage.

Maybe the magic act is to stand up in one piece in front of the audience, all packaged with the taffeta dress and the rhinestone earrings and the bracelets and the satin pumps and the makeup and the corset top, the whole paraphernalia that makes me feel like I'm going to war, but not a war of shoot, shoot, shoot, more like a seduction campaign. I detach the mike in a very precise gesture, very controlled, and place it near my mouth, just so, and I pitch my voice, there's only one instant in which to breathe and feel the bristling darkness, the whole that could swallow me, and throw that pitch, the first sound, which will be my first step to balance that void, to pull them on my side, and my voice will be in the middle, taut between their world and mine. And at that very instant I'm dead sober. It's as if a veil has been lifted. My voice soars, a bit tight, but pitched right, I start to feel the pull and I adjust the tension. Like casting a kite in the wide blue sky. I hold the mike so tight it hurts my knuckles. The mike stand holds me together. If it didn't support me I would collapse, fold over and drip on the floor.

The first time I noticed Johnny in the lounge, his tall, gaunt body in a leather jacket leaning over the railing, was at that exact moment, as I was pulling the mike from its stand. I locked eyes with him and I sang the whole first song without losing sight of him. I knew I had him when he leaned forward on his elbows against the railing at the back, holding his cigarette in his closed fist.

I feel the strength of my voice right from the start, pushing through the tightness. I position it a bit deeper, wait until it reaches the right fullness, then I push it out. It comes straight out of my guts. Hundreds of hours of breathing exercises and mental concentration techniques to get that channel open. But not to pour myself out. I've got to keep the tension, that damned tension. The power I have to exert to rein in my voice makes me tremble. My voice seems so much stronger than my body. As if my body could barely contain it, could be shattered by it.

At first I hear the room. It rustles. It's opaque. It breathes so hard I think my voice will never pierce its stirring life. The sound goes up, extends around the mike, but the room is like a curtain of smoke I can't penetrate. The voice comes right back at me, like an echo, as if the audience was refusing to catch it. They're not sure they want to play yet. Until my voice makes its way to the other side. I release the grasp on the mike just a notch. The voice expands, it flows, it reaches out.

Afterwards, when it's all over, when I've curtsied to the audience and smiled to the applause and a few fans have come to congratulate me, I wonder how the real great artists feel when they're performing, what immense power rises into them and what tremendous craft they must have developed to unleash that power and control it at the same time. But it's a thought that never lingers too long after a performance, I usually joke around with Angelo after I get back into my street clothes and with Felix, the pianist, who's taking a break backstage, smokes a cigarette. He puts his arm around my waist and leads me into a tango as the house canned music plays Carlos Garda. Felix cracks me up. He languorously tilts his head back and keeps a straight face with his tight trimmed mustache and his hair slicked back, his heavy eyelids half closed. I giggle. We swing to and fro at steep low angles, we swoon backward over our arms, forward over our feet. When the music stops we're in stitches. I kiss him on the forehead and wipe the sweat with the hankerchief I find tucked into his jacket pocket. If only you liked women, I tell him with a mock sigh. You'd be the perfect male.

Angelo and Felix are buddies. Angelo is Puerto Rican, Felix half Cuban, half Colombian. They're Latin accomplices. On weekends they stage sumptuous parties at Felix's place, to which they invite me and Mimi. Felix cooks all morning, sometimes starts the night before. He cooks chicken, rice and beans, elaborate stews, salads of avocado and kiwi. Twenty, thirty people show up and when the party is in full swing he sits at his piano and plays piano-bar music while everybody gets down to serious stuffing and drinking. Once, at a Christmas party, he asked me to sing while he played. We had a huge success. In the summertime he barbecues on the roof of his building and blends pitchers of lethal margaritas and rum daiquiris. Mimi lies down on a chaise longue or they stretch a string of pillows for her against the wall of the bulkhead. When she is fast asleep I scramble down the stairs, Mimi hanging over my shoulder like a rag doll, and carry her back the few blocks to Albertine's apartment.

Felix offers me a drink at his place and we stay up late discussing channeling and crystal meditation, Felix's recent obsessions. He thinks he was a courtesan back in Atlantis and that it accounts for his tumultuous sex life in the recent past. But he was also a monk during the Middle Ages in the Piedmont in Italy. He hopes that past experience will guide his new celibate life.

The doorman is reading the *Post* when I come back. He's completely into it, his elbows, his whole face. He lifts up his head when he hears the click of my heels. At this hour it's pretty quiet in the lobby. His face lights up in a big grin. I can tell he's got something juicy. So what is it, Morris, I ask him. You won't believe this one, he says. But of course I believe every one of them. I believe anything. They could make them all up for all I can tell. Your boyfriend lives downtown, right. That puts me on the defensive. How does he know that. What does he know about Johnny. He sees my face. Sorry, he says. I just . . . I thought you told me once. I don't believe that. He must be spying. So, anyway, Morris, what were you going to say?

He says a policeman found a dismembered body, arms and legs (what about the head? I ask) stuffed in plastic bags, just regular kitchen bags, you know, in a dumpster over on St. Mark's Place.

You know how they found out?

Beats me.

The smell.

That figures.

A restaurant employee was cleaning up the sidewalk and he thought it smelled funny, I mean, like, stench, you know, and he called the cops.

Later that night, I wonder how one can tell the smell of flesh decomposing from the smell of garbage going bad, and I think about the body, how it must have looked, if the flesh gets purple and soft, I imagine the arms together in one bag, the legs, maybe cut in half, they'd be too long, I wonder what kind of knife he or she used, a saw maybe, an electric saw, how it must've felt, like quartering a turkey at Thanksgiving, maybe, only goddamn more cumbersome. Trying to be clinical, an operator doing a job. What on earth, what fear or warped logic would lead some-one to perform such a task.

She will die

She will die. She will die. She never seems to stop being on the verge of dying. This fading. This softening. This going back to sleeping, to less food, to softer food, to liquids, to lying down, to ga-ga-ga-ga-ing in bed, to not recognizing, the brain reverting back to this clean-slate state, the circuits

worn out, flattened out, not registering anymore, they've been gone over too many times. But she knows it, she knows it. Or does she? She feels the slip into silence, and then, trying to catch on, to hang on by her fingertips, her memory, losing her sure footing. Reality receding, turning against itself, into hallucination. Mirrors crashing. She sees it coming. The perceptions changing, slipping. She sees it coming. The train hurled straight at her, going at 160mph straight up, big black loco puffing black smoke. Aahhh! The scream. But not even a scream. A faint whine, sigh? But no, not so simple. Not so obvious. Faces from the past coming to inhabit visiting bodies. Interchangeable bodies. Blurs whispering her name. Jean, her ex-husband, kept coming to her, his beard from way back, from the time they were first married, kids still, from before the war, when men were still wearing a certain kind of beard, bushy but carefully clipped, crisp black pattern around the face, maybe it's her eyes, maybe her eyes don't see too well. Jean, she screams, the passion of her youth (what was she, eighteen, nineteen? A whole era she's gone through) lighting up her sunken mask. Going backwards, the time when he took her hand and pressed it to his lips, that first time . . . Jean, I'm so glad to see you, she mutters in a small polite voice. The present pulled from under her. The present has stopped moving. A few years left for what. Reliving and reliving like a record-player needle going over and over the same groove. Or maybe it's the shapes that shift like patterns of sun on water. A state of pure fiction. When the cord has finally been cut loose from reality. The mind free to err and wander in its jungle of short-circuited connections.

The tuberose

Eva's suite at the hotel smells musty. It's dark, either because the curtains are perpetually drawn or because night is somehow its mood. The sun can be glaring outside but the apartment remains in shadow with just some strips of light filtering through. There is a couch in one corner, the kitchenette on the side with a green-speckled linoleum flooring curled up at the edge next to the carpet. She always trips over it when she is in a hurry.

I like cities, she says. Because they have a history. It doesn't matter if you see the old houses, buildings, whatever, you can feel it. It's in your bones, the smell of the city. Like a gigantic lung pumping for you. Yeah, blowing this disgusting, polluted air into your mouth. Well, it's got all the human life, too. Even American cities smell of history. I couldn't live on a ranch, for instance.

How old is history?

It doesn't have to be so old. I guess at least two generations. Places that have already been recycled once at least. It's like patina buildup.

Yeah, sleaze. Sleaze, slime, gook, grit, whatever grows on top, viscous moss.

The perfume of a tuberose, a single stem in a green glass vase on the dresser. The perfume climbs up the curtains, sweeps down the bedspread, clings to the sheets. A sweet perfume, not unlike that of honeysuckle. Sicker. Sweet-sick. The sweetness of organic things beginning to turn. The French writer Emile Zola wrote that when tuberoses start decomposing they take on a human smell. The smell of death. A heady perfume? Headstrong? *Qui s'entête à vous empuantir?* A stinker, in other words. It covers the smell of decay, of time passed without attention having been brought to it. Mixes with it. Time passed and elapsed. Left to itself. Only patched up. She thinks she sees bugs in the folds of the comforter. Shadows fleeting when she moves her toes. The door is half open. Barely so. She tries to see behind it. Is it too dark? Too much foliage? No, it's a dark street. At night of course. Badly lit up. A few cars parked along the curb. Two or three guys walking, unhurried, indifferent. Somebody is lying on the ground. He is lying on his stomach, stretched out, in shirtsleeves. The night is warm. It could be a perfect night to sleep out. But on the sidewalk, facedown, city grime in the mouth? Nobody stops, nobody turns around. Words flow around the lying body. She opens her eyes. She thought she heard the sound of her own voice. And the tuberose brought by Johnny opens up, opens wide, spills its smell, heady, as it is. Spills out its presence.

Hold on to the tuberose. Hang on tight. Go ahead. It is a cluster of white flowers. They open from the bottom up. Tuberoses are used in perfumery. They were fashionable at a certain period. But which one? And what does the word mean? A rose in a tube? A rose in the shape of a tube? The weather is dry, warm already. Spring weather. A soft little wind. Something balmy, totally out of season in the air.

The tuberose doesn't lead anywhere, even when squeezed. Would its juice taste like blood? In the bathroom next door the water runs. A toilet flushes. Steps. A pattern in the void.

She's stretched on her bed which is covered with a quilted satin spread of faded blue. She's in a black slip. Her skin very white. Her black hair up in a twisted bun. Heavy bangs. Thick eyebrows. Around one of her wrists a hefty bracelet made of Bakelite or some such early plastic matter. Black, too.

But listen, Eva's not married, Eva's had tons of lovers. What does she care? She's got a kid already. As if that wasn't enough. A kid, in her situation. Imagine. She was lucky, I tell you that. She didn't even have to pay for an abortion. I bet she doesn't even know who knocked her up.

It doesn't matter. Nothing matters. That Mimi was Frank Jackson's daughter or some guy I fucked on the run. It doesn't make any difference.

Are you expecting your period, by any chance? Because it's

what usually puts you in that mood. What mood? You know damn well what I mean. This fucking mood you're in. I don't know what you're talking about.

We always end up managing without men. They even die before us. No longevity. Who needs men anyway? S.o.b.s're just more trouble than they're worth. Price's too high. She sees snapshots of Johnny. Johnny in movement. His angles, his curves. His hips, his shoulders. She felt Johnny like a wave running through her body. It was a complete meltdown, red-alert.

In the street, winter dusk, hard snow on the ground, two shadows bundled up, talking, balloons of white breath in front of them. One is a woman, overweight, in a down jacket. She is saying, you know, I don't think I owe you any money for the rent. I cook for you, I do your laundry, I been taking care of the kids.

And me, I fuck you, thinks Eva.

This is our arrangement. He comes and goes. Me too, of course. In principle. Except I stay put. Which suits me, I suppose. I don't like to run after anyone. They come to me and then I make my move. At least, I used to. Who can afford to, these days. Johnny and I look at each other and laugh, and say, we are each other's last lovers. We're both healthy. Who's going to take another chance? It is our pledge of fidelity.

His body is slender. He has something of a teenager. As if manhood wasn't going to thicken him, but maybe just dry him out, sculpt him deeper.

We sat at a little table behind the bar, facing each other. The table was as far back as we could find, as if we were trying to avoid a jealous husband or mistress. Are you seeing someone? The question floated. It was ludicrous. He was drinking Jack Daniel's on the rocks, his usual drink, I found out. I had ordered the same. Straight bourbon has a soberness about it. Just a pure warm sharpness on the tongue. Cocktails make me think of ruffled dresses. The other tables, the customers disappeared, dropped out of sight. He was talking. He can really talk if he wants to. He was telling me stories. They didn't make sense. They were American stories, cross-country stories, New York stories. I didn't really follow. They were just a texture of sounds that I bathed in. The table was narrow. I put my hand on his. He didn't stop talking. He turned his hand palm up. Our palms together were like fire. We went on talking, drinking. Our hands were making love. Down each finger, between each finger, around the palm, wrist against wrist. They were dancing an erotic dance in the middle of a crowd. We were fucking each other with our hands and no one noticed. I bent toward him and I tasted his mouth.

In the street I had my hand on his ass. These bikers' leather jackets are good for that. The ass moves freely in the jeans underneath. Round taut muscles, I had my hand full of them. You've got a great ass, I said. He pushed his hand under my coat. Fumbled all over me. You too.

It was love at first sight between me and Johnny.

She was woken up by the sun filtering through the curtains. In the late afternoon there is that stubborn ray that plays across the bed and on one of the bedside tables. It had reached the quilt. At first she thought it was some animal moving, it was going back and forth, a gentle pulsation, then she realized it was the breeze coming in through the top window that was open a crack, and pushing the curtain in and out. She can see it now. She would like the curtains to be sewn together, or, better, a piece of pressed wood to be nailed to the window and then the day would be eliminated, these shards of light piercing the eyes.

She waits for the sunbeam to shrink and gradually fade out to turn on the lamp by the bed and get up.

She walks around her two rooms, her energy suddenly up, makes herself tea and *tartines*—slices of bread untoasted, buttered, that she dips into her bowl of tea, standing up, at the kitchen counter between trips to the stereo to put a tape on. *The New York Times* is open in front of her under the bowl and the saucer with the bread on it. Right around the edges of the saucer it says, "A man armed with high-powered rifles and handguns opened fire at two downtown shopping centers Thursday, killing at least eight people and wounding at least eleven, authorities said. The gunman then took several women and a man hostage in a supermarket, but he let the women go about one A.M. today, six and a half hours after the shootings began." The rest of the article goes on inside the newspaper and Eva will never know why this man decided to blow up his neighbors and fuck up his own life in such a radical way. Although the impulse is understandable. Let it all hang out. The rage coming up, mounting in waves, buzzing inside the ears, overwhelming, the ripples sweeping through the organs, which start discharging their juices, bile, phlegm, saliva, cunt juice, sweat, pee, shit. The boiling point is reached. The brain liquefies, doesn't control the body anymore. Melts down to its core, clutched around a sole idea, an obsession, a channel to get the rage out: the long double barrel of a rifle through which death travels from the heart. An accomplished gesture, vastly superior to that of the wild animal lashing itself against its enemy, all nails and teeth out (even though a wild animal has probably its own methodical approach to killing), the satisfaction of a performed act, the discharge of energy embodied in the perfectly hard, round and efficient bullets traveling at full speed.

The phone is ringing, it may have been ringing for an eternity, she was deep into one of these lazy afternoon dreams that won't let go, coming back from it is like emerging from deep-sea diving in slow motion, she can hear the phone, but it might as well be ringing on a different planet. She finally pulls herself upward and picks up the receiver. It's Frank Jackson.

The ironical twist in his voice, she has a built-in response to it: a knot in her stomach and her hand jumps up to her head, starts rolling and unrolling a strand of hair around her fingers, a spasmatic gesture that involves three fingers, sometimes four, an elaborate teamwork of thumb, forefinger, middle finger and ring finger busily and mechanically at work around one single curl, usually located at the nape, over and over again, forming it into a perfect curl (a gesture inherited from her own mother, who always did it in time of stress). So here is Eva, frantically twisting that one single strand of hair and tightening her stomach muscles while Frank Jackson grinds his slightly nasal voice into her ears and announces his arrival in the city and would she put him up for a couple of days.

She stays speechless for a moment. The nerve this man has. That's how he used to get her. How he used to get anyone he wanted something from. Nerve and charm. She draws a deep breath. She says, you must be kidding. He says, no, why? I'm coming into town. We used to be pretty close, you and I, if my memory doesn't play tricks on me. No foul play, he says. I'm just looking for a place to crash.

She didn't use to say no to Frank Jackson, not for years, and then she herself turned into a big, shrill, screaming NO and walked out the door.

Sorry, she says in a very calm, slow voice. You can't stay with me.

Why? You got a boyfriend?

No. I don't want you to stay with me.

Aw, come on, baby. Remember me? We used to know each other pretty well. You're not going to let me down.

No, Frank.

The funny thing is, confronted with a real "no," he would back off, or at least skirt the issue—had she only known it then . . .

All right, all right, take it easy, man, I'm not going to force you. I was just looking for hos-pi-ta-li-ty, you know? A little human kindness, for a traveler from out of town.

Cut it out, Frank Jackson, she says. You didn't need me for all these years, you don't need me now. Have a good time.

Hey, hey, don't hang up, I want to see you, man, I want to see my kid.

Shit, she says, away from the receiver, but audibly enough.

Say what?

How did you get my number?

Hey, I've got my sources.

You talked to Paco, right?

All right, I did. He's still playing the Bottom Line.

So why don't you stay with him?

Guy's living in a studio, man, with a wife and two kids. He's got no room for me.

What did he tell you?

Nothing.

Nothing? He told you about Mimi, right?

Yeah, he did.

I don't want to see you, Frank. I want you out of my life. Back where you're coming from. Back where you belong. Good bye.

She hangs up and immediately unplugs the phone from its socket in the wall.

Any minute now Frank Jackson is going to walk in with a shaven skull, or relaxed ringlets or dreadlocks and the gold ring on the fourth finger of his right hand and the smirk on his face will go right to her guts and then she'll see the resemblance with Mimi and he'll demand to see his daughter. Any minute now he is going to blackmail her, bring her past to trial, throw it in her face, use it to prove she's a fake, to deny her a present.

Any minute he's going to get his grip back on her. He's going to walk in the door and invade her space, the bastard, he's going to bring her down to her knees, down to the size of a pea. He's going to try to deface her. He's going to open his mouth and daggers will come out of it, blades woven through his speech, they'll go straight to her liver. He is going to look smooth and suave, he's going to dance around the room like a butterfly, he's going to be in constant motion. Then he'll sit and talk seriously to her, heart-to-heart. And it'll hit her and she won't know where it's coming from, because the smile will be painted on his face and she'll wonder if she did it to herself, and he'll lean toward her, his long brown hands on his bony knees, honey will drip from his mouth, and he'll say, velvet-toned, now don't get paranoid, Eva. Eva dahling.

He'll let her twitch and pant for a while, then he'll pull a cigarette out of a pack with his lips, he'll light it with an old Zippo and he'll say: and where's Mimi? I want to see her. Then, a beat, letting the smoke out of his nostrils, exhaling deeply, and: if you're not hiding her somewhere.

Punished in the dark

Eva: I was about seven or eight. I used to go to a religious school at the time, before they sent me to the Lycée like everybody else. We were living in Orléans, that was a few years before we moved to Paris. The sisters' school was a big stone building that felt cool and damp even in sum-

mer. I must've done something wrong, but I don't remember what it was. I was sent to a small room at the back of the directrice's office, which was used for punishment. It had one window with wooden shutters that were shut tight and made the room completely dark, save for thin lines of sunlight painted diagonally on the hard floor. There was no furniture, not a chair, not a table. It was just a square room with oil paintings of saints and the Virgin Mary hung on the walls that gleamed softly in the semidarkness. The punishment was to stay there alone for an hour and repent. One wasn't allowed to sit on the floor or lean against the walls. One had to kneel in a position of prayer. I didn't know if someone, the Mother Superior herself or a sister, could see or would check if I was disobeying the rule, and didn't even ask myself the question. I knelt for an hour without moving more than gently swaying from time to time to maintain my balance, my hands folded on my thighs. The thick stone walls muffled all sound and the dark shadows of the saints' robes I got a glimpse of when I looked up were more frightening than total darkness. I muttered my Hail Marys at full speed to try to evade the demons crawling around me, rampant, slimy. I closed my eyes, but the demons were in my head, they crawled all inside of me, I closed my eyes tighter, they turned into voices. The voices said, they whispered, their whispering was insistent, hissing in my ears, they said, you slut, you lie with every man that comes your way, you're a low-down tramp. You're a whore. And they said, she's a fucking bitch. And I put my hands over my eyes because there was no end to sinning and I would have to confess the voices, the blasphemy howling inside of me while I was supposed to repent and I would have to sit down, kneel, just like now, on the confessional's hard little bench, my chin over my crossed fingers, my nose on this side of the wooden grating, the father's stale breath on the other side, blowing right into me, so close to his breath but the tight lattice not allowing me to recognize his features, and I would have to tell him about the voices, that the punishment didn't clean me up, that I had to start all over again.

But you don't hear the voices anymore, right, Albertine says. I laugh. No, I'm singing now. I sing so I don't have to hear them. But if I stopped singing, I am not so sure they wouldn't still be here.

I still hear my daughters, Albertine says. I hear them crying at night when I wake up in the dark.

I hear Mimi. She's stirring in her bed. She must be dreaming. I sense her sit up, bracing herself, I'm already up when she yells, Eva! I am already standing up from the cot I sleep on when I stay at Albertine's, I've already flown halfway to the other side of the room, she's staggering toward me, rubbing her eyes. She collapses in my arms. She tells me she saw a witch, that she was dressed in black and pursuing her, that she had the face of a wolf and that she was so scary. Her body is small and bony, not bony, really, small-boned, but not as small as when she was a baby, big, in fact, in comparison, a big girl, almost too heavy for me. Her head of curls shoves itself somewhere between my collarbone and my breasts. It smells sugary and oily, a wild-animal, gamy smell. I sniff at it while I cup her in my arms and deposit her back on her own bed, pulling the T-shirt she wears as a nightgown smooth under her butt. She's as limp as a cloth doll. But when I attempt to move away from her she feels the shift, my weight removed from the mattress, and she gropes blindly for me, moaning, Mom, Mom, in quick gasps as if she was drowning, and I sit back next to her, one of her hands wrapped tightly around my forefinger until she lets go of me.

The next morning Frank Jackson is at Albertine's door. We are having breakfast at the kitchen table and Albertine gets up to answer the buzzer and there's a commotion at the door and from where I'm sitting I can't quite see what's happening, I have to cock my head in order to catch a glimpse of her large backside and one of her upstretched arms hugging the door frame as if to defend her threshold from outside intrusion and I hear the low rumbling of a man's voice and Albertine saying no way, mister, no way, and the man's voice rises above hers and I freeze. What the fuck! I get up. Mimi scrambles next to me. What's the matter, Mommy? Who's that? I plant both my fists on the kitchen table, squeezing her hand that I'm holding against it, and I say: that, my dear, is your dad.

His dreadlocks are gone. Cut, shaven, God knows. He's got a tenth of an inch of hair on his skull, marine-style, cut so tight you can almost see the skin through it, a gold stud in his left earlobe and black army boots strapped across the instep.

What are you doing here, Frank Jackson?

Shit, Eva Marquand. I've been looking for you all over town.

He pronounces "Marquand" with the stress grotesquely accented on the last syllable, distorting my name to make it sound like the end of Samarkand, turning it into an exaggerated American sound that is pure Frank Jackson: sarcastic and overbearing.

Albertine's body is still positioned between us, but he's already stepped in and she's clearly not defending the entrance to her house anymore. She's moving slightly to the side, letting me handle it, while Mimi is hanging from my terry robe, one of her arms clutching my thigh like a vise.

Frank Jackson moves on one step and leans forward, resting his hands on his thighs.

You're Mimi, right, he says.

Yes.

Her voice is firm but she doesn't release her grip.

He moves toward her as if she was a cat he was presenting

a saucer of milk to. Squats down a couple of feet from her.

I'm Frank, he says.

She doesn't say anything.

Enough of this, I say, struggling to free myself from Mimi's grasp. I take her hand and I tell her, Mimi, this is your father. So to speak. His name is Frank Jackson. I told you about him.

Nothing good, I can tell, he comments.

Fuck you, man.

Mimi doesn't say anything.

All right, what do you want?

I haven't been in town for fucking four years, man, I wanted to see my child.

Oh, for God's sake! You didn't even stick around to see her be born. What's eating you?

Nothing. Albertine, you got some beer?

Albertine has left us to our own devices and she's been busy clearing the table and making noise cleaning the dishes in the sink.

Don't involve her in this, I tell him.

I'm not involving her in anything. I'm just asking for a beer. A man can be thirsty.

Beer! It's breakfasttime.

I'll settle for coffee.

I don't have the time to answer, Albertine's already set the pot of coffee on the table and poured some in a mug, pushing the bowl of sugar next to it. I remember she used to have a soft spot for him. Sit down, she tells him. Sit down and explain yourself. He does. He sits down. I send Mimi to her room. I sit across the table from him. I tell him, you've got no right. He says, don't hold a grudge, will you. We spent time together, we can still speak to each other. I say, you fucked me over, bastard.

He pushes his chair back, balanced on the two hind legs, his hands lying on the edge of the table. He's got a gold ring with a stone encrusted in it, one of these thick high school rings some Americans like to sport way into their twenties or even thirties, way into their lives. I flash on the ring. I can't believe these hands touched me. I can't believe these hands are Mimi's hands. She's got the same blunt fingers with square nails. A miniature version. And it's because of her hands that I'm listening. He says, Jesus, don't be so jumpy. He looks at me, appraising. Weighing, rather. I curl up under his gaze. I see my hair tumbling over my face, my eyes puffed, a red spot near my chin, Albertine's oversize old terry robe of a nondescript yellowish color wrapped around me and falling over one shoulder. I get up. I'll listen, but not under his eyes. I lean against the dresser and I stare him down. He nods. He says, boy, you're nuts. I ask him if he came to see Mimi, because I really don't have anything to say to him. He pulls a pack of cigarettes out of his back pocket. Yeah, he admits, I wanted to see Mimi. Be in touch with her, he says.

And before?

What, before?

When I was pregnant, when she was born, you didn't want to be in touch, then, right?

I had my own problems.

So did I. And you knew about mine.

All right. Let's not start again.

We're not starting *again*. We're only starting. You came here. What did you expect?

How is she?

Who? Mimi? Jesus! She was fine, until you showed up.

I turn around, I see Albertine's disappeared into Mimi's room. I say, listen, it's not a grudge. There's no way. . . . You can't show up like this.

I'm here, he says.

I move toward the table. I lower my voice. It whispers like the voices I used to hear in my head, with a hissing sound. A forced whisper. A whisper that wants to be a torrent of lava, that wants to burn and liquefy, my mother used to say when you're mad, your eyes turn black like bullets, I dart these eyes at him, I hiss, how do you think it makes her feel, *hein*, not a call, not a word, she was fine without you, she never wanted to know about you, never asked a question, when they've never known their father, it's like they never had one, you know what I mean? Zap. Nothing. You don't miss something you've never known. You don't miss the snow if you've always lived in the tropics. You're hurting her now. NOW. Showing up.

Mimi's at the door, Albertine behind her, a huge shadow. Mimi's holding her toy dog, an oversize red Clifford dog that sits atop the bookshelf she uses as a dollhouse. It's so big in her arms, it covers her mouth and her nose, all you can see is her eyes. She takes the dog to Frank Jackson, not giving it to him, holding it, not quite like a present.

You want to see my dog? she asks. His name is Clifford.

Madame Rosalita

The neon sign reads *Madame Rosalita* in red script, shaped like a half moon. Below, the words READER ADVISER PALMISTRY, each separated by a dot, form another half moon, curved upwards, also in red neon letters. In the center, a pair of green neon palms are crossed, evoking palm read-

ing as well as the position of hands in prayer. The window is partially shaded by a shiny red curtain. When Eva pushes the door open it triggers a crystalline bell sound caused by a brass chime hanging from the frame. Two notes: one when the door opens, two when it closes. It's stuffy and dark inside, and no one comes to greet her. She picks up a leaflet from a pile stacked on the windowsill. It says:

MADAME ROSALITA READER AND ADVISER

If blind, sick, mute, crippled, heartbroken, no matter what your problem is, she can help you. If she doesn't help you, no one else on earth can. Are you filled with misery? Is your husband seeing another woman? Is your child sick? Are you sick? Do you have a fatal illness? Do you have a drinking problem? A love problem? Do you want the man you love to marry you? Are you having an unlucky streak? Do you want to change your life?

See Madame Rosalita before it's too late.

OPEN SEVEN DAYS—9 A.M. to 8 P.M.

Eva folds the paper and puts it in her pocket and waits some more. After five minutes or so, a young woman with eyes haloed in charcoal shadow and a long black braid down her back walks in and invites her in. They sit down in the storefront, on two garden chairs around a table stacked with tarot decks and books on magic.

Are you Madame Rosalita? Eva asks.

The girl shakes her head and turns Eva's palms open. She runs a quick finger along her lines, then stares into Eva's eyes for a long time. Eva shifts uncomfortably in her chair. Then the girl starts speaking in a quick, flat voice. Busy love line, she says—lots of men. I see a shadow from your past. A man. It scares you. You're right to be scared. This man is dangerous. He could be dangerous to you or to someone who is close to you, very close. I see . . . oh, my God. Her voice falls to a whisper. I see a dark aura around you. I think something's not right in your life. You have to act right away.

What, what do you mean, Eva asks quickly.

The girl drops her hands.

I can't tell. But I can help you. I can light candles for you if you want. To dispel the danger.

Does it work?

It costs forty dollars. I'll light the candles during the night.

What! Forty dollars, for lighting up candles! I can buy my own candles for fifty cents and light them myself.

The girl looks at her with pity.

This black aura, she says. Is very bad. Very bad news. If you don't do something about it . . .

The girl lifts up her hands in a fatalistic gesture.

Eva pulls two twenties from her pocketbook. Okay, she says. Is there anything I should do?

No! Absolutely not. Come back tomorrow morning. We'll see how it worked.

Eva has a flood dream. She finds herself in a flat countryside by the ocean. The sea has come up and flooded the country. She is caught in the water with a lot of people, trying to reach the dry land or climb into boats. She sees Albertine and Mimi, calls to them but they don't see her. Someone on a boat waves to her, mistaking her for a famous singer, and offers her room aboard. The level of water keeps coming up. But it's not a tidal wave. It's more like a gentle tide. There's no panic. The whole landscape looks like a gigantic marsh, with grass grazing the surface of the water. There are abandoned bicycles, water reaching to the middle of the wheels. It's treacherous, though. Some people walk in water up to their ankles, some are drowning. There's an eerie silence.

Eva goes back to Madame Rosalita's the next morning. The girl is again alone, her eyes even blacker and more drowned in dark makeup than before. You see these eyes, the girl says, pointing to them with two threatening forefingers. See how tired I look? I was up all night praying to God with the candles. You have a very black aura. It's very bad. This man we talked about yesterday? He wants you dead. If something is not done. . . . The girl knocks three times on the table with her closed knuckles, like the knock of the black ripper on your door. . . . You're finished. Dead.

Eva sits down, dizzy, heart palpitating.

Can you do something about my aura?

The girl lowers her voice, she says, no, not me. Madame Rosalita. She can help you. You'd have to come back at night, if you don't mind taking off your clothes. You have to give me nine hundred dollars.

What? Eva laughs. But I don't have that kind of money!

The girl drops both her hands flat on the table.

Then there's nothing I can do about it. You're going to die.

Eva stands up. She feels trapped. She's got to get out of here, breathe some fresh air in the street. She takes a step toward the door. She nods. She says, I'll handle it by myself.

The girl follows her. Eva feels her dark eyes darting at her, looking for the weak point. She puts her hand on the door handle before Eva has a chance to push it down.

Or you will lose someone who is very close to you, she says.

Eva doesn't answer. She pushes the door and steps out.

Hazy sunshine. Out of season heat wrapping itself around you like a sticky vapor and Frank Jackson's shadow a more intense type of heat surrounding her. The heat on her. Why did he come back? Not to kill her. The girl's prediction is too extreme to really alarm her. Frank Jackson is not a killer. Not in cold blood anyway. If he was to kill her, he would have done so when they were together. His threat is more . . . subtle. As if he had something on her. A key to her. She feels his presence all over town. It's like an added pressure. An eye over the city.

Albertine is pinning a piece of white satin on the mannequin when Eva walks in. She keeps a row of pins in her mouth and pulls them out one by one as she needs them.

One of these days, Eva says, you are going to swallow a pin, Albertine, and then what are you going to do? You should keep them in a cushion. That's why they call them pincushions.

You don't teach new tricks to an old horse, Albertine replies, the pins balanced on her lower lip.

Eva shrugs.

Mimi is watching She-Ra. Eva squats behind her and nuzzles her in the neck. Stop, Mom, Mimi whines. Eva nuzzles some more. Stop it, Mommy! I want a kiss and a hug, Eva says. Mimi, distractedly, not moving her eyes from the screen, smacks a peck on Eva's cheek.

Everything as usual. Eva looks for Frank Jackson's shadow, for a trace of his passage. Dirty coffee cups, cigarette butts, empty beer bottles, a sports bag left hanging on the back of a chair. But she sees nothing. The air doesn't smell any different. Albertine is pinning away, not talking. Clifford the dog has been put back on top of the shelf.

So, Mimi, what did you think of Frank Jackson?

Mmmmmm? Mimi asks, eyes glued to a Lady Lovely-Locks doll tauntingly swinging three pink-dyed locks held by blue barrettes about the screen.

The guy who was here this morning. What did you think of him?

My dad?

It's hard to take, but there's no two ways around it.

Yeah, him.

He doesn't look like a dad.

Are you upset that he came?

Back to She-Ra, who sports a gilded cape and a panoply of

gold weapons and frosted blond hair flowing down well below her butt. Eva and Mimi follow the action for a couple of minutes. Then Eva starts again:

Are you upset that he came?

Who? Mimi asks after an infinitely long time.

Your . . . your dad.

No. But you know what, Eva, he didn't even know who Clifford was. I had to show him the book. He didn't know anything.

More She-Ra. More ads for Lady Lovely-Locks, Barbie and Fruit-Rollups, Care-Bears and Sweet Secrets. Eva has an urge to smash the TV against the wall. Instead she plays with one of Mimi's dark curls, rolling it around her fingers.

I don't want to see him again, Mimi says before She-Ra winds down to her last segment. He tried to kiss me and his breath smelled funny. I didn't like that.

No, Johnny, Eva says on the phone. I can't. Something's come up. I'm staying at Albertine's with Mimi. I'll tell you. I promise. I don't want to talk about it right now. Not on the phone. Next time, when I see you. I swear Johnny. Please. No. Listen to me. No. I can't. I'll see you. Johnny, listen. Okay, good-bye.

In the dark. The receiver in her hand. For a long time before hanging up in the phone booth. Night in Times Square never quite the night. A hazy, yellowish mist. Neons above eye level twirling, pulsing, marching in squares and circles. A thick crowd she could disappear in. She wished to blend in when she first came to New York. A crowd not unlike that of Mexico City, or Bogotá. An American crowd. South and North and Caribbean mixed on the dusty sticky pavement of New York City. Dark faces, Spanish-English trailing around her. The tourists are afraid to stop in the middle of that crowd. They feel it could eat them alive, trap them like hikers in the Canadian forest attacked by a swarm of blackflies. But you can't spray deep woods OFF in the middle of Times Square. So the tourists don't stop, they go at the crowd with fast strokes. Unless they're looking for trouble. And then, 99 percent of the time, they find it. Eva makes her way down Forty-second Street, heading west, favoring the harsh lights and heavy crowds of the main drag to the darker side streets. Then she cuts up Eighth Avenue, walks a few blocks uptown and turns left.

A small Italian bar tucked away in the middle of a dark block, down a few steps from sidewalk level, its two signs, blue and red LITE and red and white BUDWEISER floating in each window. "Rock Around the Clock" beating on the jukebox as she walks in, picks up a beer at the bar, threads her way to the back, where the two pool tables sit, toad-like, their green carpet a bit faded and worn in the middle. The two overhead lamps in green-enameled metal throw two swinging disks of light surrounded by dark halos. Johnny is at the table on the right, chalking his cue, concentrating. There are about five or six guys around the table. The balls are weirdly positioned. Johnny has to walk around to find the best angle. The guys move away to let him maneuver. When he's found his angle, he leans over the table, way toward the center, balanced on three fingers outstretched on either side of the cue.

Johnny once said to Eva, when she asked him where his family was from, and after he said, from New York City and she insisted, no, I mean, where did your ancestors come from, he said, I am a bastard, part Scottish-Irish, part Russian Jew, part American-Indian. All Americans are bastards. I'm a bastard because my father did not recognize me, Eva said. That's different, Johnny said. In your case, it's your father who's the bastard.

The balls hitting against each other make this distinct crisp sound. One time. Then the ball ricochets against the edge of the table and that sound is more like a thump, more subdued, and all the eyes follow it as it moves slow motion but fails to pick up any speed and stalls right at the edge of the hole. Johnny swears between his teeth and turns around to pick up his bottle of Beck's on the window ledge behind him. Hey! What're you doing here, he says, noticing Eva. An hour ago you told me you didn't want to see me tonight.

I gotta talk to you.

I'm shooting pool, he says.

Just for a minute.

All right.

They sit down at a booth across from each other.

Johnny takes a swipe at his bottle, rubbing his lips with his hand still holding it.

Okay, shoot.

Frank Jackson's come back.

Who?

Frank Jackson. Mimi's father.

Johnny tenses up. Takes another hit. Turns around to see where the game's at.

The ex-fuck of yours who knocked you up?

She shoots him a dark look. He shrugs.

Sorry.

Yeah, it's him. I haven't seen him in years. Last time I saw him I was still pregnant with Mimi.

How did he find you? What does he want?

I don't know. But I don't want him around.

Wait. Johnny stands up, waves his bottle toward the pool table. Hey! Right here. And to Eva: hang on, be right back.

Eva watches him from the bench. Rubbing the chalk. Resting the tip of the cue on the green right up against the smooth ball. Holding his balance on the tip of his fingers. Getting ready for the shot. She hears the double sound, fails to see the result.

Johnny comes back, slides next to her on the bench, pushes a hand between her legs. His touch makes her gasp.

Listen, she says, turning toward him and putting some distance between them, this is serious. He's going to fuck me over.

Frank Jackson believed in pushing his way through life just like he believed in pushing his way through women's cunts and asses. Like a soldier strapped to his machine gun. He would've done it in your nose if your nostrils had been big enough to accommodate him. But of course he was much too big for that. Even though he had an inclination for tight orifices. His most bitter frustration was that women didn't have enough holes to shoot through. He would've been happier with a Swiss cheese. He insisted he was a romantic, though. By that he meant he had an artichoke heart, like we say in French. Every artichoke leaf another woman, and Frank Jackson's big heart (cock) in the middle, ready to fall in love with each one of them.

Eva fell for Frank Jackson's body. Long, lean and smooth with tight hips and an ass round and firm like an apple, and pale green eyes in the middle of his dark face.

What does he have on you? Johnny asks.

Nothing, really, nothing. But he's the kind of guy who won't let go.

But he dropped out of sight for years.

Yes, *he* will go, but he won't *let* go.

Tell him to fuck off. Don't let him come up to your place or to Albertine's.

He's already been.

Don't let him manipulate you. You look like you're scared of him.

Maybe I am.

I gotta go back. Wanna wait for me?

Eva gets up to get another beer and sits down facing the huge oil canvas hung on the wall representing a Roman scene in dark gold and brownish tones, with columns, perspective, men in togas and sandals strolling down a dirt road in a dry Mediterranean landscape of burned *garrigues* and olive trees. The surface of the painting is burnished and its heavy varnish cracked to simulate an antique canvas. Several of these canvases, each a variation on the same theme, cover most of the walls of the bar. After staring at the one hung next to her table for a very long time, Eva drains her beer, gets up and walks out of the bar. Johnny catches her at the door.

Hey, what's the story? I thought you wanted to talk to me.

Obviously, you don't have any time for me.

I'm shooting pool, man. First you call me, say you don't want to see me, then you show up here, now you're splitting. Wait till I'm finished. I promise I'll give you all the time you want.

No, it's all right. It's my problem, anyway.

Johnny shrugs.

Okay. I'll call you tomorrow morning. Take it easy.

Frank Jackson

Mimi *(twenty years later)*: I would've preferred never to see him. I would've preferred never to put a face on his shadow. When I was growing up, Eva never said his name. Or if she did, I lost it, it fell through my black hole. It was so hollowed out its syllables did not make a

sound. I drew a blank every time I thought about him. "Father." That was a word that, when she let herself use it, Eva never said without quotes—a deep breath before or after or a particularly clear and forceful enunciation—to make sure she had emptied it of meaning. He was the negation of a man. When Eva talked about him she defined him by insults. Asshole, jerk, wimp, good-for-nothing, *enculé*. She spat them behind her breath, the words whistled between her teeth, when she thought I couldn't hear but was hoping they would reach me all the same.

I didn't call *Dad*, *Dad*, in a soft voice to myself before going to bed. I didn't think of his absence. I didn't think anything. He was like a void around me. I was used to it. Like missing a finger or being deaf. You know there's something wrong, but you have no idea what you're missing.

When he showed up that day, almost twenty years ago, I wanted to spit him out, I wanted to puke. His big male body shod in army boots. And he had a smell. And thick lips and a long fingernail on the little finger of his right hand. Like a tool. Like a human screwdriver or knife always at hand.

I thought he was like a bear. With a lot of hair, and a beard. Now, Eva says his hair was cropped tight and he was clean-shaven. I saw him tall and wide, all shoulders and feet, heavily carrying his weight around. In fact, he is a skinny guy, tight, nervous. I closed my inner eyes. He wouldn't go through to me. I saw his hands looked like mine, I couldn't help it. Except for the long pointy fingernail and allowing for the difference in size. The shape of his fingers was similar to mine. I stared in horror.

Eva used to say, I never knew my father either. In our family, we make children without men.

She made it sound like a blessing. The dark shadows around us were threatening. We kicked them in the ass if they came too close.

I was a bastard. I read it in the books.

I kept having nightmares. There was a shadow around me and

it became larger and larger and it turned into a blackout. It was so black it was like being blind. I groped around but there was nothing to touch, I was batting my arms in the void. I moved in circles. There was no wall to collapse against. It made me feel dizzy. I had to crouch on the ground to feel something solid and when I did, it gave way under me. The instant I toppled into the blackout is when I woke up screaming. I might've liked his eyes. They were striking, almost green. But liking his eyes would have been crossing over to the enemy. His beautiful eyes were a repulsive weakness and they repulsed me.

I spied on him from behind my bedroom door. Albertine didn't see me. She had pulled out my doll basket to distract me and she thought I was playing in there. She'd gone back to the kitchen to make some coffee, more likely to check up on him, make sure he wasn't going to cause more trouble. The door was ajar. I glued myself against it. From that safe distance he looked like any stranger. Just a guy. A little loud, but a guy. Say, a new neighbor who would have come in to ask something about the building, where to put the trash, what time the mail got in, something like that. Nobody worth paying much attention to. Green army jacket, jeans, a duffel bag. I wanted to see if he and Eva would touch each other, if I could read something in their bodies.

That's what I thought about, all the time, after that: if they'd kissed, if they'd held each other, if they'd done it together. They had to, since here I was. I tried to guess if there were still invisible threads of desire stretched between them. A few years later, when I had a more graphic idea of what it meant, I imagined them making love. I know her body so well, her small, extremely small waist, and on either side the hips and the chest opening up, widening, like an hourglass. She is wearing one of her little suits that exaggerate that silhouette, jacket cinched at the waist, curving around the hips, padded shoulders, rhinestone buttons, three-quarter sleeves with a little cuff showing bracelets on both wrists. He's got his hand in the opening of her jacket. He pushes it in. All she's wearing underneath is one of her silk bras, maybe an ice-blue one lined with off-white lace. He slips his fingers under the lace. The tips of his fingers reach the nipple. He starts playing with it. She leans against the couch, lets her legs go in front of her. The legs open up a little under the tight skirt. The movement pulls the skirt even higher and she opens her legs some more. He moves his other hand under the skirt. And so on. I didn't know if I was jealous of him or of her. Or of both.

Eva: Mimi was conceived in a hotel in Norfolk, Virginia, that was mostly used by hookers and their johns. We were driving back from Miami in a rental car. We should've stopped in a motel somewhere along the road, but we had gone to town for a drink, then we saw a movie, then we had another drink, and then, it was getting pretty late, we checked into that scuzzy hotel downtown that was the cheapest on the block. We registered as Mr. and Mrs. Frank Jackson and we went straight to bed. I was hot for him at that time. We'd barely locked the door when we were all over each other, he had his hands in my panties and my skirt was riding up my legs. We did it every which way. But mostly we fucked. That's what Frank Jackson was good at. He could fuck for hours and stay hard as a rock. I couldn't get my hands off his body in those days. It felt like we had barely fallen asleep, exhausted, when there was a knock at the door. I opened my eyes. I saw there was some vague light at the window filtering through the drawn drapes. I thought somebody next door had asked to be woken up early by the hotel clerk. There were more knocks and they were clearly on our door. I nudged Frank with my elbow. He woke up with a start.

Who's that? he asked.

Police.

Shit.

He jumped out of bed, put his pants on. Went to the door, opened it a notch.

What do you want?

ID check.

Two plainclothesmen walked in. It was a movie scene: Frank bare-chested, his pants hastily buttoned, bare feet. Me sitting up in bed, clutching the sheet up to my chin.

Who is she?

My wife.

Papers.

Well, of course we were not married. They raised hell. I was a whore. You couldn't come up to a hotel room with a man, let alone a black man, in the whole town of Norfolk, Virginia, if you were not married, at least in those days. They made me get up and get dressed, meanwhile waiting discreetly behind the door. Took us to the police station fenced in on the backseat of their car, sirens screaming into the night. They wrote a report, took our pictures, mug shots, front and profile, then released us and dropped us off near our car. We had to appear in court the next morning to defend our case. We spent the rest of the night in an all-night diner draining refills of watery coffee and laughing our heads off. We stopped laughing when we got to court. A lawyer we met in the elevator told us to say we were engaged and that there would be a two-hundred-dollar bail if we wanted to walk away free. We didn't have the cash. We gave them a bad check that they accepted and I showed them my Mexican ring as proof that I was his fiancée. Two weeks later I started to wait for my period. It never came. People said, you have no proof you conceived that night. It could've been the day before or two days later. But I know. He knew it too. He said he never fucked me so hard.

Come, Eva says. In a sweet-as-honey voice. So sweet Mimi wants to drink warm milk from her breast. Eva opens her arms, Mimi slides next to her on the bed, lifts the sweater, pulls the bra down, her lips suck at the nipple, for fun. I want to be a little baby, she says. Eva laughs, softly. She says, no matter how hard you try, nothing's going to come out of there. It's all dried up. Mimi pretends to cry. Baby-talks. I hungwy, Mom, weal hungwy. Mimi remembers nursing when she was tiny, not remembers with her eyes, remembers with her body, which takes the position, all by itself. She cuddles, leans her head on Eva's curved arm, makes a ball of her legs on Eva's lap. She sucks the nipple very softly. She just lost her two front teeth, the top ones. So, there's no bite. The soft/hard touch of the bare gum against her skin feels strange and raw, halfway between innocent suckling and incestuous touch. Eva laughs. Laughing permits you to work your way between tight spots. The tightness in her throat erupts into pearly laughter. Mimi giggles. Giggling makes her loosen her grip. The nipple slips out, glistening with saliva. Her head falls on Eva's lap. The little body slumps, shakes a little. Now, she is not pretending anymore. Eva tries to lift her head but Mimi sticks it in deep. She's sobbing. She buries herself into Eva's clothes. She's rooting, like a baby, her whole body is rooting, trying to stick itself in there and be one. When Mimi finally allows her head to be lifted up, her face is covered with tears. Neither of them says anything. Eva presses her against her, the little face within the fold of her neck, the two of them fitted, curves and hollows, like two intricate pieces of puzzle.

Eva is lying down on her back, her eyes on the cut-glass shade covering the ceiling bulb. It diffuses the light with a pale glow circled with a double halo of gray. Dusk darkens the room, signaling the beginning of that long waiting time before her act starts, fear slowly tightening her guts. She only moves to pop roasted peanuts by the handful in her mouth. Her lips taste salty and dry.

Frank Jackson's case was closed—a long time ago. You slam the door and you move on. It's neat. You move to a different room of your life. You clean it up, set it up, decorate it, people it. You change your hairstyle, your clothes. Instead of being stuck with one life you become chameleon, you get reborn. Except something in this case went wrong. This wasn't supposed to happen. There was a leak from another room. And it's not just Frank Jackson appearing in the room, it's the door bursting open and all that she left behind her spilling in, threatening to smother her.

Frank, cool and smooth. His eyes, clear and treacherous. He had a little mustache then, à la Clark Gable. She freezes on the smile and examines it carefully. It presents itself in a clearly detailed manner: a bit lopsided, one corner slightly more outstretched, close-up on the pores, on the chin, from which the stubble of beard is peeking, a semidimple on either side, the mouth big, full, the teeth dazzling white, except for one, close-up on the gold front tooth. Looking for the dimple again, but the front tooth keeps flashing its angry yellow. The smile is frozen, increasingly forced. The magic is gone. But not the threat. Just then the phone rings. Hi, says his voice. What's happening? I thought I'd go listen to you tonight. What time do you start? She shudders. Tonight? Yeah, tonight. Are you working? It would be easy to say no, but would he stop by anyway, would he check out the place? And then confront her with her lie? Eleven, she says. I'm not sure I want you around. Why? Scared of me? She laughs. Scared? (*Don't be silly.*) No. Tonight may not be the best night, is all. Later in the week might be better. Why? Your boyfriend gonna be around? Don't want me to meet him? Oh, cut it out, will you. No, I just . . . I feel I'm coming down with the flu. Won't be in top shape.

I'm leaving town, baby, he says. Can't wait around till Friday or Saturday night. I wanna check you out. Anyway a throaty voice is sexier.

She sighs with palpable relief. Anything he wants if he's leaving town so soon. What was she scared of anyway? Frank Jackson never stuck around anywhere for very long. A firefly that guy is. He won't show up for another five years. The extent of the damage will have been he got Mimi upset and she herself got a bad scare. Eva smiles to the cut-glass fixture. She likes the milky light that spills around it deep into the corners of the ceiling.

Well, okay-dokay, she says cheerfully, at your own risk. If you show up before I start, I'll have the barman give you a couple of freebees. For old times' sake.

Atta girl, Frank Jackson says, for old times' sake. Boy, you and I go back a long way, right?

Yep, she says. Well, cheerio.

Later.

She hangs up. Keeps her hand on the receiver for a long time. Just a fucking scare, she thinks, stretching her legs on the blue satin quilt. An ex-lover comes back into town. Big deal! What's the matter with me? Johnny, Johnny, she croons, flipping on her belly. Johnny-boy, won't you give me a call. Won't you give me a call Johnny-darling. Now. NOW!

Frank Jackson was already there when she walked in. Both elbows on the bar, chatting with Angelo, scrubbed clean, jacket-and-tie, regular shoes. She thought he looked like a traveling salesman. A shy date, nervously waiting for her. Totally out of character. She was going to pretend not to see him, glide toward the back. Hey, he called. Hey baby! Hey, Frankie! she called back, letting herself be kissed on the side of her mouth. Angelo, give him a drink on the house for me, will you? Angelo blinked. Sure, Miss Eva. She turned around and walked toward the back of the stage, dropping over her shoulder, I didn't mean quite that early, Frank. He smiled a killer smile to her back and said, I'm having a great time. Don't you worry about me.

He was sitting in front, at a little round table slightly to the side. It was a regular midweek night, not bad, a half-full house, people scattered all around, with a few empty tables here and there. But his presence seemed to fill up the place. When she took the mike from its stand she felt his eyes riveted on her. She tried to focus on it rather than chase it away, use its energy to feed her singing. But the link established that way bothered her, it created a complicity from him to her, and whatever complicity had existed between them had always been in his favor. So she struggled with it, she tried to switch the terms, let the power of the music, of her own voice take over and keep her in control, but as the sounds formed in her chest and spilled out, she could feel her power becoming seduction and Frank Jackson falling for it.

Not bad, he said when she came to him after the show. In fact, damn good.

He put his arm around her shoulders and she ducked.

Why don't you sit down, he said.

She signaled the waitress to bring her a club soda and she rested her chin between her open palms. He lit a cigarette and cupped his glass, swirling the gold scotch one turn before draining it.

So, who's your new guy?

She turned her eyes to him.

None of your business. Is that what you came here for: to quiz me?

He lifted both hands in apology. Putting on the brakes. Backtracking.

Just curious, he said. I mean, it's just natural, don't you think?

She shrugged.

Boy, you still Little Miss Stiffy.

For you, maybe.

It was her turn to work on her drink, keeping busy squeezing the slice of lemon and stabbing it with her straw.

So, what about you? she asked. What's happening? You're the one who's been around.

I was in South America, he said. On a boat. Sailor, you know. Commercial tankers.

All that time?

No. The last three years. Before that I was fucking up. I lived in Detroit, in Chicago, I had a band in New Orleans. I was really fucked up. I had to get out. I took a boat down to Brazil, I worked in the mines there. But it was shit work, slavery. It can kill a man. I had worked my way down there on a boat. I found another one in São Paulo. On boats, at least, there's the sea around you. The horizon is infinite.

And your music?

I came back for that. I was in Chicago. I just came from there. I'm putting a band together.

Where? In Chicago?

I'm thinking about New York.

New York?

Their eyes crossed for an instant. There was satisfaction in his. Territorial, as if he was getting his due.

And the money? Where is that coming from?

No problem. I made a bundle in South America. Now I can really start a band and not have to worry about anything.

Things change.

Yeah. Can you believe it? Hey, what about you? How you doing?

The old intimacy brought back by his voice and his body so close to hers made her recoil in horror.

I'm fine, she said. I'm doing okay.

Singing good? His chin pointed toward the room, the stage. Good place here?

It's okay.

You don't seem to be doing too well.

What do you mean?

Oh, you look tense, nervous. Boyfriend problem?

Why do you keep saying that! I'm fine. At least I was until you showed up.

She pulled a cigarette out of his pack, lit it with his lighter before he had the time to present the flame to her. He sat back.

How long are you going to do that?

Do what?

Again his chin encompassed the club, and more, the street, the whole of Manhattan.

That: the singing, working at night, with the kid.

She couldn't believe it. She stared him down. It was too

much. She laughed, a hard, splintery laugh, her throat as full of it.

What's so funny?

She stabbed her cigarette butt at the bottom of her glass.

It's not. Not funny at all. What exactly are you up to, Frank Jackson? Why did you show up in my life?

Hey, chill out, will you.

He motioned the waitress for another scotch. There was a jazz band getting ready on the stage, pulling acid stringy sounds at intervals. Eva noticed the room was filling up in spite of the late set. The band was a good one the owner had booked a few weeks ago. The word had quickly got around that they were hot and people flocked in.

He lit up again.

I am not showing up in your life. I am showing up in town. Stop thinking you're the center of the universe. Still as self-involved as ever, are you?

As he pulled on his cigarette, she saw him turn into a snake, there was poison dripping from his mouth. He had come to attack her and she could feel the effects already. Fury spread into her, a ball of fire rising from her center, crackling, all the way to her toes, her hair. She felt her cheeks burn. She put her cold sweaty hands on them, using her elbows to steady herself. The fire didn't come out. Outwardly she was ice. His smile was decidedly lopsided. He hadn't touched his fresh glass. The band was gathering on the stage. The buzz of talking and drinking was getting to a pitch before the hush.

Good band? he asked.

It released her. She dropped her hands to the table and pushed herself upright.

Leaving already? We barely had any time together.

It was good seeing you, Frank. I'm glad you stopped by. Good luck with your band.

He shrugged.

I'll be back soon. You'll have plenty of occasions to wish me luck.

He was holding her hand in his. Before she could pull it he performed a half bow, slightly raised from his chair.

Maybe, she said. 'Bye.

She waved at him casually as she headed for the door. He waved back, mockingly, forcing his smile into a sardonic twist. Then he leaned back against his chair, crossed his legs and drained his glass in one shot as the band attacked with a clarinet solo.

Eva has wrapped herself in her mouton coat, holding the collar up with both hands against the gusts of wind. Winter is coming early this year, fall not even gone. Icy air rolling down from the north. The nylon on her legs feels raw against her skin. People walk head down, each body coiled tight around itself. Nobody's loitering, hanging around. Doorways are filling up with homeless men and women spreading sheets of newspapers, the better-off ones unrolling foam mattresses and piling rags on top of them to make pillows. Even the drug dealers have withdrawn into the arcades, stomping in the cold, the hoods of their parkas pushed low on their foreheads. She listens to the sound of her heels on the pavement echoing in the night. The danger of New York streets at night is nothing compared to the presence of Frank Jackson in town. Each block she passes puts her at a safer distance from him, but only leaving the country or going to the other side of the world would make her feel safe enough.

Eva's curled in her slip in the middle of his bed, having discarded her dress and shoes and nylon hose that was eating at her skin, turned it into red rashes around the knees and the ankles. She's holding a glass of brandy balanced in the cup of her hands. The TV is on at the foot of the bed, no sound, just its quiet purring and the quick flip of the images, almost reassuring this time, anything would reassure her in that room, small, closed upon itself, shades drawn tight, heat hissing in the risers, a sealed world with its TV window, the outside world reduced to simple images contained within that box, glassed in, like sharks in a tank, safely kept at bay. And Johnny lying at her feet in dungarees and a white sleeveless T-shirt showing off his round shoulders, his nape cropped tight, and the long strand of hair shading his eyes, looking at her.

She swirls the brandy around in the round glass, sighs deeply.

I don't know. It's the past catching up with me.

What past?

Mine.

Does he have something on you?

You already asked me. It's not something on me he has. He has *me*, me then. He's got that part of me I don't want to be reminded of. A part of me that's a ghost, that's not me anymore. And I know he's hanging on to it.

What about you?

What about me?

Are you still hanging on to him?

Give me more brandy, she says.

He brings back the glass, half full. She stares at the orange-brown liquid for a long moment, as if the answer was going to emerge on its surface as a clear image from a crystal ball.

He's also Mimi's father.

But he has no rights.

Not legally.

Is that what you are scared about? That he would take Mimi away?

She laughs, more a sneer, really.

No. Not exactly. But he's going to have claims on her and on me.

Claims?

She slowly drains her glass. Rotates it on the tip of her knee. Johnny moves his hands from her ankles up her legs, touches the red rashes with the tips of his fingers. A soft light stroke.

Johnny's body is a geographical puzzle. The freckles on his back sand rolling under her feet. His ass craters, and the crack a canyon, the back of his legs, from top of the thighs to the balls of the feet, a trip down a winding river, his cock a wave she will ride, holding her balance as long as possible until the crash comes.

She says: it turns you on to suck women, right?

Yeah, he says, lifting his face, his chin glistening from her juice.

You get so hard from it, she whispers.

He can do it for hours, each stroke of his tongue melting her deeper. She pulls him toward her by his hard-on, takes it into her mouth. They make a perfect circle, sex to mouth, mouth to sex. Fuck Frank Jackson, she thinks. She opens her legs as wide as they can go to let his tongue be all over her. He's taking his time, going in and out, circling, coming back, uncovering every fold. She's more naked in front of him than she's ever been in front of any man. He is after her femaleness and she wants to lay it out for him like scattered rubies glittering in wet grass: for the taking.

Take me in now, he says.

Where?

He moves her on top of him.

Where? she asks again.

In your cunt.

There are words she wants to hear from his mouth. Words he can say, swearing, holding a bottle of beer by the neck, but that choke in his throat when he's talking about the real thing. Saying them is laying himself out for her.

He thrusts himself in so deep she thinks her cervix is opening up. She circles his mouth with her tongue, again and again. When the waves start coming in fast, she lets herself ride on, not holding back anymore. They both fall into the rhythm at the same time. It accelerates gradually until it reaches its peak.

A clear pitch that won't die, echoes of it run through their bodies pressed together for a long time after that.

Men and women are dying around them. They are dying of AIDS. One day we'll have to hide to experience pleasure. We'll have to go underground. Certainly the words of pleasure will be abolished. Then pleasure itself abandoned to wild beasts or vulgar animals. To dogs, to rats, or to selected healthy men and women in order to propagate the species. For the rest of humanity, pleasure will be sublimated, subliminal, going for the sublime. The touch of two hands, eyes acknowledging desire for the first time, riveted into each other. Pleasure will become fleshless, retreat into desire.

Eva, he says. We'll have to hide for this, when it'll be forbidden to make love.

To fuck, she corrects him. Making love belongs to a higher spirituality and to pure, rapturous, early sex. Fuck is what's going to have to be ripped out of our brains and cunts and pricks. Fuck will be another bad habit to get rid of for one's health. Then people will go to F.A. to free themselves of their disease.

F.A.?

Fuckers Anonymous.

You have to remember something, Eva says later. Sex has always been dangerous for women. You could get a baby from it, you could become a social pariah from it, you could die from it.

Die from it?

If you had a brother or a father jealous of your honor who would hastily shoot you down or pass you and your lover through his sword to keep the family's name pure and clear his reputation. And, of course, you could die giving birth.

[illegible] books pressed together for a time [illegible]

[illegible]

[illegible]

[illegible]

[illegible]

Eva has a dream

Eva had a dream, and the dream was about Frank Jackson. Some of the details had vanished already. For instance, she didn't remember why he found himself naked at her feet begging her to give him back his ear and her holding a bloody ear between her thumb and forefinger and

screaming in horror. In the blur that had subsided, there remained the memory of a series of interactions between them, emotionally charged scenes culminating in this astonishing scenario: Frank Jackson's body lying facedown on a carpet (or was it a bed?) and herself moving on him with a hatchet clutched in both her hands and plunging it into his neck.

It was not a dream she could conveniently tell Albertine, who was pressing various parts of a beige gabardine fabric that she had just finished cutting against a pattern, smallish octagonal or vaguely rectangular pieces which looked like they could end up as a jacket and which she mercilessly attacked with steaming iron. It was not a dream she would in any case have told in front of Mimi, who was sitting at the kitchen table, bent over a brightly colored sheet, adding and subtracting columns of double-figure numbers with a nervous concentration.

Mummy, Mimi says, stabbing the bars of her chair with an angry heel, help me, I need your fingers to count.

Why don't you use yours?

I need more than ten. I have to add eighteen and fourteen.

You'll need more than twenty fingers to count that.

What?

Do it one column at a time. It's easier.

Mummy! Give me your fingers.

Mimi's small fingertips tapping each one of hers in turn while Eva's mind keeps severing Frank Jackson's head at the same time.

I'm not finished, wait!

But Eva can't wait, she pulls her hands away. Frank Jackson blurs. She stands up. The need to make her limbs move, to block the images that overpower her. Mimi protests furiously the loss of her adding machine. Use your toes, Eva says, which makes Mimi laugh and take off her shoes, and then bang her fists in frustration against the floor because she can't keep track of both fingers and toes at the same time.

Some tea, Eva? Albertine asks without lifting her head from the ironing board, feeling tension in the air.

All right.

What's for dinner? asks Mimi, laboring over a 2 and a 5, suddenly marveling at their resemblance.

Look, Ma, she cries. A "five" is like a "two," but the wrong way.

No. No memory can be so strong. But it is, it invades her. The dam breaks and it floods her. The memories come back as fragments, severed limbs floating toward her as if across a swamp, bumping into roots, half submerged in the syrupy waters. Like this cut-up body stuffed in plastic bags they found on St. Mark's Place. As fragments they have a bad taste. They are not fully alive anymore, they come back as ghosts. His gold tooth flashing, his prick, hard, angry, the shape of his toes, square-cut. His taste for pickles and candy bars. His laugh, incredibly alive in Mimi's mouth and the down-turn of her lips when she sulks. Didn't get it from mimicking him, couldn't have. Never saw him until the other day. It had to be in her blood. Mimi, who's now busy pasting heart and penguin stickers in her notebook and drawing trees and cats and dogs and alligators around them with balloons coming out of their mouths telling a story in shrill dialogue. And then Albertine turns on the news, and what else is new, but the same gunshots, kid that fell from a seventeenth-floor window in a project on the Lower East Side, progress of AIDS in Africa, girl victim of incest who somehow got hold of a revolver and shot her father through the heart, Republican big shot convicted of bribery, assaults on blacks by white mob in Chicago suburbs and New Orleans, Glasnost and bilateral taunting between the U.S. and the U.S.S.R. Johnny receding way back behind the general assault inside and outside of her. Vanishing to a small point of pleasure, so fine, so acute it hurts.

Wake up, Albertine taps her on the arm. Your daughter needs a bath. Dinner's going to be ready in ten minutes. We could use your hands around here. Never mind your brain and heart.

Mimi barely needs someone to give her a bath. Certainly not for the cleaning job that she can perform perfectly and intensely when she puts her mind to it, but rarely wants to and doesn't let Eva do (she's more accommodating with Albertine). She demands an audience, though: listening to long conversations held *mezzo voce* in a lilting high pitch between half-naked Ken and two or three Barbies: *no, but I don't think so, my dear; oh please, pretty please; you MUST do that, otherwise . . . oh, you have such a pretty dress! well, sir, this will be fifteen dollars. Thank you so very much!* watching jets of water spraying out of nose drops dispensers, applauding Mimi's magical transformation into a mustachioed old man by means of foam bath lather, being the recipient of tons of water splashed out of the tub followed by a wet and dripping body landing in your arms.

And then watching her eat, even though Mimi complains: you're always looking at me when I'm looking at you. To which Eva asks: what are you looking at me for, then? And then putting her to bed, listening to her read a book in a still hesitant flow, tripping over hard words, and then lying next to the fresh tight skin, not a skin really, the perfection of a taut peach-skin satin that she strokes with her closed knuckles, then the back of her hand, gently going back and forth on that place between the jaw and the lips that makes Mimi smile in her sleep, and tiptoeing in the dark back to Albertine's kitchen into the smell of a beef *ragout* still warm on the stove.

You look tired, *ma petite*, Albertine says.

I almost fell asleep with Mimi.

I usually do, Albertine admits. Sit down.

She puts a plate full of stew and boiled potatoes swimming in the gravy in front of Eva.

So? Albertine says.

So what?

Eat.

Eva starts eating, then asks again: so what?

Albertine nods.

You're not going to fool me. I know something's bothering you. What's the story with Frank?

Eva doesn't answer.

Did he talk to you?

Eva lifts her head and looks at Albertine for a moment.

About what?

So he didn't.

He came to hear me sing.

I bet he liked it.

Yep, he did.

But he's left town now, right?

Yes.

Albertine gets up, stacks the leftover dishes on the table, making several trips to the sink, showing disapproval with her backside.

If you don't want to talk about it, up to you, she says, her back turned to Eva.

He said he was going to come back, Eva says.

Albertine still doesn't turn around. Her well-padded back and shoulders are active above the sink following the back-and-forth movement of her hands scrubbing and rinsing the dishes.

He's nothing to you, *ma fille*, she says, but he's Mimi's father.

Eva gets herself a tea bag and waits near the stove for her water to boil.

I don't think he cares about me. But he's not letting go.

He hasn't changed, Albertine says, flatly, wiping the dishes now and putting them away in the closet over the counter. *Fais-m'en un, s'il-te-plaît*, get me one, too, she says again, pointing to the tea bag Eva's dropping into a mug.

They both sit down, at an angle from each other, as they've done hundreds of times, elbows on the flowered oilcloth, hands cupped around the hot mugs.

Du rhum? Albertine asks, getting a bottle from the dresser and pouring some in both cups without waiting for Eva's answer. Then she adds two pats of butter which melt, leaving an oily film on the steaming surface.

In the tea, rum doesn't burn raw like straight up, it gently warms the womb, expands out to the limbs and the chest, softens the mood and loosens the tongue, makes the body slump a bit more against the back of the chair, but it requires a blazing fire in a fireplace to accomplish its full effect, and of course Albertine's tenement apartment doesn't feature one, although she recalls the one that was constantly going in her own grandmother's farm. *J'étais juste une p'tite mioche, j'sais pas, quatre, cinq ans, p'ête bien.* She says she can't picture that fire without smelling the lard sizzling in the pan hanging from a hook in the mantel. She says she has no idea why that's what she remembers since most likely it must've been soups that were cooking in the caldron and the smell in the room must've been the acid one of green sap and the mellow one of dry chestnuts popping in the flames.

Fancy thinking of Albertine growing up in a fishermen's village, before what, twenty, thirty years in New York, first busting her butt at the Michelin plant in Jersey, then gradually working the help ladder of French restaurants, from busgirl to waitress to cashier (maîtres d's were all men), doing some sewing on the side until she took the plunge and established herself *à son compte* as a seamstress.

It's good here, though, sighs Albertine. There's not a day that I am not grateful to whomever (she makes a sign with her right hand meaning some almighty, infinite presence), fate, if you will, to've brought me here, and kept me here.

Even though you never see your kids, even though you're not so much better off than your family was?

My two kids! Leave them alone, *celles-là!* Yeah, even though whatever. I am okay, I'm taking care of my own business. Nobody's bothering me.

Yeah. I feel the same, too, Eva says, circling the flowers on the oilcloth with her forefinger. No matter how hard it is, I'm better off here than I was there. Simple as that. And I didn't run away from the potato famine or the Eastern European pogroms.

It can be bad in other ways, Albertine says.

—

But she feels and looks like a zombie. Something frantic in the eyes. A void. As if something had caved in. Instead of the healthy plumpness, fullness, a shriveling. Drying up. Each object she touches, looks at, absorbing her fear.

I think I'm going to sleep in Mimi's room tonight, Eva says. Don't bother. I'll get the foam mattress in the closet. She won't even know it.

Ah, pour ça, non. This kid sleeps like a log.

Frank Jackson was still naked. Now he was kneeling as if to pray, or beg. But she couldn't see anyone who was in front of him or whom he could be talking to. She herself wasn't there. Or he might've been going to confession. He was moving slightly on his knees. She couldn't tell if it was to move forward or just because his legs were getting stiff, to get the blood going. Wherever she was, she must've been facing him, because she could see his shriveled prick and nuts hanging between his legs. He was moving again, rocking back and forth on his knees, this time it was clear he was trying to move forward and she thought, what an uncomfortable position, why doesn't he stand up, and then of course she realized (now she could see him from the back) that he had a ball and chain fastened at his ankle and his hands were attached behind his back and the ceiling seemed to have just dropped to a few inches above his head, he was now going through a kind of tunnel, painfully progressing down the narrow passage, maybe it wasn't a tunnel, there seemed to be rays of light coming at intervals from both sides, maybe it was a hallway with a low ceiling, now the walls appeared to be made of stone, like a medieval abbey, they were slightly sweaty, actually patches of dampness were becoming apparent as he moved along (she felt like a camera following him, like two cameras, to be exact, one in front, one in back, cornering him from both angles), maybe it was a tunnel, after all, the dampness seemed to point to an underground passage, and the light could have come from slots at the top of the walls, no, she couldn't see any slots, she couldn't even see a ceiling anymore, just an upward well of darkness with these rays of light beaming down from somewhere in the middle of the night, but then the light weakened and he seemed to slow down, she thought maybe his knees were wearing out, but it was worse than that, he threw himself upon the ground, starting to crawl like a worm, ball and chain and all: the passage had shrunk to a rabbit hole, a cylinder barely wide enough for a man to crawl through, and she was the one crawling now, trying to carry her weights and feeling the sweaty walls tightening themselves around her, squeezing her in, she tried to move backward but they had shrunk at the back of her too and she tried to scream but the scream was swallowed up into the night and . . .

It's Eva with bleached-blond hair, short curls piled on top of her head, she's got a dark gray suit on. She's running along a train, she doesn't run fast enough, she's wearing her high heels, the real high ones that make her trot daintily but much too slowly. Mimi is at a window in the train. The conductor whistles. The train is beginning to move. Mimi knows the train is taking her to a place in the mountain where she's never been before. She's alone in the train. Nobody's traveling with her. She's wearing a fur coat with a little fur hood and she's too hot. The window is wide open, but it's still pretty high for her, in order to rest her elbows on it she has to stand on tiptoe and even then, she can't see that far out. The train is moving faster, it puffs in a lot of noise. There are people on the quay waving handkerchiefs and yelling good-byes, some wiping their eyes. Eva is running after the train, she's blowing kisses to Mimi, but she can't keep up. Mimi is losing sight of her, she catches a glimpse of Eva waving her little clutch bag up in the air, then nothing.

Mommy, Mommy! Mimi moans and flings her arms about.

Eva kneels next to her. But as abruptly as it came, the moaning returns into regular breathing and Eva goes back to her mattress and lies wide awake in the dark.

Mimi: at school I used to say my father was a doctor and Albertine was my babysitter (I guess she was, in a way). I made up stories about her, that she had been a chef in a fancy French restaurant on the Upper East Side and that now she was our cook and that she prepared us French specialties like *coquilles St. Jacques* and *boeuf Bourguignon* and that she did our laundry and cleaned up our house and sewed our clothes (that was not untrue either, except it was her house). They looked at me funny because how come, if I was coming from such a rich family that could afford such quality service, how come I was just like them otherwise, how come the Barbies I brought to school were beat up and kept losing their heads and how come their clothes were torn and how come I didn't have a talking doll and how come (that was the most telling point) I didn't invite them over to my big apartment near Central Park where I had a big, gigantic room and a loft bed, to play with my five Cabbage Patch dolls and my very own electric train and my life-size dinosaur and my two dogs and my cat and my gerbil. I don't think they believed me either. I realized soon enough that I might have gone too far, but it was too late. The rumor had spread in my class and then from class to class as I moved in grades and I couldn't invite anyone from my school to Albertine's place. The only (rare) visits were kids from the neighborhood or kids I used to know as a tot from the playground.

Eva didn't know any of that. I don't think she ever wondered why I didn't have friends over or why I didn't get to sleep over at anybody's place. She just found me there, plop, near Albertine, kept toasty warm and well fed. But Albertine was a good cook, that is the truth, I swear.

The way Mimi says words like . . . coyote. Just like Joni Mitchell in that old song she used to sing, way back. "Coyote." At first Eva didn't know what the word "coyote" meant. But she liked the sound of it. The pure, perfect American sound. That she, Eva, can only approximate. Amazed to have made an American child. You teach me American, she says to Mimi. All you have to do is to sit on my lap, I'll absorb it through my skin. Mimi doesn't know what *absorb* means, but she laughs. She says, I'll teach you, repeat after me: I-will-absorb-it-through-my-skin.

Having a child, Albertine once told Eva, opens up something in you that will never close up. Women are already open anyway, Eva answered. *Un peu plus, un peu moins* . . . a little more, a little less. The life juices flow to and fro. The flow, the constant flow makes you whole, never started, never completed. Like a river running its course.

Mommy, you slept here, in my room, Mimi exclaims, first thing in the morning, thin ray of light coming in through the window. Then: I had a bad dream. She sits up and rubs her eyes simultaneously. You had put me in a train that was going to the mountain and I was all alone in the train, there were all these people on the platform and the train started and you ran after the train, you were saying good-bye to me, but you were wearing your high heels, the real high ones, you know, and you couldn't run fast enough, and you tried to say something to me, I think, but I couldn't hear and I felt so sad I started to cry.

She isn't sure about the end, that she started to cry, but she adds it for effect, just in case. It works. Eva takes her in her arms and cuddles her. You called me, Eva says, but you didn't wake up. Were you very very scared?

Mimi sobs lightly. Ye-es.

But now you're not anymore?

No-o.

Your mommy is here and you're not in a train and I'm not running after the train, and I'm not even wearing my high heels. See: I'm bare feet.

No, you're not.

Yes, I am.

No, you're not.

Eva puts her bare foot right in Mimi's face and wiggles her toes under her nose.

Mimi cracks up.

Mom, stop it. It's disgusting.

Now will you admit that I am bare feet?

Eva tickles her in the neck with her toes.

Mimi's in stitches. Giggles. Rolls over on the bed.

Okay, okay, okay, she says. You win!

Mimi (2)

Mimi: Eva believed men were like drugs. She craved them, but deep down she thought she'd be better off without them. At first things were sweet as pie, then she couldn't wait to get it over with. *Bon débarras!* was her final word. Good riddance! Until she met a new one and then she

had this funny crooked smile when she pronounced his name or was asked about him as if she had to strain to keep her mouth from smiling too much and giving herself away. But they all turned out to be bastards or jerks. Later I realized she had two separate lives. Then I thought she had her bright side and its shadow. She was a mom with a shadow. Like a shadowy past, or a shadowy life. This was the way things were with us.

I think at times she would have liked to blend the two lives together. She would have liked me to live with her. At least, sometimes she fancied it. She'd decide I'd go to her place for the weekend and she'd bring some of my clothes in a suitcase and put them in the drawers of a little dresser near the living room couch and put my toilet things, toothbrush, hairbrush, barrettes for my hair in the cabinet over the bathroom sink. She'd give me a bath in the huge white porcelain bathtub that was really smooth and shiny, I still remember the cracks in the white tiles along the wall, above the faucet, she'd have bought food from a take-out place, hot food that she warmed up on her stove, homey kind of food, soup, stew, stuff like that, and she laid it all on the coffee table in front of the couch, over a piece of pastel fabric that worked as a tablecloth and she put out real plates and her silverware and glasses and real napkins rolled into napkin holders and we sat in front of each other on pillows taken down from the couch and we'd pretend this was the way we always ate our meals and that the food had been lovingly prepared by her and not just poured out of cartons and she'd make sure I ate of everything, soup, mashed potatoes, string beans, even though it was all kind of soggy and bathed in too much gravy, and then we'd clear the table together and do the dishes, and she'd pull my pajamas out of a drawer as if that was my pajama drawer and not the drawer she had just emptied of cigarette packs and matches and coasters, and she would make a bed on the couch and read me a story just like Albertine did and hold my hand until I fell asleep.

I would stay a weekend or three or four days there with her, if she had days off, and she'd take me to school and we'd arrive late, she usually overslept and I had to wake her up and make sure she gave me breakfast and that she had enough change for the bus or I'd have forgotten my homework and the teacher would scold me and I cried, so I took my clothes back to Albertine's and I cried because I missed seeing Eva, but then everything would fall back into place and then a month or two later we'd start the cycle again.

So I rarely saw her men. Sometimes they'd come and pick her up at Albertine's and I'd get a peek at the door. With Johnny it was different. Not necessarily more stable, but he was a regular. I got used to his voice on the phone and he always asked me how things were going and he brought me a toy or some ribbon for my hair and he sometimes went to the park with us or took us to the restaurant. He drove an old poppy-red Studebaker Lark he had inherited from his grandfather. I loved that car, it had this nice black upholstery with a herringbone pattern and a dashboard with wood paneling and small round buttons that I tried turning in all directions. They'd let me sit between them in the front, the three of us squeezed together, and Johnny had his arm wrapped around us along the back of the seat, and it felt warm and secure between his flesh and Eva's flesh, like one body. I liked Johnny. Mostly I liked that he was around sometimes, that he'd carry me on his shoulders in the street to get from our building to his car and that he let me order whatever I wanted at the restaurant like a grown-up even if I didn't like the food once it got to my plate and I left it sitting there. Eva frowned at me, turning her eyes into switch-blades, but he joked about it and made her laugh and he ate what was left on my plate. That was something I liked about men, when I got a chance to see one, how much they ate, and how heartily, and it was just like their bodies needed more fuel.

I didn't see Johnny very often, so I could fantasize about him, I could make him up, reality didn't get in the way. As a result of that, I was surprised that whenever I was bad or I had a temper tantrum, Eva'd say, you could be Johnny's daughter, he's as bad as you, and he doesn't have the excuse to be a kid. I couldn't imagine Johnny having a temper tantrum, that's not the way I saw him at all, and when she said that, it made me want to stick my tongue out at her, which I did, because, in any case, I didn't like to be compared to anyone, I wanted to be uniquely bad.

The hotel night guard (2)

There's another fellow, lately, I swear he's been looking for her. Kind of nondescript, by that I mean medium height, mousy-colored hair, sports jacket, youngish, so nondescript in fact that at first I didn't realize it was the same fellow. Was dressed differently, I guess, or one time was wearing

sunglasses, or a trench coat, that changes a man right away, another time a pair of dungarees, but very clean, pressed, I thought he was a guest in the hotel, just because he seemed familiar, then I realized he was looking for someone, or maybe waiting. He was close to the desk, kind of hesitant, I asked him if I could help him, but he nodded, not looking me in the eyes, kinda looking away toward the lobby, then he turned around and that was it. I didn't see him for a long time after that. Well, of course, I wasn't thinking about him, and then he reappeared one day, maybe weeks later, and I thought, here comes the weird fellow again, and it struck me just then, say it was an intuition, but I am like that, sometimes I can just . . . smell . . . things, it struck me that he was looking for Miss Eva, I didn't see him with her, nor, actually, did I ever see him around when she came down or came back from work, but I had a funny idea that his presence had something to do with her.

At first, I thought it was maybe an ex of hers, or, you know, a—how shall I put it—a client of hers? But he never asked about her, or as far as I know he never went upstairs. I asked the day man, and he didn't remember anybody like him, but, as he said to me, I see a lot of people every day, how should I know, maybe if you showed me a photo of the guy, maybe then I could tell you.

So one day I see him again, he has a newspaper open in front of him, but I have a feeling he is not reading it at all, and something clicks in me: he's using the newspaper as a cover, of course, the old PI trick. So I go up to him and I say: you looking for someone, bub? And he looks at me blankly like he's never seen me before and has no idea what I'm talking about, and he drops: as a matter of fact, I am waiting for somebody. A guest of the hotel, sir? I ask, as politely as I can. And he says, none of your business. And I say, oh, but yes, sir. Who waits in the lobby of this hotel is my business. And then he totally changes attitude, he folds his newspaper and shifts around on his feet, looks at his watch, and says, muttering, like, it's late, maybe she went down already. I'd better get going. And he walks away, not looking at me.

Of course, I have no proof. And I'm not saying he is a private eye, either. Actually, I don't think he is, a private eye would have been sharper than that, unless he's playing dumb as a cover-up. But then that gets complicated. Anyway, I am concerned about it, and I am convinced that he has something to do with Miss Marquand, and I think she should be told about it, if she doesn't know yet. So last night when she comes back from work I give her her mail and I give her a big smile like I always do, Miss Marquand is a woman you want to smile at, and she always smiles back, so it pays, but this time with the smile I lean forward on the counter and I ask her: has someone been bothering you lately, Miss Marquand, a man I mean, in the hotel? And she looks me in the eye, her big black eyes with the black makeup around them, and she looks astonished, but at the same time, maybe there was some fear there, I couldn't swear, but it wouldn't mean anything, women always think of the worst, there's always some fear in them that comes right out for the smallest thing, so it may have been just that. Anyway she says, no, Morris, what do you mean? Do you know something I don't know? I say, never mind, Miss Marquand, forget what I say. I don't want her to start worrying maybe for nothing. But of course now she wants to know, so I tell her about the man. She asks me what he looked like and what kind of clothes he was wearing and she seems relieved, like she was thinking of somebody else and this one clearly doesn't have anything to do with the one she was thinking about. But she asks at what time he comes around, and she thinks for a minute, then she tells me to call her if he comes around again and she happens to be in her room at that time, she'll come down, discreetly, and I'm supposed to point him out to her. We agree on a sign, and then she leaves and goes to the elevator looking satisfied, I think. Even though with women you can never tell. Gosh, I wouldn't want anything bad to happen to that one.

The Times Square Rapist

My teacher says that when we die we go to heaven. Is that true, Mom?

Mimi's sipping orange juice through a funny straw decorated with a little orange-colored orange in paper fanning out around the tip. She thinks the straw is neat and she takes her time sip-

ping and blowing bubbles in the tall glass. Eva's bought a bunch of them and each time Mimi comes to visit she gets an orange or a lemon or a pineapple straw and she perches on a tall stool at Eva's kitchen counter, pretending to be at a bar. They're sitting side by side, each with a drink in hand at the counter, Mimi sporting a pair of Eva's high heels, and somebody's business card rolled tight and Scotch-taped to look like a cigarette dangling between her index and middle fingers.

I don't know. Some people think so. Catholics. They think there's this beautiful place up in the sky somewhere that you go to if you've been good all your life.

And if not you go to hell.

Right.

Do people go to hell?

I don't know. Nobody knows, really. Nobody's come back to tell us.

I wish I had nine lives, like a cat.

Some people believe human beings have several lives. You die, and then you come back as somebody else. As a little boy, for instance, or as a spider. But most people don't remember what they were before.

Mimi sucks on her straw, Lolita-like, her lips pursed, leaning over the counter on her elbows.

I'd like to come back with straight blond hair next time.

What I like about Johnny, Eva writes in her notebook, is this (she thinks for a moment, sucking her pen): his cock. It's large, thick, red. When it's hard, it reaches up to his belly button. She stops. She writes: his eyes, the expression around his eyes, the green-gray-brown flickering changing color with the light. The little squinting lines when he smiles. When he gets confused and he doesn't want to show it, he turns on the smirk, self-deprecatory, and shrugs his shoulders, it's like a little dance, a pirouette he does to pull out of tough spots. The way my body stretches next to his. His presence hits me. Instant high. I don't even need to look at him. The way he runs his fingers, the tips of his fingers down my side, from the shoulder down, lingering on the waist, the hip.

Eva hears on the radio: Three women who have been raped in the Times Square area last August and September, possibly by the same man, the so-called Times Square rapist, are testing HIV-positive. It is feared that they contracted the AIDS virus through exposure from the rapist. The news bulletin describes the man as Caucasian, five feet eleven to six feet, in his late twenties or early thirties, thin blond hair, horn-rimmed glasses, about 150 pounds.

Hi, Lola? Open up for me, baby, open wide. You're so red and your hair is so black. So much hair, you have a line of hair all the way up your navel. Your asshole is full of black hair. And you're so red inside. Oh, you have your period. The blood flows out red, let me suck it up. I have it all over my mouth, my face. Let me kiss you with your blood. See: I kiss your belly. There's the bloody trace of my lips on your white skin.

Gently, Eva moves the receiver away from her ear. The voice falls into an inaudible whisper. She makes a note in her notebook. *Max, November 12. 11 P.M.*

Lola, Lola, do you hear me, are you there? the voice says, louder. She puts the receiver back to her ear and mouth. Yes, she says, I am here. I am with you, Max. Go on. Baby, he says in his hoarse but clearly educated voice, tell me you're sitting on my face, you're spreading your pussy on my mouth. Yes, Max, she repeats obediently. I'm sitting on your face, I'm spreading my pussy on your mouth. When he is finished, she unplugs the recording device that allows her to tape him and turns off the tape recorder.

Times Square. The peep shows are full of men jerking off in their pants, drooling in front of pictures of women's and men's asses and mouths out of which stick tumescent penises. The crowd wheels away, round and round the Deuce, pressing on the sidewalk. The peddlers thread their way in and out of the crowd, pushing crack, fake Gucci watches, stolen calculators, empty VCR boxes, umbrellas because the snow is turning to rain, little plastic birds; kids, barely teenagers, peddle their own bodies in the doorways.

Galoshes in the melting snow. The peculiar noise they make. In the splattered mud/slosh making waves and curvy patterns on the cement, into which the spike heels splash, splash, splash.

The huge condom ad flashes hard and fast at the top of the Allied Chemical building. It shows a bigger-than-life-size couple, shyly smiling at each other. The only way you know it's a condom ad is from the copy written underneath in sober squarish lower-case letters, saying: Are you worth dying for? and the name of the condom company underneath. For which Eva always substitutes another ad in her mind, of her own making: a huge close-up of a woman's finger delicately gloved in clear rubber, held up in front of a pair of pursed luscious red lips.

What are we going to do, now that we can't mix, drip and wet into each other?

We still do.

We're lucky.

We can wrap ourselves in Saran Wrap and only touch each other through clear plastic.

We can fuck our brains out, then commit suicide.

We can fantasize.

We can fetishize.

It's like making love in the middle of war. It's not the noise of bombs crashing they hear, but of bodies dropped one by one into the common grave.

The city is in a state of siege.

Did you think about leaving it?

And go where? No. This is where I belong. Everywhere else reminds me that the world is dying.

But the world is dying here. Right here. People are dying in the streets every day. Lying down with exposed wounds on their legs, big patches of purulent flesh and swollen ankles. People are dying in the hospitals, still hooked to their blood bag.

Their first time together they groped for each other's skin as though it were water for their bodies dying of thirst. They sighed and fell into each other's eyes like into a deep well. They sank into each other. A line traced by a finger, followed by the stroke of a palm, was ecstasy.

Now night has fallen. The reddish light from the street signs comes through around the edges of the window. There's a peculiar glow to their naked bodies as she squats above him, her full breasts heavy, her backside curving out, just a place for his hands to rest, to dip in.

That night Max called again. It seemed she had just heard his voice, it was so familiar, so close. Lola, he said, Lola, is that you? She was surprised and fumbled to adjust the recording plug on the phone, but she didn't want to turn on the light, Johnny was groaning, half awake, grumbling, who's that? She said, sorry, I was asleep, can you call me back tomorrow, just as Max launched into one of his monologues, something about her big breasts pressed into his face and she quietly dropped the receiver into its cradle, unplugging the phone simultaneously, realizing then that he had called her on her regular line, not her work line, and she shuddered, wondering how he could've found out her other number, or her real name. Who's that, Johnny asked again, as she lay down under the covers, but he went back to sleep without waiting for an answer, his hand pressed in her crotch.

The impression of a foot on sand

A stranger in a strange land. Don't you feel like a pariah, sometimes? That was Frank Jackson, back then, thinking he was damned perceptive. I laughed, and I said, yeah, I love it. I like to be the Other, an alien. That way I can spy on you, and you can't get me. He hadn't gotten it at all.

Actually it gives me a lightness, a weightlessness as if I could escape my fate. A horrible fate, behind bars somewhere in France, the drudgery routine of a life of respectability, maybe secretary in a medium-sized company located at the edge of town or a doctor's assistant, or a civil servant with the SNCF, the national train company, with excellent benefits and a pension for life. Albertine knows what I mean. She erupts from her kitchen taking her apron off, holding it by the ties as if she was going to throw it at her boss's feet. *Un pays de petits fonctionnaires.* A nation of bureaucrats. And petty minds. But smart, Albertine, oh so smart. She is back with two cups of coffee. She makes it American style, drip drip drip from the large paper filter with just enough milk to cloud it and that endearing taste of cardboard juice. She hands me one with too much sugar and I suck on it with pursed lips to avoid burning my tongue. Smart, my ass, she says. Although she doesn't exactly say that because the conversation is conducted in French, but I approximate. I am faithful to the spirit.

Pêtent tous plus haut qu'leur cul. They all fart higher than their asses, she continues. Then she throws me a sly glance from the corner of her eye, still holding her mug of coffee. But how would you know, she says, your family must've had a high-slung ass!

She thinks I come from an uppity background. She doesn't know for sure but she guesses. She says, I've got to guess because you don't volunteer anything. And I tell her, keep guessing, it's good for you, stimulates your imagination. It drives her nuts, at times, that I don't tell her my story. But I think she knows enough about me as it is. She's got my whole present laid out in front of her. More than I would have wanted anyone to know. Sometimes I think, Albertine, she's beginning to know too much, it might get dangerous for me. And what do you do to someone who knows too much? It's not that she would talk (who'd really be interested in me who doesn't already know me?), but that she knows. She's got that picture of me in her head and she's holding it up while she talks to me. And it makes me queasy. I think that's the same with Frank Jackson. He knows too much. Or he thinks he knows. I don't know which is worse. When they start knowing me or drawing their little picture of me, they start possessing me. I feel trapped inside their heads. They try to make me fit there, inside of them. And I can't breathe. I start kicking around. I see them armed with their butterfly nets chasing after me and I duck.

I like a little mystery around me, I tell her. She says: I don't even know if Eva is your real name. I am content to smile, quizzically.

I came here to erase my past. New York is a city of oblivion. Of course I didn't know that, at first. I thought I was traveling. Discovering the world.

Johnny likes that mystery. He strokes the inside of my hand and my arm, following the pale veins with his fingers, and he says, sometimes I think you had another life before this one, and another yet before that one and that you bore a different name in each one and that you lived in a different country and that you were a different person. I stretch next to him. I say maybe, but I don't remember. Johnny likes to imagine me as some exotic female emerging from the sea, like Ursula Andress in *Dr. No*, water streaming down my face, wet hair cascading over my shoulders. Or Venus in fur reclining in the shadow play of a clearing in the middle of a thick forest. Which suits me just fine. I see him as an urban warrior born of the asphalt jungle and given to romantic flights. Actually, he's from Jersey and he grew up in a brick split-level where his mother still lives with the same mustard-colored shag carpeting and oak veneer living room set with the fake tulip centerpiece in the middle of the dining room table. I was there once, on a Sunday afternoon. We took the train back and forth and had a dinner of fried chicken with potato chips washed down with Diet Coke at four o'clock in the P.M. on the kitchen table (wrought-iron stand with a brown imitation wood top) while his mother (who didn't eat because she was on a diet) chain-smoked mentholated cigarettes and showed me her latest crocheted creations running the gamut from throw pillows to flamenco doll dresses to tiny Santa Clauses to hang on the Christmas tree. Johnny and I had a fight that night on the train coming back. He said I had no respect and no understanding of the American people and their roots and that I was an uppity snotty French broad.

I liked his mother, actually. I liked her husky voice and I liked that in spite of the crochet and the dead furniture she looked like she was poised in the middle of her antiseptic-scrubbed house like in a motel room, ready to fly. She wasn't buried alive in it. She was floating above it, pushing rings of smoke and surveying the horizon. But I never went back to Jersey. I didn't have use for Johnny's past either. I wasn't sure whether it was because it undercut my vision of him too deep or whether I didn't believe in that past. It seemed so plastic I thought Johnny too had had a previous life, or his soul had been brought up somewhere else while his body was trained as a suburban boy with a doting mother.

In the snowy dusk the pink glow of Times Square filters through the half-closed shutters. Eva waits for Johnny in the dark. The room is stifling. In spite of the rampant poverty and precarious economy of numerous segments of the population, the hotel manages to pump full steam ahead, rattling its heating system, day in, day out. In the soft, moon-like light, her place seems to be flying through the clouds, the only view from her bed being the top-floor windows of a commercial building peopled with headless mannequins and dismembered arms and legs, ghostly behind the dirty glass, and a strip of white lead sky above.

Johnny brings the wet raw cold in with him. He shakes the snow off his soles on the doorstep, then sits down, with his hat and his jacket still on, to unbuckle his boots, blowing the icy air out of his lungs in noisy breaths.

Eva watches him peel himself down to his essential elements: jeans ripped at the knees, oversize shirt tucked into the waistband, thick woolen socks with a hole in the vicinity of the right big toe.

Stripped further, his body will reveal his amazing vulnerability, the soft whiteness of the shoulders, the hips, the sinuous line of the outstretched arm, long hips, folded legs, devoid of their street armor of leather and metal buckles.

But not yet. He's coming back from a rehearsal and his energy comes out staccato, wild, he paces her small bedroom, stretching his body, taking space, disappearing to grab a beer from the fridge, acting out his guitar playing, humming the song he just performed.

She watches him from the bed, where she's propped herself up on the pillows. She has this strange feeling that he is acting right now, that he is creating a scene for her, the talented musician in the throes of creativity, laying his heart bare for his mistress. When he runs out of steam, she pulls a cigarette out of his pack and lights it.

I got a letter from my mother today, she says.

You were not listening to me.

Yes, I was. I think you were good, in your part of angst-ridden young star.

He looks at her, wavering on that thin line between feeling offended or siding with her and laughing at himself.

Not so young anymore, he says, breaking into a lopsided grin. Gimme that. He takes the cigarette from her fingers. I am the smoker and the drinker. You're the one who's supposed to stay healthy.

You didn't listen to me either.

Yes, I did. What about that letter?

My grandmother is getting worse.

I didn't know you had a grandmother.

Well, I do, and a mother. And a brother, and a father somewhere although I don't know where. I just don't talk about them.

Johnny sits down next to her on the couch.

What's the matter with her?

She's very old and she's gaga. She raised me. My grandmother, I mean.

He looks at her. Her black hair is falling straight across her cheeks and all he can see is the tip of her nose and the upturned curve of her lips like points of reference in a lost face.

He stubs out his half-smoked cigarette on the edge of a candle holder and gets off the bed. His shoulders, waist and hips are outlined against the fading light. The snow has stopped. It has left a crisp layer of icing underlining every horizontal detail of the street architecture. The headless models in the window across the street are framed in immaculate white like a sadistic Christmas window displaying ripped arms and feet and torn crotches to the shoppers.

Great view, isn't it?

Yeah.

Johnny walks back to the bed, lies down alongside Eva. He lifts the curtain of hair from her face. Her eyes shine, watery.

You crying?

She says no. She says, you know, I think it's the end of the line here. There's no place else. No past, no future. Nothing.

Mimi is always asking her questions like: Mom, what did you do when you were a little girl? Did you have a daddy? Did you live in a house or in an apartment? Did you live in a big city? When did you learn how to read? What was your mommy's name? Is she still alive, why can't I get to see her? Am I her grandchild? Does she have other grandchildren? Where does she live now? Mimi asks the same questions over and over again, or similar ones. Eva doesn't know whether she forgets the answers or needs to hear them many times to believe them, the repetition giving weight maybe to distant facts that tend to have the vaporous texture of dreams. Does Mimi think Eva lived a fairy-tale life, the existence of which she cannot verify or control? Eva's childhood and the characters that peopled it have begun to take on the shades of a fiction. She now looks at them and at herself in those days with surprise and almost a sense of embarrassment to have spent so much time with people who seem, in retrospect, to have so little to do with her. Like a lack of judgment on her part. But Mimi keeps digging there, trying to extract some facts that will shine bright and true as Eva retreats, dances around them, evades. She doesn't remember the words from a song, describes one school, invents another. Even her own mother doesn't have one solid name, she has four or five, different first names, nicknames, last names, didn't use the same one from her birth to her adulthood, her father was there and then not there and there again, the dates play tricks and whole years seem to have gone blank. The whole business of what it was, for her, to be a child, becomes slippery like jelly. And then there is all that she doesn't want to tell Mimi. She tries hard, though, because Mimi's questions don't feel like an inquisition but like a serious, thoroughly honest research, quest even, reaching out to a past that rightly belongs to her, is part of her history.

Eva would like to rewrite her life for Mimi. Not to wrap it up in silver ribbons, but to give her the history she deserves. Heroic acts, quaint settings, endearing characters, powerful sweep of events. The stuff that legends are made of. Or, in a more modest scale, a romantic lifestyle, a wacko but terribly seductive bunch of people, adventures à go-go around the world. Or a solid family life. Brothers and sisters. Fond memories of summer houses. Instead, this hole, this erasure.

So, she tells Mimi she used to live in this little town outside Paris in a big white house with a garden around it, back and front. It even had a white wooden fence with a tall white gate and two chestnut trees on either side of it and a lattice with creeping roses running along the front of the house and there was a swing at the back, roped to the thick branch of an oak, and Mimi likes that description, she says she wants to see the house, where is it, but Eva turns her eyes away, she pulls on Mimi's ringlets, lifts them from her forehead where they tumble down to her eyebrows, pushes them way back and smooths the brown skin, the fine, almost invisible down that softens her temples. You saw that house, Eva says. I took you there when you were a baby. Do you remember?

Mimi doesn't remember. But we could go back, she says, hopeful.

Eva shakes her head. No. I don't think so.

Why? Why, Mom, why?

This house was sad, Eva says. It would make me sad to take you back there.

Why? Do you miss it?

No. I don't want to see it again. It was not a happy place.

Does somebody live in that house now?

Yes. An old woman, Eva says. Very old. She's all alone there.

And before Mimi has the time to ask any more questions Eva takes her by the hand, steering her toward the bathroom. Come, she says. Shall we make you up and dress you up with my scarves and my slips and my shoes and you can play princess and pretend you live in a castle and you turn all the furniture into your faithful subjects? Okay? Okay, Mimi?

Mimi drops her head down so that her curls fall all over her face and cover her eyes and her nose completely. They stop short of her lips, which are pursed into a sulky pout.

What's the matter? Come on.

Eva tries to push Mimi into the hallway, but Mimi's feet seem to be rooted to the ground. Her whole body is drooping, her neck, her shoulders, her knees, on the verge of collapse.

What, Mimi?

Mimi's curls go flying in a sharp motion of her neck. She fires these black eyes at Eva, pounding her fists into her arms.

You never want to tell me anything, she says, I ask you something and you won't tell me. I hate you. Why don't you ever tell me anything?

The old lady (3)

The old lady is watching TV from her lounge chair. It's been raised to a half-sitting position, an angle allowing the least stress for her back and neck muscles, while she's wedged in by stuffed pillows piled behind her shoulders and back, along her sides and under her seat. Among the eighteenth-century furniture, the ottoman, the *bergères*, the commodes, the faded velvet upholstery, threadbare even on the edges of the seats and armrests, the modern lounge chair sticks out with its tubular pipes encased in bright royal blue canvas, its shiny spindly legs digging into the frayed Persian rug, incongruous like a pair of dungarees at a black-tie dinner party, and endowed with a cheap mechanism in which you always get your fingers caught.

The old lady is watching a movie on TV. The movie is about . . . it is not easy to tell. A woman, two men having a heated discussion in what looks like a hotel room, one of the men storming out. Scene cutting to a dark, forbidding-looking building, an empty dark warehouse at night, again that woman with one of the men. Badly lit scene, the camera moving, shadows shifting, hard to tell a shadow from a human being. Maybe shapes lurking behind, what exactly, construction materials? theater props? Suddenly, the woman, running toward the front of the screen, her mouth open in a scream, huge eyes filled with terror. Two men—other men, previously unseen, or in any case not remembered by the old lady—come at her in close-up, grab her from behind. These huge faces threatening her, so close to the surface of the screen. The old lady jumps backward, but only succeeds in burying herself deeper into the pillows and sinks a bit more into the lounge chair. She grabs the armrests with both her hands, her knuckles white with the strain. There's confusion on the screen. People moving in all directions, somebody aiming a gun. A lot of yelling. Yelling so loud. Sirens too. Howling. Faces distorted in exaggerated anger, fear as if the souls were jumping out of them. The mouths are talking to her directly, addressing her. She puts one hand over her eyes. She cries for help. She rocks back and forth trying to push the chair back, moving it as far away from the set as possible. Even though the remote control is sitting on the armrest, at her fingertips, she doesn't think of punching the off button. She's got both hands covering her face now. She screams in panic. She calls the nurse's name. But nobody comes.

She believes she's all alone in the house. The door to the vast expanse of reception room, sitting room, drawing room, library, which separates her bedroom from the service areas (a distinct aisle containing kitchen, maids' quarters, nurse's quarters, pantry, stairway to the basement, etc.) is half open but it opens into her room, so that she's unable to be aware of a presence beyond her world, not even get a glimpse of a shadow announcing somebody's approach.

When the maid arrives, long minutes later, she finds the old lady slumped in the chair, her face buried into the cradle of her folded arms, paralyzed with terror while the final credits of the movie roll on the screen. The maid flicks off the image and asks, is there anything wrong, madame? But the old lady slowly lets her arm down and shakes her head. No, Georgette, she says gently. No. Nothing.

Would you accept chocolate ice cream from this man?

Mimi has just spotted Eva from the other end of the gym, but she doesn't run to her, she walks crab-like, her head slightly tilted toward one shoulder, her unbuttoned coat hanging down her shoulders with the weight of her backpack strapped to it.

What's the matter? Eva asks. Something wrong?

Mimi offers the side of her head, reluctantly, to Eva's lips.

I thought it was going to be Albertine who's going to pick me up.

Hey! Did I hear this? Did you actually say that? You're always asking me to pick you up!

I know. But not today.

Why?

Mimi pushes her neck into her collar, sideways, glancing coyly at Eva from under her curls.

I can't tell you.

Eva's kneeling in front of Mimi, buttoning her coat, tying her scarf around her neck, adjusting her hat. Mimi's resisting and, when Eva's done, bolts like a spring across the gym. Eva catches up with her at the door and grabs her at the wrist in a tight grip. Struggling to get free, Mimi kicks Eva in the shin and tries to yank her arm out. But Eva's holding tight. Mimi buckles under and lets herself go down. Eva drags Mimi down the front steps of the school by the wrist and pushes her against the wall. Mimi lets her legs go soft again and her body slumps until it drops on the sidewalk, legs wide open, Raggedy-Ann-like. Eva's eyes turn black. Cut it out Mimi, she yells. Cut it out!

Cut it out! Mimi whispers between her teeth. Cut it out! Mimicking Eva's voice, sticking her tongue out, kicking her feet in the air.

Eva has this urge to bash Mimi's head against the wall. Instead, she kneels next to her and attempts reasoning, something on the order of: stop acting like a two-year-old. What's the problem. TELL me instead of acting out. Trying to keep her cool, be an adult, rational, in control. Meanwhile, little fists pound her flesh everywhere they can find a soft spot, no respect for the rules of combat, below the belt or in the eyes doesn't deter them.

I'd give her a good spanking, says a voice coming from behind Eva's back. Bratty kid.

Mind your own damn business, Eva yells over her shoulder, without looking.

Oooh, bad word, singsongs Mimi, weakening her attack to savor the situation. You said a baaad word.

Like mother, like daughter, says the voice.

Fuck you!

Eva buries her nails into Mimi's wrists and yanks her to her feet. Mimi shrieks self-righteously. People turn around and watch from the edge of the sidewalk. Mimi plays up the bruised ego.

Let's go. Get a move on. Now will you tell me why all this fuss?

——

Mimi, you'd better answer me.

Albertine said I could have ice cream after school, Mimi says in a silky voice. She said if I was good.

Well, there you go. You missed your chance.

Mimi hangs her neck, sensing the battle is lost but maybe not the war. Okay, I won't have any ice cream, but can I have my cookies now, Mom? she asks in a little subdued voice.

What makes you think I have any cookies?

I know you do. You always bring me cookies.

Eva pulls them out of her purse without a word. As soon as she's got a cookie in her mouth, Mimi's mood lifts and she skips around the bus stop in tight circles.

Mom, she says suddenly, eyes opened wide, I was going to forget, oh, my God, you know who I saw this morning?

No, who?

Eva has to wait for another skipping turn to get an answer, and then the answer comes as another question.

This morning? After Albertine dropped me off? You know we stay in the gym until the bell rings, playing with the other kids?

Yeah, I know. So who did you see?

The bus is pulling up at the curb, Eva's rummaging through

her purse to find quarters or a token. Finds them in extremis, pushes Mimi in the door.

They sit at the back, Mimi takes a position at the window, checks out the street and turns to Eva.

I saw my dad, she says.

What! Where?

Mom. You're not listening. At school, in the gym, I just told you. He was near one of the pillars. He had a baseball hat on.

A baseball hat? Eva is stunned. Frank? Frank Jackson? Are you sure it was him? He doesn't wear baseball hats. At least, he didn't use to.

I think it was him.

You're not sure.

Yes, I am. I'm sure.

What was he doing?

Just looking.

Looking at you? Did he see you?

I don't know. He didn't say anything to me. He was looking at the kids. Like the other parents.

Like the other parents, Eva thinks. Of course, he is a parent. But does he have the rights of a parent? Could he just pick up Mimi and walk away with her? Who would pay attention? But would he have the guts? Would Mimi . . . ?

Mom? What's wrong?

Nothing. I was just . . . surprised, that's all.

You look worried, Mom. Was that wrong? Do you think he was going to do something bad to me?

I hope not.

Maybe he just wanted to see me.

Oh, Jesus!

What?

You wouldn't go with him if he asked you to follow him, right, Mimi?

Of course not, Mom!

Even if he offered to take you somewhere for ice cream?

Mimi looks at Eva slyly, her tongue pushing into one cheek.

I might if it was chocolate ice cream.

Eva sits upright, grabs her hand.

Mimi!

Mimi laughs her head off.

Mom! I was kidding!

I don't trust him.

I know. Don't worry, Mom. I wouldn't follow him. He's disgusting.

That doesn't appease Eva. Frank is a charmer. Nothing would be easier for him than to worm his way into Mimi's life. And if charm didn't work he would put pressure on Eva. I am the father. I have the right to see her. You can't deny me . . .

You can't deny him the right to see her, Albertine says, after Mimi's gone to bed. Maybe take her to the movies, something like that, or for hot chocolate. But that's it, no more than that. Look, don't touch. Eva says he's spying on her. Albertine says it might be natural curiosity. Actually, it was not spying, Eva says, he was in full view of the kids. He didn't even try to hide from Mimi. Next time he'll want to speak to her. So, let him, Albertine says. Turning him down will only make it worse.

But Eva doesn't think that's right. Next thing we know, he'll want a relationship with her, then he'll want to spend the summer with her. He'll be on us like the plague. He will amuse, cajole, threaten Mimi or if it fails, throw a tantrum. He is a master manipulator. Albertine groans, she says Eva is scared of Frank, that she imagines him more powerful than he is. Eva shakes her head. She says, you don't know him, Albertine, you don't know him like I do.

The hotel night guard (3)

She rang me tonight from her room. I pick up the desk phone on the first ring, and here comes her voice. There's an edge to it. Or maybe she's out of breath. She says, Morris, I'm coming down. Do you have a minute. I got to talk to you. Sure, Miss Marquand, I say. My pleasure.

Then I see her coming out of the elevator, looking around her.

She's not dressed up, she's not wearing one of her smart little numbers. She looks like she came down in a hurry, just slipped on a pair of old jeans and a sweater. She rushes to the desk.

Morris, she says with that same voice she had on the phone, kind of tight in her throat. You know this man you told me about? You said you saw him in the lobby? Several times? You thought he was looking for me, maybe, or something?

So, that's what it's all about. I look over my shoulder. The lobby is quiet. A few people waiting for the elevators. Familiar faces, mostly residents. An elderly woman sitting on one of the couches, taking notes in a calendar with a little gold pencil. She must be waiting for one of our residents. Delivery boys coming in and out. A couple of kids buying gum and comic books at the candy stand. But I don't see the fellow. I don't see him right now, I tell her. I know, she says. I mean, that's not it. Did you ever speak to him?

Yes, I did.

What does he sound like?

What does he *sound* like?

Yes, his voice. What kind of voice does he have?

Now, this demands attention. I talked to the fellow maybe once or twice, and frankly, each time, I did most of the talking. I close my eyes, I see him standing there with his mousy face and his newspaper folded under his arm, but I can't hear the voice. Nondescript is the word that comes to mind. But that won't do. I can see she is looking for nuances. Something special. I take a shot at it. Pretty low, I say, like, a deep voice, you know.

Deep, melodious?

Now, I don't know, Miss Marquand. He didn't sing no melody to me.

That got her to smile.

Why, something troubling you, Miss Marquand? Have you heard from the fellow?

She shakes her head. I can see she's worried, or is it puzzled? I promise her to keep an eye on him and let her know next time he shows up, but someone just calls me then, from the other end of the desk, to take care of some business in the baggage check, and when I come back she's gone.

Lola's men

Eva is listening to the messages on the tape. Mr. Hamamoto who likes his woman waxed and smooth like a baby lamb, Sean who likes his with rouge on her breasts and pubic hair shaven in the shape of a heart, John of the crotchless pantles, Walter of the leather suspender belt and push-

up brassiere cut low right under the nipple, making the boob swell balloon-like above the semicircle of whalebone, Lee who favors opulent pube and replete thighs, Hans who dreams of loose-tongued Valkyries, Raymond who only likes his with a certain amount of heft between the waist and the knee (who cares what they look like in the face, they might as well stick a paper bag over their head for all his intents and purposes), Chuck who waits for Mama with his diaper on, a big fat Huggie in which his dick nestles as if inside a soft hand. Oswald of the so-called ten-inch dick, Gustav of the lapping tongue . . .

Eva clicks off the machine. Business is booming because of AIDS. Verbal sex is the safest sex of all. She calls them back, the easy ones first. She plays mistress, mama, daughter, brain surgeon and elevator operator in five minutes flat, breathlessly mounting standard scenarios, the same over and over again. Mom, tell me the story of the little boy who always came between his piano teacher's titties. Pleeeease, Mom. Okay, Demion. One last time. And then promise Mommy you're going to go to sleep right after this. And you, Harvey, why don't you cover your face with a leather mask while I tie your balls up with a silk thread and squeeze them till you squeal . . .

And then Max catches her by surprise, the phone rings as she is about to lift the receiver for her last call back and she picks it up without thinking, and it's his voice, unmistakably, he doesn't even have to announce himself. He says, Lola, Lola, I want to meet you, let me come up to your room. Lola darling. Please. Please, Lola.

She says, yes, where are you, Max, in a very soft voice. He says, in the lobby, downstairs. Let me up, please, Lola.

Wait for me there. I'll be right down, she says, and she hangs up gently before dialing the desk number.

Yes, Morris's voice answers.

Morris, it's Eva. Is he there?

Who?

You know.

Oh! Miss Marquand, he was here. I was going to call you.

He wanted to go up to your room. Said he had a letter for you. I told him to leave the letter with me, that he couldn't go upstairs. Turned out he didn't have a letter, of course. I told him to leave.

Jesus. Did you see him go to a phone booth?

No. He left.

Are you sure? But before that? Wait, I'm coming down.

When she walks out of the elevator into the lobby, Morris raises his arms in frustration.

I'm sorry, Miss Marquand. He's gone.

He pushes his hand on the polished wood of the desk counter.

He said he was calling from the lobby.

Morris shakes his head.

Eva looks around at the usual assortment of down-and-out foreigners and local types affixed to the candy store or hanging around the phone booths.

Do me a favor, Morris, she says. If he shows up again, give me a ring and I'll be right down, okay? I want to talk to this guy, Max.

Is that his name?

That's the name he uses with me. But then he thinks my name's Lola.

Morris looks at her quizzically. Eva raises her eyebrows and turns around on her heels, leaving Morris open-mouthed and staring at her.

Upstairs, Eva writes in her notebook: *Max. Jan. 23, 10 P.M.* And then she prints, in large block letters, on the next line: I AM GOING TO GET YOU, MAX. And a satisfied smile breaks on her face.

A dumb accident

Albertine: When I first got pregnant, I wanted to throw my belly at them, stuff it in their faces. Flaunt it.

I wore those tight dresses. I would have liked to wear a rubber sheath to show off the shape, the hard roundness, like a big egg, that's the shape of it, isn't

it? A big egg coming out of your body. You don't think of an egg as a weapon, right? The smallest blow, it breaks, there's no sharp point protruding to attack, *pour rentrer dans le lard*, to get into the meat. But I wanted a corset for my breasts, a girdle to mold my stomach and my buttocks, my hips, and I wanted to rub against them, like a wave, dismount them, rub against their erections, but not just the men, rub against people in the street. It was so drab in the streets of Paris, then, people in dark overcoats, hats pushed down, swallowing the face, dark woolen mufflers tucked under the lapels, black berets angled over round horn-rimmed glasses, sensible shoes, a general look of reprobation. A pissed-off look. Well, it was spring, though, there were flowers everywhere, you know how Paris is in the spring. Paris in the spring . . . (singing) Ah, ah, ah! Beds of tulips and daffodils, and God knows what else, all these colorful flowers in the Tuileries, in all the parks, but they were all walking about with their asses pinched, and their mouths tight, and their shoulders stiff as if they'd swallowed a stick, and I was waltzing down the streets with my big boobs and my big belly shooting straight out, and they looked at me in horror. I'd plunge in the crowd and I'd just push the waters open with my prow, I'd brush against a hand, a hip, and they'd recoil. It was written all over my face that I wasn't married, a young pregnant wife would've had a more modest demeanor, and my hair was flaming red, curly and loose, and I was carrying high and bumping into the disapproving matrons and feeling glorious. I was a fat snake, I slithered in and out.

Well, listen, it was my revenge. I'd been knocked up and I was going to show it.

I was twenty. It was Paris, it was the fifties. The guy was a student, from an upper-class family with land in the Southwest. He was fooling around with the girls. That's what he was doing. Not that I didn't know it, mind you. And me, I knew exactly what I was doing. I had my little sideline, too. How much do you think a maid made—a maid made, English is funny, no?—in those days? Crap. That's how much we made. In a hotel behind Montparnasse? Anyway, most of us had a sideline. So I knew about men. But it was not like that with him, I had a big crush on him. He liked me too, yeah, he really went for me. For a while. He was the sexiest little son-of-a-bitch. I knew we weren't meant for each other, as they say, but it broke my heart to think he would end up with one of those well-bred bitches who had no more spunk than a slab of veal.

So I just said fuck it, *rien à foutre*. You had to have the guts, in those days, let me tell you. But I had them, the guts. So I just went ahead and did it. So I had everything, the guts, and then I got the boobs, and the belly! I was well endowed. What else could I have done, anyway? Will you tell me? A *bretonne* like me, going to church every Sunday, fasting every Friday? Look at me, still saying my prayers here in this pagan country, right here, at the foot of this bed. Like a fool. And look at Him, with his crown of thorns, the blood streaming down His face, this look of compassion, sometimes I think He's a clown. A sad clown.

It wasn't just that. I wanted it to happen. I felt like a walking time bomb. It's going to go off. Go! Go! It said SEX, capital letters. I wanted to rub their faces between my legs.

I wanted to press my belly in like a balloon and shit the fetus on their well-behaved faces. Blood squirting, placenta sticking to their polite smiles, the baby popping out like a jack-in-the-box, grinning, jumping on them like a blob covered with bodily matters. See what they really thought about motherhood!

The second time around it was a dumb accident. Didn't even know who the father was. I tried to raise the two of them, but, you can imagine. . . . I met this fellow, he was an actor, played in regional troupes, traveled up and down France. The elder one loved the country, I asked a distant cousin to keep her on the farm. I thought it'd be good for her, fresh air, healthy life. She loved horses. The second one, well, she was still little, I put her with a foster family. I didn't know what else to do. I was in love. I couldn't take a kid with me. When we split up I just worked my way to Le Havre and found a kitchen job on the first liner leaving for America.

Back in the days when Albertine first came to America, there was Times Square, the Great White Way, it wasn't the street of sin then, or maybe it was just starting, the breakdown of Western civilization, the men just back from the war, hungry for women's flesh, but it still had flash and style, the huge movie theaters with the crimson velvet and gilded wood, heavy crystal chandeliers, the noisy restaurants. And then there was Hell's Kitchen at the back of it. That's where Albertine first lived, a couple of blocks from here. It was like a little Montparnasse, back then, a Breton mini-ghetto where the new French arrivals stuck together before moving on to the more upscale Upper East Side.

Oh, that makes me think, Albertine says, pinning away. You know Eileen, right, this young woman who designs these fashionable clothes. She has a smart little shop on the East Side, on one of the side streets, what is it, Sixty-fourth, Sixty-sixth? You know who I mean? Eva shakes her head. So many people Albertine knows, so many stories, so many intimate details about people's lives, so many insights into their souls. Her stories wash over Eva and Mimi like a tide. Mimi, later, will remember bits and pieces of stories, names emerging from long-forgotten memories, little bird droppings coming out of nowhere with some tragic fate attached to them, and the way Albertine punctuates her stories with sighs and clicks of her tongue against the palate.

Yes, you know her. You do. A beautiful young woman, well, maybe a bit older than you, long black hair, always wearing these fancy turbans? She used to come here, bring me some sewing? I sewed a lot of her clothes at the beginning. Remember? She brought armfuls of fabrics, there was always some gold lamé or puce taffeta, you loved those fabrics, very special, very fancy. Like ball-gown fabrics, muslin and organdy and panne velvet. Remember now?

A floating, imprecise image comes back to Eva, of piles of shimmering fabrics in colors fit for a medieval ball and a warm, seductive smile under turbans tied high over an exquisite white forehead.

Vaguely. What about her?

She had a child, about two, three years ago?

I didn't know.

Yes, you did. A little girl. She brought her in a stroller a couple times. Cute as a button with blond corkscrew curls? Anyway I ran into her the other day, I was buying fabrics down on Orchard Street, that new place that just opened, what's it called, Stein? Not as good as whoshamacallit up the block, as it turned out, and here she was, and I asked her, how's the baby? And she said, we're starting the treatment tomorrow. So I ask, I'm such a . . . I don't know, anyway . . . I ask her, what treatment, I'd no idea what she was talking about, I hadn't seen her in a while. Turns out the baby girl has what they call a motor problem. She can't talk, can't move. It's not like she's mentally retarded or anything, she's smart, understands everything, but her muscles won't move. She has to be taught how to move, every one of her muscles in her body, the tongue, everything, can you imagine? for eight hours a day every day. There's an institute that's got a program for that. They send someone to train the baby. And on top of that she's a single mother. I can't imagine! But she hopes the baby will be able to walk one day, and talk normally. Would you believe that? What a tragedy! My God, what a tragedy! Think of yourself with Mimi.

Please, Albertine. Do I want to hear this?

This woman is brave, brave, I tell you. But life forces you

to be brave. You are a coward until you have to act brave. And then, mostly, you don't have the choice. You just do it. It's just something life throws at you. Do you think you start out brave? Something happens and you're brave, or you run away. Sometimes it's better to run away, sometimes it's better to be brave. Sometimes it's braver to run away. Whatever.

Frank Jackson takes Mimi to the playground

Mimi: Frank Jackson was in the gym, like the first time. He was with the other parents, leaning against the wall. The gym was empty. Maybe our class was the first one down, I don't remember, I didn't see Albertine or Eva. I just saw him. I wanted to hide from him, walk back the

other way. Then he came to me. He had a candy bar or something. Maybe Bazooka bubble gum. I used to always sneak them because Albertine thought bubble gum was one of those terrible American inventions, she didn't think it was proper in a little girl's mouth. Sometimes she was terribly old world. He talked to me, and then we were outside in a playground. It's like a dream, the way that memory has stayed with me. I remember sliding down the slide and pumping the swing while he watched me, sitting on a bench. I don't remember if he talked to me or how long we stayed, only that it felt strange and unreal, and that Eva showed up suddenly, screaming at the top of her lungs.

Eva: It happened on a day I was supposed to pick up Mimi. I arrive at school maybe a bit late, the bell has already rung. There's the swarm of kids milling around, the buzz overwhelming me, and I don't see her. I think maybe her class is not down yet, so I wait but they don't show and the gym is emptying out, I go upstairs to her classroom, but it's empty, all the chairs' legs up in the air on the tables. I go to the office, she's not there, I go back down, there are just a few kids playing freeze tag in the gym, outside the school buses are already gone. No Mimi. I try to keep my cool, there must be a very simple explanation. Maybe Albertine thought it was her day, maybe she came early and they're on their way home. I call her at her apartment. Unfortunately she's home, without Mimi. I rush back into the school, go to the principal's office. He has no idea where Mimi is. I wander in the hallways, then out on the street, up a little way, down two blocks, wondering what to do, my eyes sweeping the street, considering calling the cops. There's a mangy little playground squeezed between two buildings on my right.

I looked in there, and I did a double take. There she was hanging by her feet from the monkey bars, head dangling. At first I didn't see Frank. I rushed in, hollering, and suddenly I became aware of him. He was sitting quietly on a bench, watching. He didn't say anything to me. Mimi pulled herself upright and jumped down. I was so relieved to see her I ignored Frank,

I didn't acknowledge him. I grabbed her in my arms and twirled her around and around. Frank got up and came to us. He said, I was just passing by the school and thought maybe I'd take the opportunity to spend some time with Mimi. I dropped her down and turned on him: Frank, you're overstepping your boundaries. Keep playing your cards this way and you'll never get to see her. You're totally irresponsible. I can't believe the school let her leave with you, I guess there's no security whatsoever. Didn't you think for a minute that whoever was going to pick her up was going to go insane with worry? What were you thinking about anyway?

Hey, she's my daughter, he said.

I told you to lay off her.

He retreated, apologized, after a fashion, for the scare, said they'd just been at the playground for a few minutes, he hoped that he would see me walking by, he hadn't meant to frighten me, but take his point of view, Mimi's his daughter, okay right now she might be a little frightened of him, a little cold, but once she'd get to know him, the walls would come down and she would love him. Give me that opportunity, he asked. Then he offered to take us out for a hot chocolate or a soda. Mimi was tempted, she jumped up and down saying yeah, yeah, yeah, her eyes sending violent sparks of desire, but I don't like to have my arm twisted at the same time my hand is being kissed. And I told him so. I walked away dragging Mimi behind me. She threw herself into a fine fit to reward me for my strength of character, and only quieted down when I took her in for a hot chocolate and a Danish at a Chock Full o'Nuts.

The next evening, Frank shows up at the club, just as I am bowing to the applause, or at least, that's when I notice him. He's not applauding, he's leaning against a pillar, looking real cool and self-assured. I am caught off guard, for a split second I see him as my lover coming to pick me up after the performance. Angrily I remind myself that he is not my lover, that he is the man who abandoned me while we *were* lovers and I was pregnant with our child. As I walk backstage I'm having trouble casting away the feeling that has cut through my mind, an old flash emerging pure from the depths of my buried memory. He's waiting for me at the door of the dressing room as I walk out, joking with Felix, the pianist.

Go for a drink?

The feeling has opened a little trapdoor. He has touched something in me, so I agree, but if Frank knows it or not, I slam the door shut real quick.

We sit down at a table and again I have this *déjà vu* feeling, him and me across from each other.

His presence fills up the space. It's as if he's never left. His big, hearty laugh, his fingers drumming quickly across the table, nervously tapping the tip of his Camel to tighten the tobacco. He's trying to pin me like a butterfly for display. I suspend my motions. They've become contrived, a parody of themselves. I can physically sense his power over me. I pull away, he probes and I use irony back. But when he brings up the subject of Mimi, I find my resolve.

So, you're not going to let me see her, right?

I say, no, I'm not.

You're so fucking possessive.

I'm not trying to control her. I just don't want her to be involved with you. I don't think you're good for her and I don't want her to get hurt.

Every little girl needs her daddy. We had a good time together at the park. We can be friends. I like her, and I think she likes me.

You're dreaming, Frank. Men are amazing. Such big egos. You think it's enough that you show up and everybody will be at your feet? You're suffering from mental delusions.

Female chauvinist bitch!

That's Frank. If all else fails, there's always the insult to fall back on. And he knows exactly where your weak spot is. One parry used to be enough for me. I'd get up, run away, and burst into tears. This time I don't run away, but I flinch. I become very warm, I think I am going to be sick. I get up. He takes my wrist. Listen, Eva, sorry, he says. I don't mean it. I just want to love my daughter. He gets up too. We're both half bent over the table.

Fuck, I know Frank. What does he really want? Six years later he's first remembering he's got a kid, coming back to him like a little itch. Isn't that perfect?

Bored with your life, Frank? Something missing, some humanity? What happened to you? Tired of the hassles of South America? Split up with your old lady? Maybe she dumped you. You always were immensely dumpable. All of a sudden your life is empty and you remember, hey, I got a kid! You don't even know her name, but what does that matter? You don't even know if it's a boy or a girl. But never mind small shit like that: YOU GOT A KID. A ready-made little family. But shit, Frank, you can't come back, peddle your charm and expect us to embrace you? We're not your family, Frank. God forbid. You and me just fucked for three, four years, it was never anything more than that.

I see the moisture in his eyes, like a misty veil coming over. My heart sinks. Beaten dog face. I brace myself.

You're so cruel, Eva. You didn't use to be so hard. Yeah, okay, I didn't raise her. There's nothing I can do about that now, but she's my child. No one on earth can deny that. I have a right to see her and she has a right to see me.

Oh, now here we are, back with the sperm theory. What does it fucking mean she's your child? You have no right.

So what are you going to do, you won't let me see her?

No.

You're saying I can't take her to the park, to the movies? What do you think I'm going to do to her? I'm her father. Okay, it's a little late, but better late than never. This kid doesn't even have a "father-figure." I want to make it up. She has every right to have me, you can't deny her that. Think about her for once and not yourself.

Oh, the moisture in the eyes! The honeyed tongue! I know his tricks. Only what if for once they were not tricks, what if he's sincere. He actually means it, I can tell. And that's what scares me. I see passion in him. I feel pity welling up in me. Disgusting. He could have me that way. I realize he wants Mimi bad.

She's entitled to a father.

I put my hands down flat on the table. I have to fight the pity, the sentimentality, take my responsibility. Better be wrong than hesitant.

I am sorry, Frank. You are not her father. Not the way I understand the word father. You forfeited the right. As far as she is concerned, you are a nobody, coming out of the blue. A usurper.

How do you know what Mimi thinks?

It's not important. At this point in her life I decide what's good for her. Maybe you're right, maybe she needs a father. But you're not him. Maybe Johnny. He would make a better one than you, even without a drop of his blood in her.

Screw you. I disagree. I think she should be the judge, not you. Let's ask her what she thinks.

Don't you dare!

It's her life. I think we should give her a chance to choose. If she doesn't want to see me, if she says no, okay, fine. I'll leave, I'll be out the door. You guys won't have to see me again. But let her make the decision for herself.

I can't think. He's pressing too hard. I feel the pressure inside my body. The confusion, the anger, the guilt. What's he talking about? What right? Whose right?

I get up.

So . . . ?

No, Frank. Absolutely not.

You can't do this!

I pick up my pocketbook.

I'm not going to let her go so easily, he says.

I walk away. Now he's threatening me. I don't want to hear

him anymore. I walk straight back to the hotel. I don't say anything to Morris, who's waving at me from the desk, I go straight up to my place, straight to my bed, I beat on my pillow with my fists. I hit it for a long time, I want to hang on to my anger as long as I possibly can, because if I don't, then Frank may get back under my skin, everything will collapse, and I don't know what will happen then.

Madame Rosalita (2)

The window is dark, only lit up by the crossed neon palms and cursive letters of the name MADAME ROSALITA running a half circle around them. Eva crosses the street at an angle and approaches the storefront from the side. She presses her nose against the window and cups her hands on

either side of her eyes to shut out the light but all she can see is the pair of wicker chairs flanking the little wrought-iron garden table and the couch along the back wall, like a stage set before the spotlights are turned on.

She stands on the sidewalk, not able to make up her mind what to do. If someone showed up she could duck in the adjacent building doorway or walk innocently down the street.

But then the girl from last time appears at the door. She looks as though she's been expecting Eva. Her eyes seem even darker, if possible, the charcoal circles around her eyelids deeper. But it might be the darkness. Her mouth is a deep crimson and her hair swept up in a pompadour curving high above her forehead, and gathered at the nape with a barrette. Eva follows her in.

From the storefront they walk right into a kitchen, where a small dark woman is sitting at a round table covered with a checkered oilcloth. Eva figures it's Madame Rosalita and she thinks Madame Rosalita looks just like a peasant woman from Latin America, the proud Indian features softened by Spanish blood. She seems tired, or sad, possibly bored. She observes Eva without any trace of curiosity.

Siéntate, she says. Eva sits down.

In contrast with the dark storefront, the room is violently illuminated by a single ceiling fixture. It is a typical tenement room, living room cum kitchen cum bathroom, with a claw-foot tub against one wall and a run-down couch upholstered in a beige-and-brown plaid across from it. A playpen made of a net attached to plastic tubing is propped by the table, a chubby brown baby with a full head of tight black curls stationed in it. When he sees Eva, the baby grabs the top edge of the pen and utters determined guttural noises as he swings his body back and forth, saliva drooling from hunger or astonishment down his chin.

Eva takes this as a friendly gesture.

Madame Rosalita points to the girl and says: Olga. Eva says, Hi, my name's Eva, and the older woman says something else in Spanish which Eva doesn't get while the girl busies herself filling the kettle with water and setting it on the stove, then goes koochi-koochi-koo to the child, who's now vigorously chewing on two of his fingers. Olga pulls the fingers out and inserts a rubber ring in his mouth, which the child immediately spits out with a jet of saliva.

He's teething, she says to Eva.

Have you tried giving him zwiebacks? Eva asks. They really work.

Olga shrugs. He only like fingers, she says.

You come before, right? The older woman is suddenly addressing Eva's back, in strongly accented English.

Eva jumps and turns around.

Yes.

You have problem.

How do you know?

But of course, only people with problems come here, Eva thinks.

Madame Rosalita turns to Olga and makes a sign that the water is ready. Olga lets go of the child and goes to the stove to make some coffee. Eva feels like getting up and excusing herself, it was nice meeting you, sorry for the interruption, have to run now, thanks for everything, but Olga sets a plastic mug in front of her and Eva leans back in her chair.

They all sip their coffee in silence and after a while Olga gets up and lights a row of small votive candles on a dresser.

Madame Rosalita touches Eva's hand and says, I think I can help you. She is more subtle, or just more professional than her daughter, if Olga is her daughter. Maybe she figures she has Eva in the palm of her hand. Which she has opened in the middle of the table, as a peace offering. Or is she asking for money? Forty pesos, she says, extending her palm a little farther across the table. Eva apologizes, fumbles in her pocketbook and pulls out two twenties. The woman slips the bills in the opening of her blouse and stuffs them into her bra. Which seems to set off her concentration.

Behind the votive candles is spread an assortment of religious objects and artifacts, one of which catches Eva's eyes, a three-D portrait of Christ crowned with thorns, blood streaming down his ravaged face, and eyes that alternately close or open depending on the angle from which you are looking at them. Eva tilts her head from side to side to catch the two expressions of Christ until Madame Rosalita fires a stern glance at her. Eva looks down and folds her arms on her chest, waiting for the session to start. The electric switch clicks shut and the room goes dark, save for the candles on the dresser.

Eva doesn't see Madame Rosalita's hands, but she can hear them move, a slight swoosh. The old woman's face is in shadow, her hair frizzled white by the candlelight behind her. Eva's face, in contrast, is sharply illuminated and her hair blends into the dark.

There's someone in your life, Madame Rosalita starts—and her hands stop moving, as if she's found the spot where truth is gushing out of the table—someone coming back to your life, you scared of that person. I don't know if is a man or a woman. But I see a shadow around you.

Eva sips a little of her coffee, holding the mug with both hands.

Madame Rosalita switches to Spanish to ask for a candle. Olga brings one that she sets in the middle of the table, at equal distance between the two women. Blinded by the flame, Eva keeps blinking and has difficulty maintaining eye contact with the woman, which doesn't seem to bother her in the least. What she is looking for, or at, may not be in the eyes at all but in the cut of the face, in the way the features open up or close, in the history that has carved the lines and shadows like geological layers, each event of life encoded in the pores, and it is just possible that she knows how to crack the code and can read Eva's story on her face.

I don't know how dangerous this person is, but you scared of him.

Eva tries to stare into her eyes and says nothing.

I see someone walking in a street. A man. Yes. I see a child,

I think this man and the child are together. Maybe a teacher and a student. No. Wait. They don't know each other. They walk side by side. The child seems friendly to him.

Madame Rosalita's eyes don't see Eva anymore, their gaze seems to reflect back upon itself. Characters and whole scenes spring out of Eva's features or out of some glistening aura around her face and then vanish. From her hesitations and tentative descriptions the scenes sound pretty murky as if she was reading coffee grounds. But for Eva they stand out sharp and clear as if under a five-hundred-watt spotlight. She sees Frank holding Mimi's hand and taking her away, claiming her as his daughter, alternately demanding to take Mimi with him or to move in with them, sleeping on Albertine's couch or setting his quarters in Eva's living room.

You still attracted to this man, the voice says, and Eva springs to attention. This man very dangerous for you. Eva leans on her forearms. I see evil, but is not too late to stop evil. You have to stop evil in you. I see the man walk away. Oh, now I see an older woman, very very old. She is dying. Oh, *mala suerte!* Now I see you near the water with another man and the child. But you can't escape evil!

At this point the baby, who's been making gurgling noises as background music, breaks into a fit and Olga whispers to him, trying to calm him down.

Eva cranes her neck and looks Madame Rosalita straight in the eyes, but the woman still hasn't come back to earth. *Mala*, she repeats, *mala suerte!*

It must've been Olga's cue, because she appears in the candlelight holding the baby in her arms, blows out the flame and turns the electricity back on. It's the end of the show. Madame Rosalita pulls a large white handkerchief out of her cuff and proceeds to wipe her forehead and neck and armpits under her blouse as though she's been running a marathon. She asks for *agua*. Eva realizes she's hot too. She feels sweat drip down the inside of her sleeves and her hands are soaked. She rubs them on her pants. The Christ is still blinking at her from the dresser.

I can help you, Madame Rosalita announces, tossing her crumpled handkerchief on the table.

You said *mala suerte.*

I can turn the *mala suerte* around. But is going to cost you.

How much.

Cinquo ciento pesos.

Dollars?

It's less than Olga asked for originally. There might be room for bargaining.

Claro. Dollars.

Five hundred dollars? I don't have that kind of money.

Madame Rosalita lifts her hands palms up, rejecting all responsibility if that's the case.

I want advice, Eva says. I don't care about ceremonies and recipes.

No entiendo, qué dice ella? Madame Rosalita turns to Olga. Olga translates, even though Eva has the feeling she understood perfectly well. Eva waits. Madame Rosalita shrugs, makes a sign that in this case she washes her hands of all potential evil.

Eva leans forward.

You were right about the man and the child.

I know.

I could find the money, what could you do for me?

Madame Rosalita moves her hands over the table. They are short and plump with very smooth fingers and well-kept nails. To Eva they seem to move like two animals that have a life of their own. Madame Rosalita looks pensive. Eva wonders if she's such a hard-assed businesswoman as she acts. She and Olga seem to be doing okay, their apartment is small but well kept, at least they have a roof over their heads and their clothes are clean and the baby looks healthy. And in order to be able to survive in New York City you have to be hard and competitive, but still.

The old woman gets up and tells Eva to follow her.

Standing up she's really small, her head barely reaching Eva's shoulder.

Venga. Véngase. She encourages Eva with little motions of her fingers. She seems warmer, more animated now.

They walk through the rest of the apartment, a narrow bedroom serving as a hallway and a larger one, and come out into the backyard. Eva shivers without a coat. Madame Rosalita doesn't seem to mind the cold and stands on the dirt ground in her light blouse as though it were a warm summer night. She points to a stone altar at a corner of the garden looked over by a plaster Virgin Mary and a profusion of cherubs perched on the stones, some holding the horn to their mouths. There are dried flowers in vases at the foot of the altar and rows of votive candles more or less burned down. All in all, not a very sinister or pagan scene. The rest of the backyard is littered with urban detritus: an old toilet on its side, ghost-like, piles of demolition wood, a scattering of bricks, burst garbage bags. The area around the altar has been carefully cleaned up and a row of bushes neatly trimmed forming a half circle around it.

I pray for you here, Madame Rosalita says. I call up the spirit of this man. I try to clean the evil out of your life. If you know who the man is, and if you can, bring me a photo of him. And write his name down on a paper. Not tell me his name. Write the name. And you bring me an object, a personal object: a ring, a scarf he wears on his body, best, a lock of hair, but it can be difficult. Cut in his sleep, maybe?

What will you do with that?

Madame Rosalita thinks it's very funny. She chuckles.

I not tell you. Is my secret. I like you. I can see you're in trouble. Trouble of the soul. I tell you what to do when I work with what you give me.

When?

As soon as you bring me these things.

Can I bring them now?

Now? Is late.

I live in the neighborhood. I can bring them to you now.

They go back inside, tiptoe through the small bedroom where Olga is singing the baby to sleep.

Madame Rosalita chuckles some more.

Okay. You come back tonight if you want, she tells Eva. I start work for you tonight. Then you come back in three nights. I tell you what to do.

She sits down at the table and her little hands take their position flat in front of her. She seems lost in thought, not even noticing that Eva's left.

Pulling evil like a tooth

Frank didn't leave a scarf or a handkerchief from his recent visit. It would've been an incredible stroke of luck. There is a good photo of him, not like he is now, but with his long curls blazing around his face, a straight-ahead picture of him, eyes looking at you from under as if he is

appraising you and the full lips at rest, content, satisfied sensuality. The photo had been cropped to fit into a metal frame, at the time, but she thinks it'll do. Finding a personal object that belonged to him turns out to be more difficult. There are old books of his in the trunk, mostly thrillers, the hard-boiled, hard-assed variety in cheap mass-market paperback editions, their blaring covers of gold-embossed titles or lurid scenes of sex and violence scratched and dulled. They are piled in a corner of the trunk, Eva has read maybe half of them and she leafs through their tired pages pondering if they count as a personal object, because how personal were they? Frank never paid much attention to books. Books were objects he consumed and threw out, like newspapers, in a trash can, or abandoned behind him in motel rooms. The only reason Eva has them is that she picked them up behind him and read them herself, and she doesn't throw out books, even books like that. They are words on paper and they are meant to line up and eventually fade away on shelves, proudly standing up. She decides the books won't do. They didn't mean enough to Frank, and anyway, he didn't wear them against his skin. Albertine looks at her in disbelief, wrapped in her old flannel robe, her face pale and puffy from sleep. She disapproves of Eva seeing Madame Rosalita. She has no idea who Madame Rosalita is, barely remembers noticing her storefront on that block, there are so many gypsy storefronts nowadays in the city, how can they afford to open a store with the rents being what they are, she'd like to know, some Moonies or the Mafia had to be behind that traffic, and no, she doesn't believe in white or black magic or no damn santeria or whatever voodoo that Madame Rosalita is practicing, but she thinks there has to be some evil there, playing havoc with natural forces and fluids.

I thought you believed in rationality, Eva says, head and shoulders deep into the trunk, throwing piles of clothes out of it. This shouldn't bother you. Some old pagan ritual.

Albertine mumbles something in French and wanders to the

kitchen to make some tea or coffee. Eva thinks Albertine's life is not so different from Madame Rosalita's and Olga's and that maybe they would get along if they ever got a chance to meet, which she doubts.

She finds an old sweater that she used to borrow from Frank all the time and that he liked to see her wear, with nothing underneath, just that V-neck dusty-raspberry wool pullover that stopped right beneath her butt; he liked to slip his hands under it and feign surprise to find her naked skin. But she doesn't think it qualifies. She's worn the sweater a lot since then, she wore it when she was pregnant, it was perfect to fit over her big belly, she wore it over her jeans, she wore it over a bathing suit at the beach on cool days when the sun went down and the evening chill whipped you by surprise. She pulls the sweater out. She feels like wearing it again. It's definitely hers now. She sniffs it inside and out but can only detect a whiff of a perfume she used to wear a few years back.

A grayish-white T-shirt with a frayed collar rolled at the bottom of the trunk and smelling vaguely musty is more promising. She recognizes it right away. He used to wear these sparkling-white cheap T-shirts that looked great on his dark skin in the summer and he bought them on Fourteenth Street by the dozen, threw them out when they ripped and turned dull gray after a series of laundry cycles. He must have left that one behind when he left, maybe pushed under the bed. Or maybe he'd thought it was ready to go in the garbage and had left it to her to do it. Next to the T-shirt is a pair of old white terry socks and an odd green one. Albertine comes back with a steaming mug in her hand and is looking at her with a smirk, asking if the object has to be smelly to be more efficient. Eva tosses the socks away and keeps the T-shirt. I think that'll be good, she says. You remember these T-shirts he used to wear all the time?

Albertine sulks. She thinks Eva has stupidly traded her healthy Gallic skepticism for a ridiculous American gullibility. You're making a fool of yourself, she grumbles. This country has brainwashed you. You came here too young, you were still susceptible to influence. You didn't get a chance to solidify your beliefs. And now look at you, pushed this way and that. Falling for a fad. The prey of quacks, like they all are. Throwing your money away on charlatans.

What do you want me to do?

But Albertine has already resumed her work, her massive back bent over the sewing machine, letting the steady whir of the electric motor and the flow of an iridescent blue silk cascading from the presser foot down the side of the table carry her answer to Eva.

Nevertheless, giving Frank's photo and his T-shirt to Madame Rosalita is like getting him off her back. It's not so much that Eva believes in a result, but for three days and three nights someone else will worry about him and she doesn't have to carry the burden and the relief is immediate.

Eva stayed at Albertine's for the night and held Mimi's hand long after they were both asleep. Mimi was thrilled. She fitted herself into the curve of Eva's body, first resting her head on her shoulder, then complained that it was uncomfortable and slipped into the fold of her arm. Eva was already asleep, lulled by the warmth of their bodies next to each other. When she woke up much later, she realized she was fully dressed and that her right arm was numb from clutching Mimi's hand. She undressed, slipped her naked body under the covers and tried to pull down Mimi's bunched-up flannel nightgown without waking her up. She wondered if it was a bad habit to sleep in Mimi's bed when she stayed over at Albertine's, if Mimi would get dependent on it and if she would end up having trouble sleeping on her own, or if she would want to sleep with Albertine. Then she wondered if it mattered either way. She always thought Mimi would come out all right if she was meant to. It was a load of crap to make the mother's every move responsible for a child's outcome. If the mother was made to feel responsible, though, then the child would invariably blame her. Eva thought in Mimi's case if she turned out fucked it would be because of Frank Jackson's disappearance. Or his reappearance. Take your pick.

Eva recognizes Frank Jackson's fingers in Mimi, the shape of his mouth, his long legs, the shape of his eyes. She carefully runs her palm around Mimi's buttocks (how close to a lover's a parent's touch can be) and up her back, trying to remember Frank's body, and finds the texture of his flesh. Mimi has united them in her body. She is the link between Frank Jackson and Eva that can't be dissolved. Eva thought the same way about her own mother when she thought about her at all. Links that won't be severed are like ball and chain. But she doesn't think of Mimi as her ball and chain. Mimi, on the other hand, might see her that way when she grows up. Mimi coughs and grinds her teeth. Then she thrashes about and kicks Eva in the leg, one of her closed fists lands on the wall. She seems to be fighting a dream enemy. When she wakes up she'll say she dreamed of a witch but Eva believes a witch is a convenient password to cover night terrors that might be too close or too dangerous to give a name to. Mimi grinds her teeth again. Eva gets up and lies down on Albertine's couch, wrapped up in a spare blanket. Mimi's nightmare is too much for her to bear. Sometimes you need to concentrate on your own demons.

Madame Rosalita's storefront is always quiet and mainly deserted. Eva walks by it every time she gets a chance, slowing down and glancing at it casually, but she only sees Olga once, sitting on one of the rattan chairs with the baby crawling at her feet, and making little come-on signs with her index finger as soon as she establishes eye contact with someone in the street, usually a woman. Eva turns her head away, keeping her eyes downcast, and hurries by.

At Mimi's school, all is clear. Eva relaxes, thinking Madame Rosalita's efforts have already taken effect, and she practically runs to her appointment on the third night.

Olga looks pretty gloomy when she comes to open the door but Eva thinks it's the darkness, again, that deepens her black makeup. Eva goes straight to the playpen and squats near the baby, poking him in the belly with her finger, cooing with him in Spanish.

Then Madame Rosalita comes in from the backyard, looking harried. Ah, she says to Eva, throwing her hands up on either side of her ears. This is hard, very evil. Eva looks at her like a patient who was starting to feel better and who's just been told he was terminally ill. I try to reach this man's spirit, the old woman goes on, but it slips away from me, very cunning, very wicked. She sits down and motions to Eva to sit down too. Eva's turned pale, her heart's jumped to her throat. Madame Rosalita looks particularly intense, her eyes burning embers, the rest of her face sallow and drawn. I've worked day and night for you, she says. Her hands, again, drawing silent patterns on the table. Eva thinks she looks it, too. Imagines her working at the altar in the corner of the backyard, freshening up the candles, concentrating on Frank's photo until his eyes would come alive and he and she would start a dialogue; burning incense in her bedroom till the fumes made her dizzy and she had visions of Frank and Eva and the shadows of their life playing around them. Eva can imagine the strain on the woman's energy. Who now seems to have sunk deep in her thoughts while Eva stares at her hands.

There's something I can do, Madame Rosalita says finally, breaking the silence. But that would require your presence. I'd have to work with you. Also, it would cost more money.

How much more?

She shrugs. Two, three hundred. Maybe five. Depending on how many seances. And you still not pay me.

Eva makes a sucking sound between her lips.

I don't have that. I told you.

Again, the hands thrown up. Well, in this case. . . . The hands go back down on the table, serve as a lever to help lift Madame Rosalita's small body from the chair.

Wait, Eva says. Maybe . . . would you accept a down payment?

Every time the question of money comes up, Madame Rosalita seems to lose her grasp of English and turns to Olga. When the translation comes through, Madame Rosalita has an indulgent smile. No, *carita*, she says, sweet as honey, tough as steel underneath. I already did you a favor, remember?

What would I have to do?

She laughs.

No, no. We don't talk about these things. You have to decide.

She's already on her way to the stove, busy with other thoughts, other plans.

Think about it, she says. But don't wait too long. You're in trouble, girl. Don't waste no time.

The hotel night guard (4)

I saw the man again last night. This time he was wearing sunglasses, the old-fashioned kind that you clip on your regular glasses. I didn't think they made those anymore. He was leaning against the wall of the lobby, near the candy and cigarette stand, reading the back page of the *Post*. I could see the front-page headline from the desk. It said: SWORD MANIAC CHOPS EX-LOVER'S HEAD OFF. And underneath was a blurry gray picture half hidden by his hands. I walked to the stand to buy my own copy and read the rest of the story. The photo was that of the woman's head in a pool of blood. A small photo of a pretty and smiling young woman was inserted at the right-hand corner of the page, so that both heads, the dead and the alive one, were of about the same size and side by side. There was also a photo of the sword used for the decapitation, lying on the sidewalk. The crime weapon. I didn't get a chance to read the story, though, because the man, my man, folded his newspaper, tucked it under his arm and walked up to the desk.

Yessir, I said. May I help you?

I believe so, he said. I am looking for a, a Miss Eva Marquand. I believe she lives here. Would you give me her room number, please?

I couldn't believe the man's nerve. I told him we didn't give tenants' room numbers, at their request. He asked, what about deliveries, and I asked, what about deliveries? He said he had something to deliver to her. So I go, I don't see no flowers, no package. He goes, it's a letter. I put my hand out. I say, give it to me. Letters get delivered at this desk. We put them into each tenant's cubbyhole. No need to go up in the rooms. He's patting himself right and left, digging into his pockets. I think I've misplaced it, he says. I say, sure, sure. I point to the cover of the *Post* with the girl's head swimming in its blood, and I go, sure you've misplaced it, as sure as this girl walked away from here with her head on her shoulders. Take a powder, buddy.

The beach house

Down in Dallas
Near the palace
I met a boy who was so cute
I loved his hugging, I loved his kissing
As we sat in his little red coupe
He said, tell me, confidentially
How much do you love me?
I love you honey
I love your money
Most of all I love your automobile.

Right, Johnny says, driving his red '58 Studebaker, one hand on the wheel, his other arm resting on the seat behind Eva's back. That's how I got you—with my little red coupe. It never fails. I can always count on my little red coupe to get the girls. It's easy to figure out women's psychology, don't you know? But that part about the money, I don't know about that. He bends to kiss the corner of her mouth. I guess I just look rich. Leather jacket, hole in my jeans. Army boots. A rich déclassé. Fooled you.

She pinches his cheek, hard. You're cute, she says, but you didn't. Money is not what we modern girls are after. I thought you were a walking sex bomb.

Damn right. And still ticking.

Better be, bub.

I love you baby
I love you maybe

Johnny puts his hand over hers. Feeling better?

Yeah, she says. Great.

And she does. She does. They're off for the weekend, seashore retreat in the dead of winter and Mimi is asleep on the backseat, covered to her eyes in a thick army blanket. The road spirals under their wheels. Eva thinks it's like straddling time.

They ride that highway. They ride it for a long time. It's as if the gray asphalt is absorbing them. They drive eastbound, across Long Island. The landscape is a dazzling white. White on the treetops, white on the lawns, white on the sloping hills. The white is crisp and pure like meringue. But if they pissed on the snow it would turn yellow.

Wanna stop?

No, keep going.

Keep going and don't turn back. If only there was a way never to retrace one's steps, never to have to eat one's dinner at the same table twice. When she first came to America Eva didn't just stick to the United States, she wanted to see both continents, North and South. She traveled through the Andes and down the Amazon, all the way to the bitter winds of Tierra del Fuego. She soaked up the new world through her skin. She went from New York City to Los Angeles and from Los Angeles to Tijuana and across Mexico and through Central America to Panama and then from Barranquilla in Colombia to the heart of the Andes until she boarded a boat at Leticia, the source of the Amazon, down to Manaus, and from there motored her way through the jungle and the rubber plantations of Brazil and hitchhiked down to Buenos Aires and across the pampas where carcasses of dead horses lay along the highway. She went as far south as the road could go before making her way back through Chile, Valparaiso, Santiago and up the Pan American Highway, cutting across Colombia to Caracas to fly back to Miami. She developed illusions of immortality. When you don't see the familiar faces against which to measure your aging, time disappears.

I need to go pee-pee, Mimi whines from the backseat.

We'll stop in a minute. Hold on.

Can't. Need to go now. Right now.

The first time they went to the cottage, the "beach house," Johnny called it, it was summer. They had arrived in the late afternoon. The low-riding Studebaker had banged on the rocks and ruts of the dirt road that cut through the woods to the bay. The hedges on either side were overgrown with honeysuckle vine. The ground was littered with yellowed honeysuckle blossoms. The hot, moist air smelled like heady perfume of only one note. A note you wanted to suck in through your nostrils in great gasps. Eva had felt drowsy. The sugary smell filled her like a rich dessert. She let her arm dangle out the window against the side of the car and her hand brushed against the bushes. Her fingers raked a fistful of blossoms that she sniffed before pushing it under Johnny's nose.

Smell this. Isn't it incredible?

He sneezed, shoving her hand away with his wrist.

What are you doing? I'm driving!

She pushed the flowers back in his face.

Close your eyes. Guess what it is from the smell.

He sneezed again and the blossoms scattered over the dashboard, raining on his knees.

Cut it out! Can't you see you're giving me a fucking allergy attack? What's that stuff anyway?

Honeysuckle. Don't you know?

Oooh, that shit is strong.

It's an aphrodisiac.

No kidding?

She dropped her hand to his crotch, feeling for the bulge.

Too bad, she said. Didn't work.

The car scraped bottom in the dark. No honeysuckle this time. Just the dirt road, bare and hardened by the frost, and naked branches whipping the car windows. The bungalows were half hidden in the woods, the edges of the roofs catching the moonlight. The cottage was the last one down the road, hidden by a thick row of bushes, on a strip of land sandwiched between the bay in front and the lake in back. They woke up Mimi and made their way to the back of the house following a narrow path, pushing overgrown weeds aside, carrying duffel bags on their shoulders. A pool of light glimmered beyond a clump of reeds.

Woooh. Look at the lake, Mimi.

Mimi grumbled.

The kitchen door was locked. They walked back around the house to the front porch and dropped their bags on an old wicker couch.

It was a wood-frame cottage from the forties with knotty pine on the walls and musty furniture that felt damp and looked like it hadn't been sat in in years. But there was a fridge and a big cooking stove with a lot of chrome around the edges and blankets stacked on the bed in one of the two bedrooms and a showerhead suspended above the bathtub.

Each place she inhabits takes on the shape and smell of Eva's fear. Objects soak it up like sponges. This time, the wainscoting on the walls, painted in faded almond green, seems to close in on her. From the kitchen, you can see the lake iced with moonlight. A splash of white, swallowed by the jagged shadows of the trees.

They huddle together around the stove stocked with wood they've found in the back of the house, rubbing their hands to get the blood going, still wearing their coats, Mimi leaning against Eva for added warmth.

Johnny pulls out some sandwiches from his bag and a six-pack of beer.

Jeez, I'm starved.

Eva joins him at the table and they both eat silently, quickly, sucking beer from the cold cans.

Want a sandwich, Mimi?

I hate ham sandwiches.

Eva shrugs. That's all we have.

They finish their food, crinkle the wax paper, pick at crumbs, polish off the beer. Mimi is watching them from the couch, one leg thrown over the armrest, looking sulky.

What's the matter?

I'm hungry.

There's a half banana left over. Want it?

Huh huh.

Johnny wipes his mouth with the back of his hand and stands up.

I'm going down to the beach. Anybody care to come with me?

The beach is down a short sandy slope, about thirty yards

wide, bordered on either side by docks of bleached-gray wood. The night is cold with the moon a forlorn sliver of a crescent (look, Mummy, Mimi says, it looks like a cut toenail), and stars like shards of diamond in the pure sky. The beach is littered with spaghetti-shaped algae and half-crushed shells and a few discarded plastic bags. Two soft-drink cans are bobbing on the edge of the water, scraping the rocks with a clanking noise at each lap of the waves. Mimi bends to pick up tiny shells that glow softly in the moonlight with mother-of-pearl colors, orange, flush-pink, bluish-gray. Look, Ma, she keeps saying, look how beautiful they are. LOOK! She flourishes a handful in front of Eva's eyes before stuffing them in her coat pocket. Eva and Johnny, their mufflers wrapped several times around their necks, are standing side by side, their arms hanging along their bodies, their fingers barely touching. To Eva it seems as though they are swaying in the cold air, their feet shifting in the elastic sand, their heads lolling in the wind like winter-stripped ash trees.

It's like being on the moon, she says, shivering, pressing herself against Johnny, circling his neck with her arms. Icy and desolate.

Mimi comes back with a handful of shells and when she sees them together, throws the shells angrily on the sand. She tries to pull Eva and Johnny away from each other.

No, she says, no. I don't want you to do that. Don't touch.

Hey, Mimi, stop it.

But she doesn't stop. She hits them with her closed fists, little hard pellets raining on their arms, their backs.

Johnny pulls himself out of the embrace, grabs Mimi by the wrists, sends her swinging in big, widening circles around him. But she's not game. She drags her feet on the sand, using them as brakes. She yells, stop it, I hate you. He lets her go, steps back, stiffly looking over the dark expanse of water.

Mimi, cool out, will you, Eva says. I think we should go back. It's real late. Come on, Mimi.

But Johnny's not making a move. His hands are deep in his jacket pockets and his heels dug deep into the sand. His body barely moves, vibrates almost imperceptibly. His face reflects his tension, the features pulled downward, his mouth almost set in a childish pout. Eva puts her arm around his shoulders, an uncomfortable position for a woman who is smaller than her man, and one that cannot be convincingly maintained for any length of time, and anyway Johnny shrugs her arm away.

What's the matter?

But Mimi's all over her again, stuffing her pockets with more sandy shells, and not only shells but rocks, bits of dried seaweed (judging from the texture), unidentified objects and matter, and the more Eva tries to stop the invasion, the more Mimi gets possessed by a collecting frenzy, dipping her hands into the sand and coming up with more and more strange and heavy and wet natural or man-made objects until Eva pushes her away, half laughing, half mad, causing Mimi, brooding silently, to go to the edge of the ocean, the tip of her sneaker teasing the waves, as if she was considering walking into the sea never to return. Meanwhile, Johnny has retreated to the edge of the beach, his back to them. Eva thinks he's sulking too until she realizes he's opened his fly, pissing in the bushes.

When she goes to bed, Eva finds Johnny already asleep. She cups his body with hers but he doesn't wake up.

The next day, it's raining. Steady unrelenting rain. Johnny's gone to Bob's, a local bar he noticed on the way in, to watch the afternoon game on the bar's satellite dish, taking the car with him. Eva is tempted to take her shoes off and walk in the rain. Go off and melt in the fog. The steady pitter-patter of rain. She listens to the sound, her nose to the door. The rain breaks on the outside screen and blurs her vision to an impressionistic rendering of various shades of brown framing a lead-gray lake. What's left of the deck shines with pools of water. Mimi is reading a book aloud to an imaginary group of kids. Eva gives her ten minutes before her concentration starts wavering and she calls for attention. For most of the day, Mimi's major contribution to conversation is: I'm bored, Mom. I have nothing to do. What can I do?

Mom, will you play a game with me?

Mom. I'm cold.

They build a fire in the wood-burning stove. They huddle in front of it, Mimi at Eva's feet. They find old children's books on a shelf and take turns reading them aloud to each other, Eva taking over when Mimi stumbles on the words.

They go out for a walk along the dirt road and look at the cottages in the woods, most closed for the season. They watch the rain pass to sun and the sky drain of clouds. They follow the path of the sun over the lake. The light is pale and uncertain. Mimi clutches Eva's hand. They traipse down to the beach and toss rocks as far as they can into the bay. Mimi squats near the water and dips her hand in it to judge the temperature. She squeals in mock pain. It's freezing cold. They sit on the breakwater, legs dangling, and watch the seagulls and the sun set in a cold mist.

Isn't that pretty? Eva says in a distracted voice. And it is. The winter light, as if coming from a long distance. The icy pink of the sky at dusk.

I'm cold, Mommy, Mimi says. They huddle together in their winter coats. To Eva it seems that spring should've started already in the city, that they're caught in eternal winter, frozen on that little tongue of land. Frozen in space, frozen in time.

It's night when Johnny comes back, pushes the wooden door. Eva hasn't bothered to turn on the light. She is sitting cross-legged on the rug in front of the stove. Mimi is asleep on the couch. He sits behind Eva and wraps his arms around her. Eva slips a quick look to Mimi. Carrying her to her bedroom would be too risky. The movement, the change from warm to cold might wake her up. Let's go to the bedroom, Johnny whispers. But that would be leaving the warmth of the fire. Eva feels trapped in the strategy of domesticity. Not Johnny, though, who is dipping his hands into her sweater and reaching for her nipples. She puts her hands on his, cutting him short. He pulls back, rolls over on his side, lights a cigarette. He tells her he has an idea for a song, says it takes place during the fifties, a love affair that turns bad. She stretches in front of the fire, lays her head on his hip. Tell me about it, she asks. I can't yet, he says. It's just an idea.

That night, after Eva took Mimi to bed, she fell asleep next to her. She woke up at one o'clock and found Johnny lying on the couch, snoring, his mouth open, the fire cold in the stove.

They drove back the next morning, early, a bright, crystal-clear day, the sun in their eyes, the radio on a rock 'n' roll station. In the backseat, Mimi quietly drew doodles and princesses with her Crayolas for two hours. Eva fell asleep. They ran into traffic on the BQE. The profile of the city was sharply edged against the hard-blue sky. It was as if they'd never left.

[illegible] and puts his arms across [illegible] the sheet. He pulls back, rolls over on his side, lights a cigarette. He [illegible] [illegible] says a rather quiet [illegible] during the [illegible] [illegible] that night. She [illegible] her [illegible] on [illegible] it, he says. I can't [illegible] it. [illegible]

[illegible] she fell [illegible] [illegible]

They came back the next morning, early, a bright, cold [illegible]. On the way to their room, the radio on a news broadcast, [illegible]. In the back seat, Mimi quietly drew her jacket around [illegible] with her [illegible] fell asleep. [illegible] The [illegible] of the car was [illegible] the [illegible]

Motherhood

Eva: you don't want to believe it when people tell you, but I swear, when you've had a kid, it's never the same again. The buck doesn't stop at you anymore. You become part of the human chain. You're just a dumb link. You do to her what your mom did to you. History repeats itself, except

the background shifts. This time it's the drought in the Midwest and AIDS and African famine. Then it was de Gaulle and the Algerian war.

Meanwhile you stand behind the child, her thick curly black hair swells like a bush around her head, from the back you can't even tell it's a human being, what with no visible neck or shoulders or even the shape of a skull. You grab the brush squarely by the handle, you hook it into the hair and you pull down. The child screams and insults you with a torrent of four-letter words. You go at it again. You manage to brush through a quarter of the mane accompanied by only groans and whimpers. Then you move to the other side. There's a tangle there that you can't even see, but it's so thick it feels like a bird's nest. Animals could grow in there. Lice, fleas, rodents. The texture is semivegetal, halfway between jungle underbrush and sheep fur awaiting shearing. Before the brush even gets a chance to attack the nest, a harrowing yelp and a blow to the dead center of your tit makes you jump in agony, holding your chest with both arms folded over for protection. The child is on you, the furious mass of hair hovering alarmingly in your field of vision. She manages to land a mean kick on your shin. You leap up to your feet, still armed with the heavy-duty boar brush. A wide-open mouth gapes at the level of your ribs and fists pound everywhere they can reach. You bang the brush on top of the skull. The child goes down, hollering pain. You want to go for the kill, but you get hold of your senses and only toss the brush across the bathroom with the speed and might of a hardball rocketed across the diamond at a major league baseball game. The brush goes *bang!*, splits in two halves, the handle slides behind the john, the brush itself lands at the child's feet. You collapse on the floor near the child who has now turned into a pack of sobs, clutching the prickly brush against your chest, and you start laughing hysterically.

Mimi lifts her head toward Eva's laugh. Little face swollen and striped with tears. Sees that Eva's laughing at her face.

Deep insult registers in the eyes that turn black. Then, unexpectedly, the downward mouth starts quivering and stretches into a big laugh. Mimi tries controlling the laugh, attempts to restore the sour look in her eyes but she gives up; the laugh rolls over her and up and down her belly, and they fall all over each other, once in a while gasping for air.

Spent, Eva catches her breath and starts getting up. But Mimi's already on top of her, delivering a quick punch to her jaw. Eva looks stunned.

You hurt me, Mom, Mimi says, the offended look back all over her face. You hit me on the head!

Then, crossing her arms against her tight little chest: You abused me!

So, you just go on. Feed the child leftover spaghetti with a glass of milk and two carrot sticks, hoping enough protein and vitamins, somehow, will find their way into the slender body that shoots up every so often its couple of extra inches under the demential mass of overgrown hair. You serve the food, barely deserving the name of dinner, at the kitchen counter this time, no time for elaborate rituals of napkin rings and place mats on the coffee table. Looking at each other like two female wolves, claws at the ready, and later when teeth are brushed and nightgown pulled over head, wrap her into your bed for human warmth, sensual bonding and to avoid more tears. Watch her drift into sleep, the body gradually relaxing, little palms stretching on top of each other under the cheek, a smile hovering on the lips. And succumb yourself, lie down on top of comforter just for a minute, drift into a dreamless sleep, a state of oblivion, both hands squeezed between the folded knees, the two side by side, the little one and the big one, in a perfect parallel, same profile resting on two identical pillows in a mess of tangled hair.

The ring startles Eva, who was drifting to sleep, and her arm shoots out to the night table to pick up the phone before Mimi gets a chance to stir. At the same time she tries to decipher the time on the clock radio. It is a little before eleven. She feels woozy as if it is the middle of the night.

It's Frank.

Hi, he says. What's happening, babe? Did I wake you up? He has his warm, solicitous voice.

She says, wait a minute in a low voice and goes to the living room to pick up the other phone.

I am back in town, he says.

She doesn't answer.

What's the matter?

A cold anger has suddenly jolted her out of her sleepy daze.

And you're calling me to tell me that?

No. I am calling to ask you to reconsider, about Mimi.

There's nothing to reconsider. I told you what I thought.

I want to see her.

Frank, I told you, I can't do that.

So let me talk to her.

She takes a deep breath.

She's not here.

Just then, Mimi's thin white shape appears at the door, a waif in a long white oversize T-shirt hanging down below her knees, one fist rubbing her eyes.

Just a minute.

Eva puts the phone down, kneels in front of Mimi and holds her tight.

Did I wake you up? she whispers.

Who are you talking to? Mimi asks.

Nobody. Just a friend.

Are you having a fight?

No. I mean, no. We were just talking, you know. I was just talking loud.

Is it Frank Jackson?

Mimi, go to sleep.

Were you talking about me?
Why are you asking?
Were you talking about me?
No.
Mimi hits Eva softly against the shoulder.
You liar. Liar, liar. Stick your head in fire. Wash it off with bubble gum and . . .
Come on, Mimi. Go back to sleep. *Va faire dodo. Il est tard.*
. . . take it to the cleaners. Liar, liar, wash your head in gravy . . .
Come on, Mimi!
. . . and take it to the navy!
Eva pushes Mimi toward the bed and carefully covers her with the comforter.
In the dark, the partially drawn curtains frame the mannequins across the street. A faint light comes from the back of the floor, someone walks to the window, dismounts the arms from the pale waxed torsos and piles them in a heap by the side of the window, the arms protruding at strange angles from each other, hands sticking out, fingers pointing upward or outward and accusatorily through the glass pane. Eva pulls the shades down and tiptoes back to the phone. She picks up the receiver and says Frank? in a hushed voice.
But the line is dead.

The next morning, the headline on the *Post* clamored:

THE BROADWAY RAPIST IS HIV-POSITIVE!

The paper was folded on the desk in front of Morris and Eva couldn't read more. She was late taking Mimi to school. Later in the day, at the Follies, a copy of the *Daily News* lay on the toilet floor. She picked it up and read the details of the story. Eleven women raped by the so-called Times Square Rapist (because each assault was performed in the vicinity of Times Square) in the last thirteen months have suddenly turned out HIV-positive.

The evidence of the HIV factor was too much of a coincidence, the paper reported, not to be related to that common occurrence in the women's lives, since they were all at low risk as far as AIDS was concerned, six of them married with a stable life and the other five not drug abusers and with steady boyfriends. Eva wondered if the Times Square Rapist was aware of being positive himself, and, if so, was raping women with the added intention of inoculating them with the AIDS virus as a bonus, like the syphilitic libertine in Sade's *Philosophy in the Boudoir* who fucks Eugénie's mother to purposefully infect her with his disease.

She thought of the giant condom ad, hung high in the haze of the cold gray day, the finger sheathed in rubber held upright in front of the lips.

She went to Madame Rosalita's storefront that night, carrying a bundle in a brown paper bag. The girl opened the door to her and took her directly into the back room, where Madame Rosalita was waiting for her dressed in a flowing black gown. Eva had her money ready in a purse, all four hundred dollars of it, sharply negotiated, in cash. Olga took the money away without a word. Three tall candles burned on a dresser. A kind of massage table was set up in the center of the room and covered with a black fabric that fell all the way to the floor. Eva was told to get completely undressed and lie down on the table. It was warm. She closed her eyes. It felt like she was at the doctor's office, waiting to be examined. Madame Rosalita had something burning in a little caldron, not incense, something thick, spicy. She was bent over it mumbling unintelligible words. It was laughable, the *mise-en-scène* so obvious, out of a self-help witch manual. The steaming caldron was passed over Eva's body accompanied by a new litany. Eva was waiting for the cocks to be brought in, their throats slit or their heads cut off, or doves' entrails simmering in a dish. Instead came Frank's photo and his crumpled T-shirt. They were given the hot caldron treatment. At that point Olga, now enrobed in a similar long black gown, had joined Madame Rosalita, and they were chanting around Frank's effigy, the fires furiously turned up, in a way that didn't sound good at all for him. Eva was beginning to get a little chilly, but here came the caldron again, passed over her head, over her chest, over her navel, the chanting rising to a pitch, burning the hell out of the evil spirits, then the caldron was taken away and a smell of burned fabric rose from the fire. Frank's T-shirt was going up in smoke. Eva sat up in alarm. Madame Rosalita was holding the photo to the flame. Olga held her back firmly. It was a beautiful photo of Frank. Eva was surprised at the strength of her feelings. Here was a man she wanted to neutralize and possibly eliminate, and she wanted to keep his photo. Madame Rosalita dropped the print in the crucible. The edges curled up black and sizzling, with an acrid smell. Eva let go and fell back on the table. If it had to be the necessary sacrifice, so be it. In any case Madame Rosalita seemed satisfied with the session.

Albertine is furiously stitching a strip of grosgrain at the hem of a taffeta skirt because the dress is due tomorrow at noon. Her mouth is tightened on a piece of blue lining like a dog's fangs around a bone. She groans, her foot clamped down on the electric pedal, as the edge of the shimmering fabric zips past at top speed under the presser foot.

The fabric flies. It grows wings. Eva marvels at Albertine's sure hand. Even from where she is standing she can tell the stitches are razor straight, the hemline as if traced by a ruler.

Can you finish it by tomorrow?

What? Albertine asks in a whuzz of motor just cut short but spinning until it slows down to a full stop.

Sorry. When you're holding one end of it you want to do it in one shot till the other end, that way you hold it steady, it goes straight plumb, otherwise thread does curlicues. Oh, I'll be done. Work till one, two o'clock in the morning, finishing touches in the morning, you work miracles at night, nothing interrupts you, you go bang, bang, bang. I used to do my best work at night, with strong lamps and a pot of coffee going on the stove, clients called me the miracle lady because I could turn a dress overnight. Bad for the eyes, though, let me tell you. Couldn't do it now, even if you paid me triple rate.

Albertine looks up at Eva and laughs. Oh, boy, you look like a sheet. A dirty sheet just pulled off the mattress, she chuckles. Don't tell me you went to see that voodoo woman again? You did, right? *Seigneur*, Eva, don't be surprised if you bring it upon yourself. If you absolutely need to do something like that, you'd be better off burning a candle to Saint Joseph in church.

Albertine's seen it all, nothing fazes Albertine. Or if it does, she keeps it all well locked up, ten thousand miles under the surface. You develop tough skin on your soul, she says, like calluses inside your hands. Otherwise how can you go through life with baby skin that bruises silly at the weakest blow? But you're a tough mama, Eva. You just don't realize you are.

Albertine (2)

Mimi: Albertine drunk. At times. She was an on and off kind of alcoholic. On the wagon. Off the wagon. This is something that you'll find Eva will have trouble admitting. If she mentions it at all. Up until now, Eva will say: yes, she had a fondness for the bottle. She liked to have her red

wine at dinner or the occasional glass of rum, but an alcoholic? No, I wouldn't say that. But I remember finding Albertine asleep in the big Naugahyde wing chair, all dressed in yesterday's clothes, mouth wide open reeking of liquor, and I had to shake her awake, and the days I found her like that her eyes were red and unfocused and her face looked all fat and bloated and she complained of violent headaches. She'd say, ah, I felt sick last night, couldn't even drag myself to bed, I had a horrible migraine. And look at me this morning.

It didn't happen very often. But even at six, seven, I could recognize the smell of liquor on someone's breath. Looking back, and thinking about that period, which I would roughly date as the time Frank Jackson came back to New York, it may have been a rare occurrence, but then it seems that something changed in her daily behavior. That may have been later, when she started getting antsy about getting older and was New York a good place to grow old, etc. She was fatter. Her eyes were watery, she would lose her patience with me and her mood would swing without reason. I remember looking for construction paper to do some art work, or some art material, and I opened that closet where we kept odds and ends, wrapping paper from previous Christmas presents, balls of string, empty boxes flattened on their sides, shopping bags carefully folded, things like that, and I couldn't find what I was looking for, so I pushed the stuff out of the closet, the way kids do it, just flanked it out on the floor, and there were some liquor bottles in back, and it was obvious to me they were hidden. I took them out to look at them, read the labels, inspect the amount of liquor in each. Albertine wasn't in the apartment, I wouldn't have been so bold otherwise. She often went down to the second or the third floor to visit one or another of her neighbors, exchange some gossip, borrow a couple of onions or a stick of butter for the cooking of dinner, return a magazine she had borrowed. She'd leave me for twenty minutes, half an hour maybe, it seemed long, but not long enough to be threatening and I knew she was in the building. Sometimes I didn't even realize she wasn't around for a while, I was so engrossed in dressing up my Barbies or fooling around with the tape recorder pretending to be a hot rock 'n' roll singer, although she must have poked her head in my bedroom door to tell me she was going to be out for a little while. Anyway, I looked at those bottles and they were just dumb bottles, some half empty, some full, and there was nothing special about them, they looked like other liquor bottles I had seen in liquor cabinets, at Eva's for instance, those tall bottles she kept at the end of her kitchen counter, except Albertine's bottles were tucked away behind this forbidding entanglement of paper and boxes, and even though they could've been just spares (and they might have been a stock of unused bottles put away and forgotten at the back of that cabinet), I had a sense of something forbidden, something sinful, another layer of life adults don't show to children, a darker side of Albertine's round cheeks and sharp black eyes and quick hands ready to slap my bottom if I didn't follow the straight and narrow path, the side of her that prayed for Jesus kneeling down at the foot of her high perched bed, her skirt and apron tucked tight under her thighs.

Eva always said Albertine just liked red wine like all the French do, they like to have their wine every day, they drink it like Americans drink milk, and I wonder, I wonder if I made it up, or if I was the only one to know.

The old lady (4)

The old lady has been taken to the hospital. She barely eats. She has lost all appetite and pinches her mouth when a spoonful of food is offered to her. It becomes more and more difficult for her to walk across the sitting room with its ghosts of furniture floating in the dusk under the white

sheets. They use a wheelchair now to take her to the dining room at the other end of the villa, past the mahogany-paneled hallway, past the library with its faded emerald velvet curtains drawn in front of the wooden shutters sealing the light as if it was some form of radiation that had to be kept out at all cost, on to the dining room where the long table is set for one with a narrow tablecloth covering one end of it. She is wheeled to the table and a large white linen napkin tied behind her neck.

The food has been ground or pureed or mashed and the nurse feeds her with a small spoon, always a little too fast. The old lady pushes the nurse's hand away, a piece of food falls on the nurse's lap. The young woman curses and angrily drops the spoon on the plate. Then she cleans the food from her blouse. The old lady laughs unexpectedly loud and says, you have to be more careful, Denise, calling her by somebody else's name, you're going to stain your pretty blouse. The young woman darts a murderous look at her and pushes more pureed meat into her mouth. The old lady purses her mouth again stubbornly and moves her face back and forth against the spoon. Eat, screams the nurse. If you don't eat you're going to die. The old lady just looks at her with her mouth shut tight.

At the hospital they put an IV in the old lady's wrist, the skin is like rice paper, the vein rising pale blue under its clear surface. The IV brings her food. After a few days her cheeks flesh out, her eyes light up, she can hold the spoon by herself and she eats with better appetite.

Come, my baby, she sings softly after her meal. Come my little one, come and nurse. She sings a French lullaby.

Dodo, l'enfant do
L'enfant dormira bientôt.

Her arms close on an imaginary infant and she rocks gently from side to side. She remembers the words, all the words perfectly.

Ferme, ferme, ferme vite
Ta paupière si petite
Dodo l'enfant do
L'enfant dormira vite
Dodo l'enfant do
L'enfant dormira bientôt.

(Go to sleep, child
the child will soon fall asleep
close your eyelids quickly
your tiny eyelids
go to sleep, child
the child will sleep quickly
the child will soon fall asleep.)

Max

At a table right in front of center stage, the man who was hiding behind the *Daily News* now folds the newspaper in half and sets it in front of him. He always drinks whiskey, straight up. He holds the glass with a hand that has a small round black ring circled in gold on the little finger.

His trench coat is carefully folded on the back of his chair, and everything about him is modest, manicured and measured. His clean-shaven face, his balding hair combed back, his sports coat, the crease of his shiny navy trousers. His face is blank, the expression as if ironed out. It took a long time for Eva to notice that the man kept coming back to the show and always sat in the second row, sometimes way to the side, sometimes right in the middle. Actually she didn't notice him first, it was Felix. They were in the dressing room waiting to be waved on stage by Angelo. Eva was sitting at the makeup table applying lipstick. Felix was standing by the curtain, looking at the room.

Here comes mystery man, he said.

Who's that? Eva asked distractedly, pursing her lips to fill up the heart shape of her upper lip.

What? Don't tell me you haven't noticed him?

Who? Eva mumbled through her clenched teeth.

Your fan, darling.

She saw him when she pulled out the mike. Drab and blank. Holding his glass. Waiting for her to start. He was gone before the end of her set. By that time she'd forgotten about him.

Felix kept track of him. I didn't see him this time, Eva would say. He was here, oh, he was here, Felix would reply. He was on the side, by the door. He always leaves before the end. He's too shy to come and talk to you. I think he is in love. She'd giggle. Oh, please, Felix. Gimme a break. I swear, Eva. This man is consumed with passion.

Eva has taped all of Max's messages on one single tape that she is playing on her cassette deck. Max's voice is filling up the room. It booms from the stereo loudspeakers.

Beautiful dark eyes, it says, *lift your skirt and go juicy in my mouth.*

Show me your ass and shit on me.

My dick is fifteen inches long. I want to stick it in your ass.

Eva is drinking a cup of tea that she holds tight between her hands, pacing the room back and forth on her bare feet silently.

You have the biggest tits. They're huge. You push them in my face. You push them in my mouth. I can't breathe. Stop, Lola, stop, I'm dying! My huge cock is buried between your boobs. It shoots up in your mouth.

The voice is breathy but mostly clear, the words spoken close to the mouthpiece, more whispered than spoken, as if the speaker didn't want to hear himself too loudly. His words come out of the loudspeakers in a hush.

Lola. Your cunt is moist and hairy. Lola, let me stick it in your ass. Lola, I can't see your face. I can only see your pussy. It's all over my mouth. Lola, stick your fingers up mine.

Eva clicks off the tape and rewinds it. The voice doesn't bring any memory of other voices. It is curiously disembodied. She tries to put that voice in the mouth of the mystery man, the man with the blank face and the *Daily News* and the trench coat, but fails to produce a click, a connection. She looks for him in the lobby, but there are only residents and a homeless woman who attempts to settle down on a couch opposite Eva and drink something from a bottle wrapped in a brown paper bag, until Morris kicks her out.

I wasn't fourteen, actually, when I came to this country. I have this need to cover up, twist things a little. Maybe to keep the upper hand on life. I was seventeen and a half, on the dot. And it wasn't fate. It was desire, or was it inspiration? I was caught necking with Boris on my mother's bed, but that, in itself, isn't an explanation. I dreamed of living a romantic life, of being an amazon in the free world. And it turned out to be my fate: Frank, Mimi, Albertine, the Angel's Follies, you. And now I'm caught in my fate.

Johnny. At first she thought he was the opposite of Frank. Loose, laid-back. Where Frank was angular and hard-assed, Johnny was moody and slippery. Johnny could be real hard-assed too in a sort of volatile and uncontrollable kind of way.

But Johnny made her feel different. He put her into a slow, dreamy state, from which she woke up in shock, tied in knots when his mood turned.

Johnny is lying on his mattress scribbling notes with the TV on for background vibes and he just waits for her to come to him, dropping his notebook, stretching his arms out and smiling, offering himself. The smell of him is all over the place. His trace, animal tracks. She likes his mess, his cups of cold coffee left on the floor, on the tables, she wants to put her lips to the brown rings inside the rims, rub her hands on the heaps of dirty socks and underwear or lean on them as if on a pillow. He waits for her to take him, do what you want with me, whichever way you want. She helps herself from his body, stuffs herself with it. Life has noticeably receded with him, to a distant fringe of consciousness. She goes at it in a dream, forced chores she performs in a dazed state and tries to get rid of as fast as possible.

On the house phone, Morris tells her a gentleman is asking for her in the lobby. It's not Max, it's Frank, in full regalia of hard-core all-male paraphernalia. Doc Martens boots, black jeans, torn T-shirt under heavy army parka. Morris is definitely impressed. Frank and he look like two old pals, shooting the breeze, slapping each other's palms. High five! Frank has turned on the seduction. He could make buddy-buddy with anyone, an old lady, a dog, a tadpole. Eva tenses up. It usually means he wants something.

He's all smiles, waiting for her, his elbows set like wings behind him on the desk.

Hiya! Extra-wide smile showing super-white teeth. Hey, what's happenin'!

Hi! Anything for me, Morris? She stretches her hand toward her mail cubbyhole.

No, Miss Marquand, Morris says, regretfully.

Frank drapes his arm around her shoulders.

Come, let's have a drink.

She pushes his arm away. I'm busy, she says. Walking past him toward the elevator.

I need to talk to you. Seriously. I'll go up to your room if you don't want to go out.

No, she says, sighing and turning around. Let's go out.

It's supposed to be the end of winter, but the wind is sharp and cutting, the cold nips at your neck. They walk side by side, hunched against the wind. It feels like it could snow again, Eva says. Frank curses about the weather, says he doesn't know why he came back to the city, at this time of year he should be in South America, not freezing his ass on these mean streets.

They go to the local bar and sit at the last booth, near the pool tables, right under the big painting of the Garden of Eden, the one with Adam modestly covering his crotch with his hand. Eva looks for Johnny in the crowd, relieved not to see him. Frank stretches his fingers out, the school ring squat and shining on his index finger. The ring reminds Eva of the mystery man. Frank taps his fingers rhythmically for a moment, looking Eva squarely in the eye. She looks back at him. They stare at each other for a while. Frank breaks it up first and laughs.

Boy-oh-boy-oh-boy, he says.

She just arches her eyebrows. Bullshit.

Hey, you in-ti-mi-date me.

He gets up and pushes through the crowd to play the jukebox. When he comes back Sam Cook's "You Send Me" fills the room.

Okay, so shoot, Eva says.

She always felt Frank had the upper hand. Well, not at the beginning. At first, she called the shots. She just had to walk into a room, she knew she had his number. He was an enthusiastic audience for the swing of her hips, the curl of her lips, the pitch of her voice, her foxiness, as he said. All she had to do was put herself into motion and she had him. He came running with his tail straight up between his legs. She stroked him there and he wanted to dig it into her anywhere he could. And then all of a sudden, he had the upper hand. She didn't remember how it had happened. He was fucking her his way, they were going to his favorite restaurants, they were hanging out with his friends, she was wearing the clothes he liked, he made out with every girl in sight. Don't be so uptight, he'd say. Cool out. You don't own me.

So, she says. Shoot, Frank Jackson.

He met this girl at a party. She had straight red hair, big blue eyes and a large mouth. Look at that mouth! What a mouth for blow jobs was the last thing Eva heard him say before he followed the girl into a bedroom and came back half an hour later pulling on his crotch with his cupped hand.

He liked white girls but he also liked black ones. I just can't stand bitches, he'd say, wrapping an arm with a silver cuff at the wrist around some pretty girl's waist. He himself was black and white and red all over, 100 percent pure mulatto, he said.

He's looking at Eva with a funny look, from under up. His sad look. His beaten dog look. Bad news.

Listen, he says gently. I really want to get to know Mimi.

No, she says.

He puts his hands up. Peace offering. The silver cuff slides a little up his arm. It's the same old cuff, the one he told her he bought at a jewelry dealer on Canal Street when he was eighteen years old. He doesn't even remove it to take a shower or go swimming.

No. Listen. Listen to me. I don't want to take her away from you.

She's already shaking her head and flames are darting out of her eyes. No way. No way.

Listen to me. She is my child, she comes from my sperm, you're her mother. I'm not saying I have any legal rights because I don't, but humanly, humanly, you know, between you and me, two human beings trying to do good, trying to do what's right.

She chuckles, guffaws. Cut the bull, Frank. Who's trying to do good to whom? Not you, not me.

I want to see her. I want to have a relationship with my own daughter.

She bristles at the word. The word doesn't pass too well from his own lips. This is a man who's more comfortable with female words like cunt and tits than daughter. But he manages to say it straight.

Eva keeps her head down. Tapping Frank's box of matches on the old worn wood of the booth table. A small slim matchbox that bears the name of a jazz club up in Harlem on a purple background. She slides it open. Inside, the matches are slim too, with an elongated white tip. She strikes one and watches the flame shoot up and work its way down the wooden stick almost burning her fingers, before dropping it into the ashtray where it ends its course abruptly.

You want to see her, she says, it's going to cost you. Five hundred a shot.

He laughs, not knowing if she's serious or not.

I'm serious, Frank. Look at it this way: a new form of child support. Rent-a-child.

It sounds like blackmail to me, babe.

She shrugs. He asks for another scotch.

I'm not saying I want to act as her father at this late date. I said I wanted to get to know her. You know, like, spend an afternoon with her, take her to the movies, to the ball game.

The ball game!

What's wrong with that? She could use some of that stuff. Make her a real American. Take her for ice cream. Take her for a roller-coaster ride in Coney Island. Okay, not even that, not even that far, just round the corner to Nathan's, go for a hot dog with her. Walk around the Deuce and take her to one of the old movie theaters where my grandma used to take me when I was a kid, popcorn, all that shit. Just talk to a six-year-old. See what's she's got to say. Maybe her and me got things in common, who knows?

Eva is staring at him with mock astonishment and a growing sneer.

Stop it, you're going to make me cry.

His hands fly up again. Listen, it's up to you. She's your daughter. She belongs to you.

No she doesn't, Eva screams. Asshole! No she doesn't. (Heads turn in their direction.) But she sure as hell doesn't belong to you.

Well. So she don't belong to nobody. So what are we gonna do?

She toys with the matchbox again. Up goes the flame, down it comes, until the match turns black in the ashtray.

Problem is that I don't trust you, Frank Jackson. What you're saying makes a whole lot of sense, but coming from your lips, your lips change the meaning of words, if you know what I mean.

I am trying to be straight with you. You're giving me shit.

Maybe.

She slips into her coat and picks up her pocketbook and slides to the edge of the booth.

Maybe I'm giving you shit and maybe you don't deserve it, but somehow I think you do. So see you later.

Frank didn't turn around to watch her leave. He stayed for a while looking at his hands spread out in front of him, his back a little slumped. Then he gulped down his drink, left a bill on the table and walked to the men's room.

Coney Island

Manhattan looked like it was going to sink under the weight of its buildings, Albertine says. Crammed full to the very edge, and then I found out that they had built embankments on top of the marshlands to widen it. Midtown, you felt like you were at the bottom of a pit, walking,

your neck screwed up to see a patch of sky. I figured God couldn't see me, so little in the shadow of the skyscrapers, and he wasn't going to mess around with my life. I still feel that way. You don't play by the same rules here. Naughty children playing in the mud, nobody says anything.

Which reminds me. I think you're screwing up, gorgeous, if you want my advice. The man called three times again last night. Aren't you going to do something about it? Let him see her, have some heart.

Nope.

Eva's leafing through a fashion magazine and she turns three more pages slowly, studying each outfit and accessory with full concentration before making her next move.

I put a curse on him, she says, casually.

Albertine turns around from her stove. Sweetbreads tonight. She's just blanched them. And now she's melting butter in a double boiler. She turns around holding the pot in front of her like a weapon, then turns back and sets it down again because you've got to do it quick, every second counts.

What are you thinking about? You fool! With that . . . that voodoo woman? Don't you know it's going to come back at you?

Eva shrugs. No it won't. Nothing will happen, more than likely. Nothing at all. I will just have wasted my money.

Play with fire, burn yourself, Albertine mutters, starting work on the carrots and the peas. She covers the sweetbreads with a top to keep them warm and wipes her hands on her apron.

I got a letter from France today, she says, rummaging around on top of the dresser amidst loose piles of bills, coupons and catalogues.

Here.

She hands Eva a piece of paper with fine blue lines that looks as if it's been torn from a school notebook. The handwriting is slanted backward, big and a bit shaky.

It's from my daughter, Albertine says, sitting down across from Eva.

What daughter? You don't have a daughter! Are you talking about me? Mimi asks, poking her head in the door, lips slashed with purple lipstick, turquoise eye shadow lavishly spread on upper and lower eyelids, three dressed-to-kill Barbie dolls pressed to her chest.

Eva waves her away. *Allez va, va.* Go play. No. It wasn't you we were talking about. You're not the only daughter around. And Mimi: clean up that face will you. Dinner is going to be ready.

What does the letter say?

Read.

I can't read this handwriting.

It's my elder daughter. She found my address, I don't know how. She said it took her years. She wants to see me.

What are you going to do?

I don't know. I think she's making a mistake.

Do you want to see her?

Mimi! Come and set the table. Come on, girl! *Merde*, the vegetables are going to be overcooked, I can't stand them limp.

Albertine pricks a fork through a carrot stick and quickly turns the gas off. She pushes the sweetbreads into a dish and pours sauce over them.

Ready. Let's eat.

Do you want to see her?

Albertine pensively sucks the sweetbread juices off her thumb and middle finger, nodding her appreciation.

I don't know, she says. You're supposed to feel that bond, a rush of emotion, come my daughter, come to your mother's arms. Come back to my womb, you know, something stirring in the groin, the heart, the breast, wherever these things are situated. But it's an old story for me. All that it'd be stirring, I'm afraid, would be dirt and mud. Nothing so very noble.

Really? Not even curiosity?

Okay, I'm ready, Mimi yells, her usual tone of voice, storming into the kitchen. I even washed my hands. Look. She holds the palms up to show streaks of color slightly washed out by the soap.

Okay, set the table, please.

This is always a big affair, to have Mimi set the table. She waltzes out of the room as soon as the word table is pronounced. She comes back and gets involved in a coloring book, spreading furious patches of green and red until she is physically forced in front of the kitchen cabinet to take the tableware out.

In front of the sweetbreads which she quickly judges yuckko, Mimi announces she wants to go for a ride, a roller-coaster ride, at Coney Island. Eva asks what gave her that idea. Mimi answers that Frank Jackson said he would take her. When? Eva asks, suddenly shot through with alarm. But Mimi won't say. She keeps repeating he'd mentioned it to her when he came to Albertine's, that first time. Albertine and Eva exchange looks. Albertine shrugs, meaning, go ahead, why not? Let it go.

Please, Mom, Mimi is pleading, the same way she'll plead for a new Barbie doll or to watch a special show on TV. Please, Mommy, please Mommy please Mommy please Mommy. Pleeease!

You don't have to go with Frank Jackson. I'll take you, Eva says.

Both of you! Both of you! Both of you! Mimi chants, a devilish glint in her eye.

Albertine shoots Eva a meaningful glance.

And Mimi emerges victorious, as usual.

So here we are, like a happy family, getting off the subway, last stop on the D line, Brooklyn, the air just as nippy as the last few days, the wind blowing in hard gusts straight from the ocean, thick with oil and iodine. The three of us walking in a line, Mimi in the middle, winter coats tight around our waists, heads bent to cut the wind. Frank has a spinach-colored muffler wrapped twice around his neck and tucked into his army jacket. He walks with quick jerky steps, his usual gait. Mimi takes two steps for his one. She's dead serious, for once, doesn't chat away or run ahead, one hand stuck into her coat pocket, the other one squeezing mine tight, not her usual style. Maybe she's wondering if this outing was such a great idea. I'm not wondering. I know it's a terrible idea.

Frank is now a little ahead of us. We cross the boulevard, now we're moving in a diagonal line. He is the first one to set foot on the opposite sidewalk. There are people standing in little groups outside the food stands. He could weave his way through the groups and walk out of a stand the back way, or walk straight into the amusement park, disappear behind a Ferris wheel. I wish he would. But no such luck. He turns back and waits for us to catch up with him. Mimi walks right into Nathan's hot dog stand, her chin barely reaches the metal counter. She positions herself in front of one of the machines that wheels the dripping sausages on a turning bed and looks at them longingly. Before I can say a word, Frank's already pulled out his wallet and pushed a few dollar bills on the counter. How many you want, one, two? He buys one for her, one for himself, offers to cover hers with mustard and sauerkraut, but she stops him in his march forward in the direction of the ketchup and mustard machines. No, no, she yells. I want mine plain. I *hate* mustard.

I watch from a distance, leaning against the wall. There are the eyes, and then the bodies: small, round, sticking out, high-slung ass; long legs; long fingers; the curl of the earlobe. You don't pay attention to earlobes. But here they are, from that angle. Eerily alike. I shouldn't have come. Leave them alone. But I don't trust him. I would never do that.

Now they march outside. Frank tries to take her hand but she pulls back and waits for me. You don't want a hot dog, Mom? she asks, her mouth full of a brownish gooey substance. No thanks. I have more civilized tastes. The back way leads directly to the amusement park. The roller coaster lurks high and foreboding above us against the steel-gray sky. The park is practically deserted on this weekday, Mimi's only free afternoon from school. Clumps of teenagers stomping their feet and slapping their ribs like they're waiting to score some dope or mug an old lady, and a few lone kids kicking soda bottles and old newspapers around looking for trouble. That doesn't faze Mimi, who is clapping her hands as the first car of the joyride comes to a full stop in front of us. I remember last time I got on one of those infernal machines was in Frankfurt, Germany, where my mother had sent me in the hope that I would pick up the language of the Teutons and I had gotten into a wheel that comes to a vertical when in full swing and the only thing that keeps your body up is the centrifugal force. My pockets emptied themselves, keys, cigarettes, and a gold cigarette lighter, a Dupont lighter, present from my first boyfriend, and which I discovered (the lighter, not the boyfriend) hours later in the grass underneath the machinery of the wheel. When I came down I swore it was going to be my last ride. Famous last words.

Mimi is jumping up and down in the cold dreadful wind, while Frank Jackson gets the tickets, presumably for the two of them. Mimi's already sitting in the car, strapped in behind the metal bar. I'm standing by the track thinking, I really loathe these rides, if I'm getting on it, I know I'm going to die. Frank is now turning toward me, asking, you coming or not, he's got extra bills in his hand, he is offering to pay for me. I tell him I'm thinking of taking a walk. I don't want to admit those things scare the shit out of me. In front of Frank I want to be fearless, the knight in shiny armor. Mimi's screaming, pumping her arms up and down, the only part of her body still free, begging me to come with them. I look around me. I could leave them alone at it, walk around the park, go to the shore and stroll up and down the boardwalk. From here I can see the seagulls gliding low and uttering their cries of doom. Frank is now strapping himself in the car and suddenly it occurs to me they're sitting in the first car with Mimi in front, and if there's an accident she'd be the one to topple over and break her neck or get smashed under the following cars coming at a hundred miles an hour or thereabouts. I tell Frank to sit Mimi at the back but she kicks her feet and screams, no, no, I want to see. The ride operator says it's time to go, am I getting in or not. I wonder if these rides have to follow a schedule, like a train, otherwise, what's the rush, since nobody's waiting. Mimi's still kicking and pumping her arms up and down demanding that I join them, and I think, what the hell, if I sit in back of her and something happens, maybe I can hold her tight and protect her, or else we'll die together which is better than being witness to her death. I grab some money from my pocketbook and hand it to the attendant. Frank starts getting up, offering me his seat. You can sit in front, he says, you'll see better. I say no thanks and squeeze my body into the back. The attendant makes sure I'm strapped properly and walks to the cabin where he's going to maneuver some levers and send us to our death. I think of Jesus sweating and bleeding our sins out of his wounds on Albertine's purple velvet and I mentally burn a candle to his thorns. Wish me luck.

The beginning is a piece of cake. It's the ride going up and it's the slow train to freedom and I breathe for about two minutes thinking that there's nothing to get excited about, it's actually almost fun, maybe my memory of that German ride distorted reality. We go down a short hill and that's okay, Mimi's in stitches and I keep screaming, hold on to the bar, Mimi, hold on to the bar! And then we're going uphill again, and downhill and that's fine, if a little rocky, and then we go uphill again and the hill doesn't seem to end, it's so steep you have to hold on to the metal bar in order not to fall backward. Mimi turns around to exchange a look with me, I notice that Frank hasn't made a move toward her, he's sitting stiffly by her side, not that there's much room to move, but it seems to me he's making a point of not touching her, of avoiding any gesture that might be misinterpreted or inappropriate, but I don't wonder anymore because in a split second we've reached the top of the hill and we're falling down like stones, propelled at full speed down a quasi-vertical, the pull of gravity multiplying our speed as my heart flies into my mouth and I hear Mimi screaming, Mommy, Mommy in panic and Frank's arm juts sideways to grab Mimi's little body and I can't believe everything's over, that I'm dying in a roller-coaster ride at Coney Island, the most stupid way to end your days, or at the very least have a heart attack, when we suddenly hit bottom in a clatter of metallic jerks and I hear Frank sigh wow! as he turns toward me and asks me if I'm okay. There's no time to answer, we're back on the upswing again, very fast, using the downhill momentum we've gained and then again we're going down, we're tossed up and down, my eyes are permanently shut and a scream of horror half choked in my throat. Mimi seems to have recovered from the first steep chute and I can hear her giggle from a faraway distance as if I was deep underwater losing my breath and she was safe on the shore, I think Frank laughs with her. I feel the back end of the car lift up again preparing for a new chute but something is holding us back, could it be brakes? The car comes to a full stop and I open my eyes to see the bored ride attendant shuffle his feet toward us and lift the metal bars first from Mimi and Frank and then from me. A small crowd of people are gathered in line along the tracks waiting for the next ride to start. Before I can extract myself, Mimi is all shouting mouth and bright eyes. That was fun, Mommy, that was fun, wasn't it, Mommy? But it takes all my composure to hold myself together, to walk to the back of the little cabin and squat and throw my tripes up, carefully avoiding my shoes and my pocketbook.

The beach is swept by sharp gusts of wind that seem to be getting even colder now that the sun is going down and the litter, scattered around our feet, seems frozen in the dirty sand. Mimi runs after the seagulls and complains there's sand in her shoes while Frank and I are left standing side by side facing the spread of lead-gray water like a couple of bored parents watching their kid frolicking by the ocean. To look at Frank and me that way is such a disturbing thought that I step away from him and he must've sensed it because I catch him glance quickly at me and he says, appreciatively, she's a good kid. I bristle. It's almost as if he had said, we've got a good kid here. The implicit "we" is unbearable to accept. Yeah, she's a great kid, I reply, with a detached tone intended to separate her from "us." Truly, I don't think she belongs to me either. I know parents who, when people compliment their children for their beauty or their intelligence, say "thank you" as if the compliment was addressed to them. I never felt that way about Mimi. Mimi happens to have been born through my body and I am in charge of her and of course that creates ties, but it's a temporary business, a matter of sixteen, eighteen years at the outside until she is ready to take off.

Now he puts his hand on my forearm and says, gently, you did a good job. She's okay. I shake his hand away. Please, I say, between my teeth, thinking, don't go sentimental on me or I'll puke. He walks a few steps forward and squats, pouring sand from one hand to the other. Then he suddenly jumps up on his long legs and throws a rock into the ocean. Mimi turns around. Do it again she says, do it again, and he obliges. Throws flat rocks and makes them ricochet two, three, four times over the surface, hitting the waves that come breaking with a mustache of dirty froth at the edge. Mimi picks up a bunch of pebbles and tries her hand at it, but hers sink as soon as they hit the water, so Frank picks flat rocks for her and takes her hand and teaches her the correct method to move the wrist and shoulder. He is patient. From this angle I can see the skin around his chin is less taut than it used to be, it's a little looser around the eyes. I look at him coldly, observing the effect of aging, even a few short years, but instead of being vindicated that he is not indestructible, I feel a softening, a letting go of my body and bend to pick up a rock myself and silently move next to them and toss it from a low angle, shoulder, head going down, wrist at hip level, always throw from the hip, same way you always shoot from the hip, my brother used to say, and mine splashes and hits the first wave head-on and bounces off it to sink a couple of feet farther. Mimi claps her hands. Good, Mummy, she says, that was good. I pick up another one. Frank comes behind me and adjusts the position of my right foot. Like this, he says. Better. Now go ahead. But he's thrown me off balance and my rock sinks. I am mad at him, I feel like Mimi when one of her endeavors fails and she whines, it's your fault, look what you made me do. Let go of me, I say, let me do it my way. We both toss our rocks at the same time. Mine goes farther than his, one more ricochet. He laughs. I laugh. Mimi gets antsy. You're doing it better than me, she says. It's unfair. Stomping her foot and turning her back to us. Then we all realize the wind is dying down and the rain is coming, lazy odd drops to begin with, splashing wide brown circles on the sand, but we don't have an umbrella, so Frank and I both get hold of one of Mimi's hands and we run across the beach across the boardwalk across the amusement park all the way to the subway where we arrive soaked and exhausted but briefly burst into giggles before Mimi turns on the whine and announces she's hungry and she won't make one more step, proceeding to prove it by letting her knees go soft and trailing her feet. So Frank buys her a bag of cookies and I can see she's ready to sell out. The child makes me sick. No dignity.

Frank is on his way downtown, so Mimi and I get off first at Times Square where we buy a cheap umbrella before charging into the pouring rain and Albertine is expecting us at the door, a pot of hot chocolate heating on the stove. As she helps Mimi get undressed I see her eyes questioning me but I make a point of not saying a word, waiting for Mimi to narrate our outing, curious to find out what she's made of it.

Mimi's pretty sly. She muses over her hot chocolate asking for additional sugar and something, anything, to eat, she's starved, she's going to be sick if she doesn't eat something right away, and answers Albertine's questions with groans and downplaying the afternoon like it was some kind of boring and utterly predictable routine. But then, when we've given up trying to extract any more reaction from her, she says, I had a real good time this afternoon, is Frank Jackson going to live with us?

No, Mimi, I say, trying to keep my self-control.

Why not, it would be fun, she says.

So, the afternoon was a success, Albertine says after Mimi's been put to bed. With that scowl on your face you'd think it was a disaster.

I don't want to talk about it, I tell her.

Oh, no? Why not?

I change the subject.

Tell me, Albertine, what are you going to do about this letter you got from your daughter?

Her face turns sour, but she got the point.

We both just sit there with scowls on our faces, looking at each other.

So, are you going to meet her or what?

I don't know, she says. I really don't.

Waiting for Johnny

Johnny gets up. Twelve noon pushing one P.M., hung over. Mr. Coffee lightened up with a drop of milk. He just gave up smoking, one of the fifteen times this has happened, and feels his movements as if held back by the old cigarette/lighter/fingers/lips/ashtray routine, still encoded in his body.

His whole system is off, he paces around, looks for something to hold between his fingers, grabs the telephone, sticks his finger in the dial, whirls it furiously. He organizes his day, what's left of it, and his evening, his night. Errands to run, people to see, appointments to arrange, messages to return, but not Eva's, not yet at least, rehearsal in a warehouse in Brooklyn.

Johnny is always in a rush. He reads the sports section of yesterday's *Daily News*, drinks another cup of coffee, dials three phone numbers, shaves, cuts himself with his razor blade, walks around the apartment with a towel wrapped around his hips and tiny pieces of toilet paper stuck to his chin to absorb the blood, looks for papers on his table, which is covered with letters and unmatched torn envelopes, cards, magazines, invites to various outfits and clubs, Xeroxed fliers, newspaper clippings, spiral notebooks, half-toppled stacks of cassettes, loose sheets of white paper scribbled with telephone numbers, names, addresses, doodles in black ink and fat lines made with Magic Markers in pink, red, green, doodles that tend to run into the margins, onto the edges of the sheets or immediately attached to the last letter of a word, starting as a simple flourish and developing into elaborate cartoonish figures, faces, or even complete scenes, revealing a certain talent for drawing and for caricature. He finally finds what he's looking for, the place where he's supposed to meet a client for a carpentry job, an obscure address way downtown, one of these name streets that lose themselves against the West Side Highway, short streets, sometimes no more than a couple of blocks of industrial warehouses swept by the wind, broken-down sidewalks with strings of delivery trucks parked along the curb.

Johnny always walks or bikes in the city, if he can manage it. Leaves his Studebaker over in Jersey, near his mom's place, avoids the train at all costs, and forget the bus, too slow, sluglike, can't be bothered. In the wintertime, with the snow and patches of ice on the streets, he leaves his wheels in the basement, anchored to the sewer pipe with a chain and a padlock strong enough to hold together a herd of buffalo. He trusts his rubber soles better. He zips up his leather jacket, pulls up the collar, slaps on a pair of leather gloves and a pair of earmuffs and skids away on his white high-tops. Johnny likes to feel the street as he walks, not just the hard, bruised cement under his feet, but the buzz, what's happenin' today buzz, who's in town, who's hangin' around on the street corner, what's the latest, who's the greatest, rumors rushing down from sidewalk to sidewalk at the speed of light, people's fates changing so fast in New York, upward or downward, this gyre sucking them, spitting them out, it's like taking the temperature of the city, things are bad, things are better, things are going down.

He walks across town, arctic wind blowing into his face, whistling through his hair, under his earmuffs. He feels the energy of the cold wintry air running through his body. The gusts of wind get stronger as he comes closer to the river. They slap around the edges of the island in great blasts eddying at every street corner and it gives him the powerful sensation, here, in the middle of one of the most urban cities in the world, of being part of the elements, of being one with nature. He could almost check his weapons, his multiple-blade knife folded inside his sock, the vise grip he keeps in the inside pocket of his jacket as a potential club but that he's only used once—to attempt to fix a leak under the bathroom sink. There are also his keys, and the brass buckle of his leather belt that can be pulled out in a split second to swing at any attacker if all else fails. One doesn't go down into the Manhattan jungle without proper protection, even though these days the best protection might be a thin rubber pressed flat as a ring in a tiny foil pouch. His clanky armor might turn out to be obsolete, yet it is good to feel the primitive textures of metal and leather so intimately pressed against his body, imparting to him some of their magic. It gives him something hard and secure to hold on to in the midst of the murky waters he navigates most of the time.

Eva imagines Johnny lying on his mattress, his arms stretched over his head, or gathering his energy and zipping down the street, running late, meeting a hundred people well into the night, bursting with creative ideas that somehow all turn against him or deflate like tired-out birthday balloons or working his ass off at a construction job, which gives him these tight, well-rounded shoulders. She craves him like she craved a jar of little French *cornichons* or a tall chocolate milk shake when she was pregnant, the kind of craving that spreads like fire centered somewhere around your guts eating at you, that doesn't leave you peace, that colors your thoughts red and they leap around you like demons with long canines and split pointy tails. It's pure lust, but lust can go a long way and it starts getting to her seriously so that the Frank Jackson question dims on the edge of her consciousness, leaving a numb stale pain that doesn't require any action.

One thing about Mimi living with Albertine is that Eva has plenty of time to hang around and torture herself and waste her time till she gets sick of it and long after and this is precisely what she is doing right now, walking up and down the Great White Way with its trashy lights and its neons bleeding into the wet pavement and Mr. Macho Man up there smoking a Winston as if he was exhibiting his dick between his fingers, not even noticing his lungs are rotting away, checking out the porn theaters with their juicy titles and the peep shows and the three-card monte smooth operators with their ever-winning sidekicks, but she only stops near the chirping bird vendor, the old guy who sits at the corner of Seventh and Forty-fifth with a clear trash bag full of plastic birds and a bucket of water and he shows you how to dip the birdie into the water and stick its tail in your mouth and blow into it and the birdie will whistle like a real bird, you can hear the old guy demonstrating his wares a whole block away. So she stops to look at him and she can't resist buying a pink bird for Mimi after he demonstrates to her the proper way to get it to whistle and then she walks downtown to Macy's to try on a few dresses and find some way to spend her money.

After a few more days of intense withdrawal, she figures there would be no harm in checking out Johnny's local hangout, go in for a beer and see if his buddies have seen him, or if he's been shooting pool, casually, nothing heavy, but no Johnny. One of his pals, named Bruce, a guy with a beer belly and a fat handlebar mustache, is reading the *Post* at a booth and she waves at him from the bar, pours some beer in her glass and starts chatting with the bartender. This is not something she usually does, she hates beer and she hates going to a bar alone, but the TV hanging above the counter is delivering a barrage of black-and-white images which look like an old "Twilight Zone" episode and the bartender starts commenting on it and engaging her in a conversation which keeps her busy for a little while, and then all she has to do when she goes to the ladies' room later is walk past Bruce the *Post* reader and say hi and ask him, did you see Johnny lately as if she could care less and he grumbles, from the depth of his belly, think he got a big construction job uptown, big money, one of those movie stars' apartments on Central Park West, forgot the name, anyway, no, he hasn't been around, 's'working too hard. Then he asks how is she doing and she says, fine, and she asks him how is he doing and he says okay, I guess, and he fingers his *Post* and she says, okee-dokee, see you later, and makes her way to the bathroom with studied indifference even though he's facing the other way and can't see her, but you can never be too sure.

So she decides to give Johnny a couple of extra days before taking further action, imagining him dropping dead on his bed after a fourteen-hour day with sweat burning his eyes and not enough strength to take a shower. But it's time for her gig at the Follies and she can't help hoping he's going to show up like that first time, at the back, leaning against the banister, a cigarette sticking out of his closed fist, and getting hot for her. But all she sees is Angelo running around, a Budweiser dangling from his fingers, and a pretty quiet house and later, when she's busy getting ready in the dressing room, Felix walking in, saying, guess who's here for you tonight, darling, and her heart jumps in her chest and she wildly hopes for a second that it's Johnny until he says, Mr. Max, my dear, mystery man in person, in the front row tonight. Eva wonders if that means anything, and she feels like punching him in the face for the bad news but she notices that his eyes are watery and his cheeks red and when she touches his hand, it feels burning hot. Felix, you're sick, she says.

I know, I feel like shit. I think it's the flu.

You shouldn't be here. You've got to take care of it.

I know. I can't wait to go home. So, what's happening with Johnny anyway?

Why do you ask?

Don't know. You seem concerned and I haven't seen him around lately. Is everything okay?

This is not the time to talk about that because she's going on in about ten minutes and she likes to blank out before she gets on stage, a sort of mental vacuum cleaning, but she knows Felix will be on her side, and she can't resist so she tells him Johnny's drifting away. And he asks her why and she tells him it's because of Frank Jackson coming back to town and that she can't handle it very well and Johnny can't handle it or her at all and Felix sees she's on the verge of breaking down so he puts his arms around her and presses her against him, there's so much love there it's almost frightening. He hugs her one more time and shakes his head. Johnny's a jerk, he says, letting her go. And, changing into a street voice: Johnny don't know what he got.

She laughs. No, he don't, she says.

Felix is right. Max is sitting right in front in her field of vision with a cocky air about him, the way he's holding his chin in his hand and thrusting his shoulders forward and he gives her the creeps. She forces herself not to look at him which is distracting because every time she wants to establish eye contact with somebody in the room she has to sweep over or around or through him and she can feel him staring at her intensely. But when she looks for him after her set is over, he's gone.

Johnny comes over that night, late, she was getting ready to go to bed. He calls from the lobby, and she can tell he's drunk. There's a nasty edge in his voice. And the urgency.

Johnny, I've been looking for you all over town. Where have you been?

Let me up, okay?

He sits across from her, slumped into one of the armchairs, his leather jacket still on, knees apart, his elbows propped on his knees, his hands dangling between his legs. His shock of hair falls angrily over his forehead.

She looks at him from the couch, curled up in her kimono, playing with a little plastic coaster, turning it around between her fingers and tapping it lightly against the coffee table.

So, what's on your mind? You play dead for a week and all of a sudden you show up at my door, you don't even call before coming . . .

He pushes the long strand of hair hanging across his eyes, slicks it back and stands up, gets a beer from the fridge, drinks some of it from the bottle, comes back, leans against the door frame. He looks stubborn and tough and vaguely lost.

Who's that guy you were with the other day at the bar?

What guy? What other day?

Don't pretend you don't know what I'm talking about. I was shooting pool. You didn't even see me.

She laughs.

What! At the bar? You mean Frank Jackson!

Whoever he was.

Johnny, you're ridiculous.

He tosses the empty bottle on the kitchen counter.

I thought it was over between you and him.

Between me and him? You must be kidding. It's been over for six years, almost seven, since I was pregnant with Mimi. It's not over, it's . . . ancient history.

What does he want from you?

Eva gets up, tightens her kimono around her.

He wants Mimi, that's what he wants. He doesn't want me. He could care less about me. But anyway, Johnny, it's none of your fucking business.

It is so.

She goes up to him, finds a pack of cigarettes and a lighter in his pocket, lights one.

I thought you quit smoking?

He shrugs her off.

Forget it, Johnny, it's not worth it. You're way off base.

You're a fucking jerk.

You too.

No, you first.

You're a bigger one.

Eva moves on him with her fists.

Get out of here. I won't get insulted in my own house!

He deflects her punches with his forearm.

Hey, cut it out! You're going to burn me with your cigarette. You could use a little practice if you want to fight.

Come, she says, pulling on his belt and popping the little brass button from its hole and unfastening every one of the metal buttons from his fly, you're going to pay me back. She lifts his T-shirt over his tight stomach, hooks her hand into the opened jeans and pulls him to the floor with her. He lands on his back, his elbows planted into the olive-green carpet. She straddles him, pulls the jeans and the waistband of his underwear down and goes fishing for his cock. It pops out moist, red, and half turgid from its nest of tight reddish curls. They both look at it. She flatters it with the tip of her tongue, runs light fingers from the balls up to the upper ridge, then back. It swells and hardens, now proud and demanding, its veins gorging thick and purple. She administers it a couple of tiny slaps as if she was trying to get some color back on a cheek. Johnny relaxes his head on his crossed hands and opens up his legs to give her free play. But she pulls back and puts her hands on her thighs. Why are you stopping? he asks, thick-tongued.

I want you to seduce me. I want you to do everything I like. I want you to be moist and hot and make me wet and drive me over the edge.

He smiles a drunken smile.

I will.

He half lifts himself to reach for her but she pulls back some more.

No, she says. Not like that.

How, then?

She gets up and comes back with a pair of satin ribbons that she hands him.

Stay like this, she says. Keep your clothes on and tie my wrists up to the legs of the table. I want you to play rough with me.

He looks at her for a moment, not sure she means it.

These phone calls you're making are getting to you.

Don't worry, she says. You'll get your turn.

He ties her up loosely to the wrought-iron legs.

You found me lying on the floor with just this flimsy nightgown on and you open my legs and you go down on me and there's nothing I can do because my hands are tied.

He bends over her and starts licking her and she moans and groans, keeping her legs tight, pulling on her ribbons and kicking him in the groin. Then gradually she opens up a little.

Now, she says.

He slaps her and she thrusts her pelvis forward.

Again.

Again.

He slaps her more and enters her.

She twitches under him.

He thrusts himself deep into her.

She pulls on the ties that bind her.

Untie me now, she says.

He pushes forward, his whole weight hammering upon her.

No, he says.

Please, untie me.

No.

She pulls on the strings with all her might. The pale blue ribbons stretch and cut into her skin, against the thin vein that runs like faded ink along the wrist ligaments. The pain makes her curl her lips.

Please, she says. Loosen the ties. I want to touch you with my hands. I need my hands now.

No.

He slaps her across the face. She screams.

He goes deeper into her. He hits against the cervix. She needs her hands, her elbows for leverage. She can't meet him. She bites his lips. She tastes the blood on her tongue. He thrusts himself with fury.

Johnny, she says. Slow down.

But he is too far gone. He pumps her like an inflatable raft. She tries to loosen up one of her thighs to slip away from him but he's got her in a tight grip. The edge of his leather jacket rubs against her hips, irritating her skin. She pulls harder and only succeeds in sliding the coffee table closer to her on one side, bringing her wrist close to her mouth. She twists her neck, trying to pull at the string with her teeth. No, says Johnny, slapping her again. Leave it alone. She manages to pull the string out and then pulls the other ribbon with her free hand. Johnny grabs her wrists. You bitch, he says. She pulls her hands free and digs into his shoulders.

Johnny grabs her by the wrists and slaps her again. He says, you asked for it, you wanted it, you can't say no, you can't go back now.

She says: you can always go back. I took the wrong turn. This is not what I wanted.

Sometimes you can't turn back. You turn around and you don't recognize the path you came from. It's overgrown with strange vegetation. There are exotic birds you had never seen before in vibrant blues, reds, yellows, greens. They chirp and land on a low branch above your head. You extend your arm toward them, they fly away with a mocking laugh, you are left touching the leaves of a catalpa. You find yourself in the middle of a thick forest. There's no path where you're coming from, only a narrow passageway in the bush ahead of you, you can barely distinguish a few feet of it that lose themselves in the thick jungle. You take a step in life and everything turns upon itself, a man you can't see is grabbing you by your coattails and pushing a knife between your shoulder blades in the dark hallway of your building and walks with you into your apartment and rapes you, you are sixteen years old and you get pregnant with your boyfriend or a guy you met at a party, you quit your job after you have a fight with your boss and you cannot find another one, you move to a bigger, more expensive apartment and you lose a big contract and you can't meet the rent, your father is dying of cancer, you meet a guy and fall in love with him and move to Hawaii to live with him. You begin to hallucinate. The trap closes upon you. The walls are stretching. The blue of the sea is threatening. You walk in Waikiki alone at night and see shadows following you. You go to Morocco and you get lost in the medina of Fez, try to retrace your steps and make mental pictures of alley corners and architectural details, but dusk is falling and the merchants are closing shop and pull the wooden shutters that are all made of wide planks painted dull gray or faded blue and you can't tell one from the other. You find respite for a brief moment in the spice market that stays open the latest but you don't know how to come back to your hotel from there and the spice racks all look the same to you, an endless succession of piles of golden-yellow turmeric, rust cayenne, vermilion saffron, slate-blue poppy seeds, brown cumin and cinnamon, and they, too, gradually get covered by the wooden shutters, and the maze seem to shrink and to darken, the sky has turned a deep navy and by the narrow patches of it you glimpse above the maze, you see the Shepherds' star shining hard and you sit down out of exhaustion on the cool blue and white tiles of a doorway.

No, Johnny says, you can't go back. Or is it Frank? It all started when she got knocked up by Frank and decided to go ahead with it, and now life is making a loop upon itself and comes back to ask for its due.

You're going to cough up, bitch! You were on the run, now you've got to face up to it.

That's not true, I wasn't on the run. I was here, I wasn't moving from here. I am working. I am raising my kid.

Raising? You call that raising a kid?

I am doing my best.

Women get caught in the end.

It's Johnny who's slapping her. He's fucking her too hard. She can't come that way. He's tearing her cunt. She wonders if it's bleeding. She notices he hasn't removed his cowboy boots. They bang against the carpet.

You played with fire, he said.

You played with me, remember, Johnny? We played together. Our bodies played together.

He sits down on the couch and bends to pull his jeans over his boots. You fucked up, he says. You fucked me. You fucked us up.

She stands in front of him in her silk robe, her arms crossed on her chest. She looks at him coldly. He has this strong voice and he can back it up with his fists but behind that it's just the wind.

And how did I do that?

You allowed your life to be taken over by your fears. You allowed this guy Frank Jackson to bully you.

I freaked out. People freak out. It's human. Frank Jackson did bully me. I didn't allow him to do it.

You fucked up, he says. You lost me.

The old lady (5)

The old lady is sitting in her wheelchair, slumped, rather, bone collapsed upon bone. There isn't much muscle left to hold her erect. Her body is shrunken to the size of a child. Under the blanket—mohair, red-and-maroon check—are two ghosts of thighs, they look as if they each would fit into the circle of a closed hand. She is asleep, her neck folded over her collarbone. Of her face, only the forehead and cheekbones stand out, with the eyes closed at the center of the deep cavity. She is taking her after-breakfast nap, even though it's already three o'clock in the afternoon, and there's no way to awake her. No matter how much Eva and her mother lean over her, talk to her, she is lost in neverland.

They wait a long time, they have tea and fruitcake, the commercial kind, not like the one the old lady used to bake, was famous for: tender, light, with just a few clusters of raisins, candied cherries. They don't mention the cake of olden times. They eat and drink heartily, chatting about the weather and Eva's shopping. They have turned on the TV set in an attempt to wake up the old lady, and their conversation is riding over a string of wisecracks badly translated from an American sitcom. The old lady still doesn't budge. None of the wisecracks reach her. Look, Eva says, her hair is all plastered on her forehead. She'd hate to see herself like that. She gets up and runs her fingers through the old lady's hair, slicking it back, giving it a hip, almost jaunty turn. Then they turn off the TV because the loud, stupid voices are driving them nuts.

Finally, Eva's mother tries to pour some cool water between her lips and the old lady fusses and gurgles like an infant surfacing from deep sleep, except it's less charming. Her eyes open and focus somewhere above the TV set.

It's me, Eva says, it's me, Eva. Do you recognize me?

The old lady chuckles softly.

The maid brings a bowl of beef and string beans ground to a brownish pulp, with a teaspoon stuck in it. The old lady's missing all her front teeth—the gums are beginning to rot—so she's got to be fed soft food. She opens her lips obediently. Eva asks her again, it's me, do you recognize me? between two spoonfuls. After a few more questions the old lady chuckles again. She mumbles, yes, I know who you are, yes, still staring at a spot over the TV set.

Did you show her the roses?

Eva's mother brings down the vase of roses sitting on top of the set. There are a dozen roses the color of a spring dawn, pinky peach.

Do you like the roses? I brought them for you.

The old lady laughs gently and nods. Yes, yes. The smile lingers and the eyes come out from hiding, a ray of sun through the haze. Yes, yes, she says. The roses are brought to her, she touches them with a limp hand, grazes the petals, one leaf. The smile is still stuck to her face, pale now, fading. She's like a candle with a tenth-of-an-inch-long wick and not much wax left around it, the flame flickers, fizzles out.

You have to eat some more, now, open your mouth.

The old lady opens up, barely. Her breath smells sour, maybe they don't clean her teeth, maybe it's the smell of old age, it's started rotting away inside? But she swallows, the food goes down, fuel to keep the flame going.

There are tears running down Eva's cheeks as she brings the spoon to the old lady's lips over and over again. The tears are silent and she speaks through them. You know, I came all the way to see you, and I brought you these roses because I know you like flowers. Here: look at these photos. See this one: it's Mimi, remember Mimi? You saw her when she was a baby, a year and a half maybe, she was running all over the place, maybe she was two, the terrible twos, she was grabbing something, something precious, fragile on a coffee table, and you said, she ought to get a spanking, remember? *Cette enfant a besoin d'une bonne fessée*. And Mimi kept repeating, *fessée*, *pas d'fessée*. Remember? The old lady nods. The smile has vanished. Maybe just some light in her eyes remains. You have to force the food into the mouth now, until the bowl is empty, *comme un sou neuf*, Eva says. Look, clean as a whistle. The old lady's eyes are hazed over again. The chin sinks back into the chest. She's gone, retreated somewhere deep within, the old brain tired, its grooves run to the ground, its wood smooth and polished to a shine.

Eva runs to the bathroom, blows her nose, wipes her face dry.

Good-bye, she says, holding the old lady's hand in hers, a light pack of bones, she kisses her on her cheek, she presses her frail shoulders against her chest. Eat well, she says, you have to eat well. I am going now, I am flying back to New York in three hours. I promise I'll come back and see you soon, I promise, I won't stay so long without coming, not so long as this time. I'll send you photos, I promise.

Albertine's photos

I have decided not to answer her, Albertine says.

Who? Eva asks distractedly.

That daughter of mine, remember? The one who sent me the letter?

Eva pricks up her ears.

Why?

Too much water under the bridge. It would only bring pain to both of us.

How do you know?

I know. I can see it already. The expectation, the awkwardness, the disappointment. Better she keeps the dream.

For you, maybe, but what about for her?

For her. For her more than for me. I can take more disillusionment than a kid. I am an old horse.

They didn't talk about it anymore. It seemed to be an open-and-shut case. But Albertine appeared to be under stress, more short-tempered, or prone to absentmindedness. And Eva thought she started showing her age. The peachy complexion of a former redhead was turning pasty and her lines were deepening. These things happen of course. Aging doesn't come evenly, but proceeds by leaps and bounds in between long plateaus when a person remains the same physically or even seems to regain some youth. The reverse of the growth pattern of a child.

One Sunday morning, hearing them talk about Albertine's daughters, Mimi asked to see photos of the girls and Eva was surprised to see Albertine go to the dresser in her room, come back with a thick gray envelope, an envelope that had been many times folded and unfolded, its creases deeply marked and caked with dust, and extract a bunch of old black-and-white photos with scalloped white edges that she passed on to Mimi and Eva, describing them and the circumstances in which they were taken in detail. Eva had never seen those photos.

What memory you have, admired Eva. I wouldn't remember about half of where and when my photos of Mimi were taken. And it's only been a few years.

I don't have so many that it would be a problem to remember, Albertine said.

There were about eight or twelve of them. The most recent ones had been sent to her through a common acquaintance.

There was a rather stiff studio portrait of the elder girl, with creamy cheeks and a well-behaved hairstyle, and the other photo was a snapshot, taken on the run, a bit blurred, of the younger one in profile, wearing a raincoat and walking on a sidewalk among passersby. I can't even tell where this was taken, Albertine remarked. Maybe Brest, I am not sure.

Who took this one? Eva asked.

Albertine shrugged.

I don't know, she said. But Eva had the feeling that she did know and didn't want to talk about it, as if it would have been revealing a secret.

Frank Jackson rang Albertine's bell later that day after Eva had left. He showed up at the door holding a red box of chocolates shaped like a heart as if it was Valentine's Day, even though it was at least three weeks past, and leaned against the door asking if he could stop by for a little chat, a visit. As nosy as a cat, Mimi ran behind Albertine to catch a glimpse of the visitor. She stayed behind her, half hidden behind her large hips. I brought you this, Frank Jackson said, dangling the box of chocolates. Mimi appraised it with favorable eyes.

Eva's not here, Albertine said.

That's okay. Can I come in?

I'm working. Albertine hesitated. Okay, come on in.

They had coffee at the kitchen table, Mimi a glass of milk and a cookie. They talked about old times, back when Frank and Eva had met, and Eva lived in Albertine's building and sometimes he'd pick her up and they'd have a glass of wine at Albertine's before going out. Mimi listened, she paid attention to every nuance, color of voice, turn of phrase. She tried to read their bodies, imagine the past that was evoked between them, suggested in their silences, their gestures. Imagine a past before she existed. Albertine made fresh coffee, offered some doughnuts from a box and announced she had to get back to work. Frank suddenly turned to Mimi, who was sitting on the floor surrounded by an army of Barbie dolls with fierce hair and garish ball gowns.

Wanna go out for a walk with me?

I don't know, Mimi said, not lifting her eyes from her dolls. I don't think Albertine will let me.

Frank, Albertine said.

What?

I don't think Eva . . .

Hey, you know, go for an ice cream, see a movie. . . . She'll be out of your hair. What do you say, Mimi?

Frank, forget it.

Come on, Albertine, don't be so uptight. Just down the block or something. What are you worried about?

Mimi, want to get a hot dog at Nathan's? Remember how good they were at Coney Island? I bet your mom never takes you to eat hot dogs at Nathan's.

Yes, she does, Mimi protested.

Liar. She hates hot dogs.

Mimi shrugged, considering her dolls.

Or go to the movies. I saw *Cinderella* was playing at the Loews.

I already saw it.

Albertine watched them, her fists on her hips, nodding.

Can see it again. Then we'll go for ice cream. What's your favorite ice cream? Mimi looks at him. I bet . . . let me guess. Frank makes a face and rolls his eyes. Mimi laughs, a little strained laugh. Let me look at your eyes. Do you know I can guess people's favorite kind of ice cream just by looking at their eyes?

Mimi rocked again, timidly. Her eyes alternately stared at Frank and at the carpet at her feet.

She shook her head. I don't believe you, she said.

Well, you'll see. You'll see I can do it. Wait until I guess your favorite ice cream and then you'll believe me. Ready?

Mimi didn't say anything.

Frank squatted close to her, the way he did the first time he came, close, but not too close, and he looked straight into her eyes. She blinked and giggled.

Let me see. What color are your eyes?

She closed them tight.

Now don't close them. I can't see. I can't guess if I can't see your eyes.

She opened them, real quick, and closed them again.

Not fair, he said.

She did it again, open-close, open-close, real fast, then opened her eyes wide as saucers.

Good. Now let me take a good look.

Hmmmm. He licked his lips. Squinted his eyes. Shook his head.

Let me see again.

Mimi opened her eyes even wider.

Okay, I see now. Brown eyes. Big brown eyes. *Chocolate* brown eyes. Your favorite ice cream is: CHOCOLATE!

She laughed. She said yes. She said, how did you guess?

He stood up and took her hand. He said, that's it, that's the magic.

Albertine had been busying herself at the sink, then clearing the table to prepare for her sewing.

So what do you say, Albertine?

I guess there's no harm in it if she wants to. You want to, Mimi? Albertine asked.

Mimi looked sideways.

I guess.

You guess? Do you want to or not?

Mimi nodded. Yes, I wanna.

All right, go ahead. But don't keep her out too long, you hear me, Frank?

Don't worry.

Mimi went to get her coat and Frank helped her into it.

But, wait, she said, putting her earmuffs around her ears, if I had had blue eyes, then what kind of ice cream . . .

Rockin' Robin

Mimi's chocolate–chocolate-chip ice cream is dripping from the sugar cone in her hand. She runs after Frank, trying to keep up with his long stride. Where are we going? she wants to know. How is the ice cream? he answers. He abruptly stops in front of an arcade of video

games and walks right in, Mimi in tow. You like playing games? She nods vigorously. Yeah, yeah. Just like your mother, he says. Finish your ice cream first. She offers him some. Can't finish it fast enough. Then they stand side by side in front of a motorcycle game, there's a taped loop with a little newspaper boy on his bike who keeps crashing into a truck at the same intersection. Frank drops a quarter into the slot and they take positions at each wheel. Mimi's boy avoids two manholes, falls off into a third one and rams into a car. Frank's flies down the highway and takes turns at breakneck speed. Mimi's bites the dust, explodes across the screen. Frank laughs loudly. Mimi doesn't think it's funny. He says, let's play together, and he steps behind her, placing his hands on hers on the wheel.

Mimi and Frank are coming out of a theater on Broadway, laughing. It's dark already, the lights flash in their eyes. Frank pulls a stick of chewing gum from his pocket and offers it to Mimi. He makes her wrap her muffler two times around her neck. So did you like the movie? Frank asks. Did you think it was funny when the fat guy bit the ear of the pretty girl and she squealed? Yes, that was funny, and what about the time when she pushed him in the swimming pool with all his clothes on, and the time when he was naked and the bell rang and he opened the door and all these people showed up at the door? Mimi's in stitches. She continues: and he was so embarrassed he had to hold a photo to cover his penis? And all the time his girlfriend was hiding upstairs? And he put a photo in front of his penis? Oh, we already said that, Mimi says. What are we doing now? Frank looks at his watch. I don't know. We still have a little time. You hungry?

They cross the street to eat at Burger King. An old woman stares at them while they wait on line. Frank shifts uneasily and takes Mimi to eat at the other end of the restaurant. After a few bites Mimi puts her hamburger down and yawns. I'm tired, she says. I wanna go home.

That's all you're eating?

Mimi's head rolls over her shoulder.

Let's go now. I'm not hungry anymore.

Not even for the French fries?

Mimi shakes her head.

Listen, I have to stop by at my place first. We'll take a cab and then I'll drop you off.

No, I wanna go home now.

Come on, Mimi, let's go. I've got something that I got to pick up at my place. It'll only be a few minutes.

Where do you live? Is it far?

Nah. Just a few minutes.

In the cab Mimi decides to sing a song. She kneels on the backseat, pretends to hold a mike in her hand and swings her hips. The song goes like this:

Daddy's on the bottom
Mommy's on the top
Baby's in the middle
Saying get down, Pop!

Frank listens to her, straight-faced, and asks her if she wants to be a rock 'n' roll star. It's in your blood, girl! But she yawns, disinterested already, slouches, puts her head on his shoulder and falls asleep.

The cab stops in a dark street in Long Island City. Frank carries Mimi asleep up the steep flight of stairs to the third floor and lays her down on a couch. Mimi wakes up to see Frank making himself a cup of coffee. Backlit, in front of a kitchen counter covered with dirty dishes, he is a strange man, his black hair cropped so close to the skull it looks like it's shaven. There are long shadows on the kitchen wall among the pots and pans arrayed above the stove, and a thick darkness is enveloping her. Mimi screams, Albertine, MOMMY! Frank turns around, grins his big grin, perfect white teeth, one gold cap, crinkly eyes. Hey, relax, he says, coming toward her. What's my little girl scared about? Had a bad dream? He sits next to her on the couch, puts a soothing hand on her forehead, her temples. Go back to sleep, he says gently. I still have a few things to take care of, go to sleep, I'll wake you up when it's time to go. Are you warm enough? He spreads the blanket evenly over her legs, pulls it up to her neck, covering her arms, her shoulders. Mimi nods, emits a few grunts, floats back into oblivion.

Frank sits in the dark, across from her, on another couch, a coffee at his elbow, smoking a cigarette. Mimi's still asleep on the couch, she's kicked the blanket off to the side, one of her legs has slipped and rests, balanced at the edge of the couch. The light from the street runs across the couch, catching some of Mimi's hair, one of her fists thrown back above her head and the top of her exposed knee. Frank sips his coffee, at times shifting his legs from his left ankle on his right knee to his right ankle on his left knee. Mimi's face is buried in a pillow, he can barely see it. He stares at the spot where he guesses her mouth is, her nose is. He strains to listen to her breathing, the barely audible whimpers she makes as she changes position in her sleep. It's late. He's going to let the night run its course. He stretches his legs, places a pillow under his nape to make himself more comfortable for the wake. But he keeps his head facing Mimi, he forces his eyes to stay open, not to stray from the area of shadow where her face rests. Her features become more distinct after a while, the frail curve of the nostrils, the fullness of the lips slightly apart, the soft line of the chin, of the jaw, fading into the cheek. At times, during the night, he will get up and squat before the sleeping body, not touch it, just look at the small fingers, relaxed on top of the cover, her foot sticking to the side. He only touches her hair, very lightly, the mass of tangled curls spread out on the pillow. He leans over her, brings some hair to his nose. He sniffs at the musky smell. But mostly he remains seated or lying down. He smokes cigarettes to keep himself awake. It is very important that he remain awake. He makes himself a fresh pot of coffee. Sometimes he stares at the red ember of his cigarette butt, shading it with his fingers, lest Mimi wake up and notice it.

Eva's looking at Mimi's little cot and her toys scattered around her bedroom and her dirty backpack open and overflowing with drawings and unfinished homework. Albertine has long since gone to sleep. Eva sits cross-legged, her back against the chest of drawers. It doesn't occur to her to lie down and try to sleep. She has kept the little duck lamp on near the bed and half expects, hopes to see Mimi's body appear in the bed, asleep, rolled into the comforter. Albertine finds her wide-eyed, clasping a dress of Mimi's, at six o'clock in the morning, when she gets up. The night is turning gray. She brings Eva a cup of hot coffee and drags her to the kitchen.

I'm sorry, Albertine says, sitting at the table with her. I never thought, for a minute . . .

I know. It's not your fault. Why do you think I wouldn't let him come near her? That's Frank Jackson. Can't trust him. I knew, I knew something was going to happen.

Albertine starts work on her mannequin, pinning away at a peacock-blue faille. Eva hangs on to the last remnants of hope: she hasn't gone to sleep, it's still night. Mimi can still come back.

It is still dark when Mimi wakes up for the second time. She's had a fitful night. Frank can testify to that, he hasn't let her out of his sight for more than a minute. Okay, maybe two when he went to take a leak, several times during the night. She rolls over, stretches her arms behind her head and immediately sits up and stares at Frank. What are you doing here? she says. She looks around her, struggling to keep her eyes open. Where are we? Frank squats next to her.

We are at my place. Remember, last night?

You were supposed to take me home.

So I was. I decided to let you sleep. You were sleeping like a baby. Didn't want to wake you up.

Mimi shrugs. Yawns.

I'm hungry, she says. What time is it? Can I call my mom?

Come, he says. Let me give you some breakfast. Toast? Glass of milk?

It was like slowly getting the news of a lethal disease. Eva came back, and they still hadn't showed up, not a word. She and Albertine went to look in the street, visited the ice cream parlors, waited outside the movie theater playing *Cinderella*, they waited in theater lobbies playing any film that could conceivably be seen by a child, short of a porn flick, they checked out Nathan's, Burger King, McDonald's and Popeye. They called everyone they could think of who knew Frank Jackson, even casually, anybody who had met him or had been hanging out with him. All the girlfriends or former girlfriends Eva had heard about. Anybody he had been known to have worked with. Anybody in New York, anybody in Chicago, his former employers, all his musician pals Eva had heard about or had been told about. His parents. Of course nobody knew where he was, or nobody was talking. That first evening, Albertine kept saying he'll be back. He'll bring her back. Don't worry. He promised. But Eva was convinced they were on their way to South America, he'd taken her on one of those boats he used to work on. She called the major navigation lines to find out if there had been ships departing for Buenos Aires, or Santiago or São Paulo, or Barranquilla or Caracas or the Guyanas or any South American harbor, small or big, and if she could see the list of passengers, and she briefly felt the thrill of a private eye on a hot track, but she drew a total blank. A woman who was an acquaintance of Frank Jackson's said she had just gotten a call from him about some sheet music Frank had lost and couldn't locate. He sounded perfectly relaxed, the woman said, and no, she hadn't heard any child in the background, and he hadn't seemed hurried or harried or otherwise stressed.

—

Your place is weird, Mimi says, surveying the loft from the kitchen counter, the two beat-up couches facing each other and the dusty emptiness, the piles of cartons stacked along the walls.

You live here? she asks. Can't quite believe it.

Why not?

It doesn't look like somebody's place.

What does it look like?

I don't know.

Her hair is a mess from the night. Matted, rising wildly on top of the head. He wonders if he should do something about it, realizes he doesn't even own a comb, and what about giving her a bath?

It's not my place, actually. It's my friend's place. He's letting me use it.

What day is it? Mimi asks.

Monday, why?

I don't have my backpack. Are you taking me to school? We'll have to stop at Albertine's to pick up my backpack.

You're not going to go to school today.

I'm not? Why?

Come, he says. I want to show you something.

He takes her to a Cassio keyboard hooked up to amplifiers and computers.

You know what that is?

A piano.

Yes. A piano. But a very special kind of piano. Want me to show you how it works?

Okay.

He shows her the panel of electronic keys running along the keyboard. Each key corresponds to a different sound, he explains to Mimi: a violin, birds chirping, a guitar, drums, a dog barking (wow, wow), and so on. Press any one of these keys and then play the piano and . . . I'm not telling you. You'll see.

Okay, okay. What do I do?

Little hands are ready to go, already bouncing off the keyboard, throwing out a ruckus of wild notes. Frank pushes the bird key and the notes turn into a bird concert in the forest at dawn. Thrilled, Mimi tries each key in turn and produces the sounds of an orchestra gone berserk.

A half hour later she walks away from the Cassio and drags her feet to where Frank is reading a newspaper at the kitchen table. I'm bored, she says, looking over his shoulder at the paper and trying to decipher the headlines. Don't you have to go to work?

I'm a musician, he says. I don't work during the day. I work at night.

Are you going to work tonight?

No, he says. Not tonight. I'm not working tonight.

I'm bored. I have nothing to do. Why can't I go to school?

Aren't you having fun with me?

No.

He screws up his face in mock hurt, pretends to be on the verge of tears.

Stop it. This is not funny.

So what do you want to do?

Do you have a TV?

A TV? What for? What do you want to do with a TV?

Watch it, silly.

Frank points to one of the computer screens.

That's a TV. You can watch it if you want.

It's not a TV. It's a computer.

So there you are. No TV.

Frank goes to a bookshelf and scans a few titles. He pulls one out.

Here, he says, handing Mimi a paperback collection of the comic strip "Little Orphan Annie." You can read, right?

A little, Mimi says.

You're going to like this. Look. Here. Come here. See this little girl. You know what her name is?

He sets Mimi up with pillows on one of the couches and brings a lamp next to her.

You're all set. Now go ahead.

But five minutes later Mimi looks up from the book and asks: does my mummy know where I am?

Eva: I stayed home, wearing an old robe, eating whatever was in the fridge, which was mostly cheese and leftover spaghetti and a half loaf of bread on its way to being stale, not making my bed, not taking a shower or combing my hair, lying on my rumpled sheets or on the couch leafing through old fashion magazines, reading fragments of previously read novels, pouring over the *Guinness Book of World Records* and ancient issues of the *National Geographic* I had once found piled in front of garbage cans outside Albertine's building, the Real Estate section of last week's Sunday *Times* and stacks of Macy's and Bloomingdale's catalogues, the cheap kind that come with the Sunday papers, even a book of stupid cat jokes someone had given me though I never owned a cat. When I was done with them I went to sleep, and woke up an hour or so later exhausted by dreams of doom as if my body was tackling a bout of malaria and my wakeful state was barely distinguishable from hallucinations caused by illness.

In one corner of the loft, or warehouse, rather, is a spread of nuts, bolts, most of them rusted, brass and glass door handles, porcelain faucets. They are arranged in concentric circles, with repeated patterns of shapes, materials and colors. The circle is located at the back of the loft, past the kitchen, to the side of an open space leading to the bathroom. Mimi's almost too busy commenting on the lack of a bathtub to notice this odd arrangement when she trips on a loose bolt that has rolled off the circle and practically lands in it facedown. What's that? she yells. Watch out, Frank yells back. He explains it's a sculpture of found objects that his friend—the one who owns the place—is working on, that one day it will be big enough to fill up a whole room and that she has to be very careful not to disrupt it, not to move the tiniest little bolt. Not even one? Mimi asks. She grabs a handful of bolts. Not even picking up this one and putting it here, and taking that one and putting it over there, and that one . . . ? Frank screams. Damn kid. I told you not to touch it. Now, where was this one? Put it right back. Mimi holds the faucet in her closed fist behind her back and swirls round and round with a wild smirk on her face. Frank tries to grab it from her but she's as swift as a ferret.

I'll give it back to you when you let me call my mummy.

Frank shrugs.

The phone's out of order.

I don't believe you.

She runs to the phone, picks it up, dials Eva's number. Frank watches her, his arms crossed over his chest, doesn't attempt to stop her.

Hi, Mummy, Mimi says. It's me, Mimi. Yes, me, Mimi. No, I'm okay. I'm with Frank Jackson. No, I'm okay, I'm okay. Mummy. I want to see you. I want to go home.

Mimi turns to Frank Jackson.

What's the address here? She wants to come and pick me up.

Frank looks at her, doesn't say anything.

You don't believe me?

She talks back into the telephone.

Mummy. Can you talk to him? He doesn't believe me. She hands the receiver to Frank. Here. She wants to talk to you.

He still looks at her without moving.

Mimi gets impatient. HERE. Talk to her.

Frank picks up the phone.

Hello, he says.

The line is dead. He listens for a moment, and, very gently, places the receiver on its cradle.

I told you the phone was disconnected, he says.

Mimi throws herself on the couch, sobbing.

That's not true. She was talking to me. You hung up on her. It's your fault.

Mimi, you couldn't have talked to her. The phone's been dead for days.

Dead? Mimi asks. How can the phone be *dead?* Phones are not people.

Listen, Frank says, sitting down next to Mimi. Listen to me, Mimi. How would you feel about spending a few days with me, like . . . like a little vacation. Not go to school, go to the movies, play video games, go for a ride . . .

Mimi sits up, interested. Her face is a mess of dirty wet streaks on a background of swollen eyes, swollen nose and flaming red cheeks.

What video game?

I don't know. I can hook one up on one of those monitors. Let's go to the store. You pick it. But first, let's wash that face. You can't go out like this.

They took the subway to Manhattan and came back with a Nintendo video game system, and on the way back got groceries down the street, at a little bodega that didn't sell any fresh produce except plantains and yams and straggly bunches of cilantro scattered on the counter, but they bought spaghetti and a jar of tomato sauce and Cheerios and milk and some white bread and a stick of margarine and some Bustelo coffee and a pack of cigarettes for Frank and a pack of M&Ms for Mimi, and they came back, their arms full, and plugged the Nintendo right away and played a mean game with the little guys breathlessly trying to escape fire-breathing dragons and piranha plants until Mimi collapsed, complaining of starvation. Frank prepared dinner while she wrestled her way through a pile of back issues of *New York* magazine and *Newsweek*, her shod feet propped on the coffee table. They played Nintendo again after dinner, but she had lost her touch or fatigue kept her from concentrating, so she retaliated by giving a couple of frustrated kicks to the desk on which rested the video monitor, and burst into tears. Frank tried to read her some of "Little Orphan Annie" but she buried her head in a cushion on the couch, her fists on her ears, and sobbed nonstop until she fell asleep.

Eva is sitting on the couch surrounded by all the magazines she's been reading all day long. She savagely shuffles them around, then picks them up one by one and tosses them across the room, using more speed and more strength each time, just as Johnny shows up at her door, holding a bouquet of red roses.

What are you doing here? How did you get in?

Morris. He told me you were in.

She keeps tossing the magazines as far as she can. She even manages to hit the opposite wall with a hefty September issue of *Harper's Bazaar*, which seems to give her some relief.

Johnny's standing by the door, quiet as stone.

Mimi's gone, she says, in the silence.

I know. I heard. I'm sorry.

She turns to him.

Who told you?

You didn't return my phone calls, so I came. Morris told me. That fucking Frank Jackson. What happened?

She looks at him, pulls a handful of pages, crumples them, and tosses them around.

The bastard! He's out of his fucking mind. That's the scariest part. Only a maniac would do that. He's got that streak in him. He picked her up at Albertine's, sweet-talked her into letting Mimi go with him, and never returned her. It's like a headline on the third page of the *Post!* We've been to the cops, they're no help, we've looked everywhere, called everybody. Nobody knows anything.

Her teeth clenched, she tosses a new magazine or a handful of ripped pages at each word.

So that's it. And you know the worst? She was driving me crazy lately, she's a handful, you know. I couldn't wait to be on my own. The little that I take care of her, sometimes it's too much. And now I'm dying. I want her back. I love that kid. It fucking hurts. It's like he took my life. It's like he bled me to death. My blood. That's why they call children their blood. My blood, your blood. I always thought it was so phony.

She pitches more magazines. She tears them page by page. The pages fly in all directions. Without weight they float for an instant and drop gently about her like leaves, some on the coffee table, some at her feet. The carpet is covered with a brightly colored sea of paper.

Johnny tiptoes through it, goes to look for a vase in the kitchenette. He finds a clear glass carafe at the back of a shelf and stuffs the flowers in it, then leans against the counter.

Eva throws the last of a handful of pages from a destroyed *Vogue* magazine and they fly all over the table, one lands in front of her. It features frail and racy blond models lounging in summer dresses in the cool shade of an oak tree on the grounds of an old Louisiana plantation.

Eva watches them pensively for a moment, then grabs a bunch of them and crushes them in her fists.

And I want to kill Frank Jackson, she says.

Johnny waited for Eva's rage to be spent. Her face distorted and wild, she got up, stepped on the blanket of magazine pages spread all over the room and trampled them furiously, then threw herself on them and made big balls of paper with her fists, sobbing in big gasps. Her breathing slowed down and she was silent, hugging armfuls of paper against her folded body. Johnny picked her up in his arms and carried her to her bedroom. She was crying, softly. He drew the shades down and sat on the bed next to her, awkward, holding her hand till she fell asleep.

Frank Jackson meant to give Mimi the time of her life. For three days they were frantically active, rushing from Nintendo to a show of *Sleeping Beauty* to a spin on the merry-go-round in Central Park back to the hot dog and the cotton-candy stands of Coney Island, up the Empire State Building, down the Hudson River on the Circle Line and back to Long Island City in a cab, Mimi refusing to put her two feet in front of each other after a day of intense activity. Then she decided she was going to stay "home." But to keep Mimi busy within the confines of a dark warehouse without a toy or a TV in sight was beyond Frank's power of endurance. The morning was barely over when Mimi turned into a wild beast caged in. She moved through the loft, kicking up a storm, leaving a trail of books, food, kitchen utensils and assorted objects behind her, then threw herself on her back, arms and legs pumping up and down like a turtle trying to get back on her feet, except she had no intention of getting up, she savored the moment and kept it going until Frank bodily removed her and took her out for a walk. They picked up a couple of Barbie dolls at a local store and Mimi finally settled down with the teased-hair beauties. Then there was the question of the itch she developed in the vulva area due to the lack of bathing facilities. She got whiny every time she went to the bathroom. They devised a way of sitting her on the sink so that she could clean herself more thoroughly. Frank left her alone until she was done and came back to help her down. He couldn't find a solution to Mimi's hair. He'd bought a brush and tried to run it through her curls but her screams were so piercing he was afraid someone in the building would hear them and suspect something was wrong. They tacitly decided to leave the hair alone and it quickly started to twist into dreadlocks.

Eva only cries when she's alone. And then she cries from rage, biting her pillow and banging her head against the wall. Her tears are hot and bitter, they burn her cheeks. She throws her body on the floor as if she wanted to imprint herself into it. She wishes it'd turn into red lava and scorch the universe as it liquefies. When she has an audience she favors wrath. She'll throw dishes into a kitchen sink and watch the horrified expressions with delight as the porcelain breaks apart. She'll tear paper to shreds, and sometimes, on extreme occasions, scissor fabrics and clothes. She once lifted the glass top of a coffee table and tossed it on a flagstone floor. She never forgot the delicious sound of broken glass as it shattered in myriad splinters. She would have grabbed a hammer and finished the job by crunching every single piece until they turned into a bed of crushed glass, if only she had found one handy.

How long are you going to keep me? Mimi asked, perched on a stool in front of the bathroom mirror, attempting to tie a ribbon around her hair.

Have you ever been out of New York? Frank answered. He was sitting on the toilet, clipping his nails.

What do you mean?

Out of the city. Have you been anywhere else in the country?

I've been at the beach, I've been to the mountains, too, Vermont, I think. I don't know where else.

What would you say to taking a little car ride, out in the country?

In the car? For how long?

Don't know, couple days. Maybe more, show you America.

I seen America. We are in America.

It's so big. You've only seen a teeny little bit of it.

Who's going to drive?

Me.

And who's going to go?

You and me.

She jumped down from the stool, pulled Frank by the hand.

Come, she said, let's play Nintendo.

Enter the realm of fear

She's entered the realm of fear. Tears and fear. Screaming, endless fear. The violence is unbelievable. It tears her apart. She thinks of taking Johnny's Studebaker and driving on and on till the end, till there's no more land. Before they hear of Galileo, kids think the earth is flat. They ask: do

you fall off at the end of the earth? Eva would go as far as she could go and fall off. She would go over that edge and be sucked into the void. The pain can't be hammered out of her brain, pulled out with pliers. Some people knock off the pain with drugs but she holds still, feeling it working its way through her nerves, her muscles, tightening her neck, her back, marching to the center of her body, gripping her at the chest, digging into her stomach, her liver, her uterus, her gallbladder, her spleen, lodging itself in the belly, making her buckle at the knees. I can't stomach it, she thinks, squatting in front of the toilet and embracing the cold porcelain with her arms, trying to puke it out. Waves come up her throat, but only a filet of spit lands on the side of the bowl. The beast is so firmly encroached she feels its claws digging into her flesh.

She makes frantic phone calls, three, four rounds of calls to the same people, her people, his people, the police, radio and TV stations. She tells them it's much more important than the arrest of the Times Square Rapist but they politely send her to another office. She screams till she gets hoarse. She walks the streets of Manhattan scanning the crowds for that flash of light in Mimi's eyes. She combs the city, on foot, street after street. She has calculated that if she covers every square foot of the island she has a fairly good chance of running into Mimi and Frank, by pure statistical hazard. She starts at South Ferry, working her way east then west, back and forth, blessing the grid structure for being able to canvas the streets without having to retrace her steps more than half the time. She walks until night falls or until she has to go to work. Any day now Mimi and Frank will cross her path. And if she misses them she can always start all over again. Southward, this time.

Eva: Albertine doesn't cry, Albertine drinks. I don't want Mimi to know. I found her one day passed out on the couch in the middle of the afternoon. I could see her from the door. The way her mouth was open, her arm hanging down. It spelled bad news. I went straight to the window, opened it for air, and put a cover over her. I picked up the empty bottle and the glass and took them to the counter, threw the bottle away, cleaned up the glass. I kept Mimi with me the next few days, until my next gig. I didn't say a word to Albertine. For a while I stopped by each day after school to check up on her, but everything seemed normal, or she was shrewd enough not to be caught by me. We just went on as before. I didn't have the choice anyway. For months everything was fine. And then it happened again. I had stopped by at her place to pick up a pair of earrings I had left behind a few days before and she was sitting at the kitchen table, a bottle of red wine in front of her. Her eyes swam around before she was able to focus on me and all the muscles in her face were slack, her cheeks hanging down like bags of skin. It was around the time Frank Jackson showed up in New York. I confronted her. She denied everything. Said she was just finishing her lunch. Always had a glass of Gallo with her cheese. It was eleven A.M. What was the point of rubbing it in? Trying to get her to go to AA? Days of confrontations and fights? Getting Mimi involved in something so sordid? I couldn't put up with it. I dropped the subject. I told her, think of Mimi. Whatever is going on, please think of Mimi.

Felix didn't come the last two gigs. He had to be replaced. A guy who was okay but played too fast and mechanically. Nothing like the kind of feeling Felix can display. Angelo is yelling at him on the phone. He says, man, you gotta take care of yourself. How long you been dragging that cold? Go see a doctor. Eva stops by at his place. She hasn't been there since last summer, since that big party he had on the roof for the Fourth of July and she had to carry Mimi asleep all the way to Albertine's. It's the afternoon. He half opens his door. He's in p.j.s, his eyes swollen with sleep or too much marijuana. His shades are down. It's pitch-black in his studio. *Qué tal*, man? she asks him. You sleeping? Sorry to bother you. I brought you some fresh-squeezed orange juice. He takes the paper bag to his chest but doesn't let her in. It's that flu, he says. It's going around. Can't kick it. It's that end of winter beginning of spring time. Viruses running around with little wings at their heels. Any news from Mimi?

Winter is finally beginning to break. There are even a couple of balmy days with a little smart wind that curls around your knees and makes you want to open your collar and bare your neck. Eva sheds her gloves and scarf and sets out on her quest thinking today might be the day. She starts at West Street and walks across all the way to the FDR Drive and the East River Park. Walking along the East River in a park that is so skinny she can see both sides of it at once, she fights off despair. The playground is empty, the park desolate, a couple of joggers huff and puff past her. This is the time for Frank and Mimi to appear to her now, out of the blue. Eva follows Johnny's advice and sees them cut across the baseball field, two tiny silhouettes that she cannot identify yet, one tall, one little, they walk ahead of her on the promenade, she presses her steps. The silhouettes dissolve into the water.

That night at the Follies Angelo pulls a long face. He is not himself. He's slouched at the bar looking concerned. He tells Eva Felix is in the hospital. His lover just called from the room. He has a 106-degree fever. Eva feels as if doom is closing in on her. It's a bad cycle, Angelo says. We'll just have to wait it out. Everything will be okay. Eva thinks that Angelo has taken up America's mindless optimism, repeat after me, everything will be okay, everything will be fine, everything will work out, a ritual, like an incantation. The religion of positive thinking. But when she calls Felix up at the hospital the next day he sounds okay. The fever's down, he says. They think I might have pneumonia. I'll be out in a week. They're pampering me like a baby. She stops at the hospital after her walk through the streets and brings him magazines and fresh-squeezed orange juice. He's already sipping spinach and carrot juice and he's got a fat bottle of After the Fall grape and apple juice on his wheel-on table. Well if you don't get out of here with all that healthy stuff, I don't know what's the matter with you, she tells him. But his eyes are bright with fever. She touches his hand lightly. It's burning hot.

Eva's final attempt at magic

Eva found out Frank Jackson occupied the back of a loft in a Long Island City warehouse. She took the subway to the first stop out of Manhattan in Queens. The warehouse was located in a deserted street, at quite a distance from the cluster of renovated brownstones that make downtown

Long Island City look like a section of Greenwich Village. The building looked empty. There was an unpainted gray metal door with a bunch of old bells with loose wires running across it, and the windows were caked with opaque dirt and grime. Eva rang the bells and the building remained silent. An alleyway ran along one side and she tried to get to the back, but the whole first floor was a blind wall. She called Frank's number from a pay phone outside a deli. A recorded message came on, said the line was disconnected. She went back to the warehouse.

It was nearing dusk. A few people walked past her in the direction of the subway, workers mostly, having just finished their day. Eva rang all the bells again, then sat down on the metal step, her arms hugging her knees. She imagined Mimi lying in the dark, sedated, on a mattress or bound and gagged on a cot and Frank Jackson watching her, chain-smoking cigarettes, knowing that Eva was downstairs and waiting for her to leave. Waiting forever if necessary, he had the patience of a snake. But Eva could outwait him any time. She thought if she stayed there long enough, Mimi and Frank would materialize in front of her, she would hear Mimi's little chatty voice and skidding crescendos and Mimi would jump into her arms, she could feel the softness and tightness of her small body, the gamy smell of her hair, and Frank Jackson would watch sheepishly and walk away.

She stood in front of the door and knocked on it until her knuckles hurt. Then she took her keys out of her purse and banged against the metal door. She stepped back and screamed Mimi, MIMI, MIMI, her hand cupped around her mouth to carry the sound upward. There was a dim light shining in a couple of windows. MIMI, it's me, Eva! Do you hear me? MIMI! She picked up some gravel from the side alley and threw handfuls of it against the windows. Her voice was getting hoarse. The whole building remained utterly silent.

A shadow appeared in the pool of yellow light at the edge of the pavement. A young black guy in dungarees and bomber jacket stopped and peeked at her through the darkness.

You looking for someone? he asked.

She was startled.

I . . . I'm looking for a friend. I am concerned about him. He hasn't been answering his phone. I was wondering . . .

The man looked painfully blank.

Are you from this neighborhood? she asked. Maybe you've seen him. He is black, light-skinned, blue eyes, very short hair, very striking, a musician, he wears army-navy kind of clothes.

No. I really couldn't say.

He is with a little girl, six and a half, brown skin, lots of black curls. She's wearing a red winter jacket and a blue skirt and . . .

He put his hand on her arm.

I've never seen the guy, he said. Sorry I can't help you.

After he had walked away, she felt the cold in her bones and started to walk back to the subway, thinking a door had closed behind her and she didn't recognize the room she had gotten into.

Of course the cops said there was nothing they could do. And how could she be so sure anyway? She tried to keep her cool. She said, I'm telling you he has my daughter with him and I'm telling you where he lives. It's a tip. I'm tipping you off. Can't you go knock on his door? Not without a search warrant, no ma'am. She screamed at them, they said no ma'am, we can't do it. She took a cab to Johnny's and sat at his kitchen table in front of Mr. Coffee dripping and told him she found Frank's place. He said, forget the cops, man, cops in this city cruise the streets, all they do is hassle the homeless and black folks, every street corner you see three police cars screeching to a halt, three pairs of cops spilling out and a black kid flattened against the wall with his arms stretched over his head while they frisk him. So what do you expect? But look, that place where Frank's staying, it's a warehouse, right, nobody lives there at night, we can break in. Eva thought it was a great idea.

They got hold of a crowbar and Johnny made sure he had his plastic hospital card with him in case he had to trip the front door. Those locks are so easy, he said, most of the time all you have to do is slip something between the door frame and the door and the catch pops back like you had the key. Really, Eva asked, how come you know that? He said it was common knowledge on the street and anyway he'd seen it a zillion times on TV. They put the pry bar in a plastic bag and took the subway a little after ten P.M. The street was deserted. The yellow pool of light was deepening the pocket of darkness around the stoop. They went to work right away, and miraculously Johnny popped the door just like he said he would.

On the first landing was an old wooden door with a rotted lock. Johnny knocked on the door several times, loud. When they were sure nobody was in, he pried it open. It made an awful creaking noise before it gave. Inside it was pitch-black. Eva fumbled for a light switch, couldn't find one. They walked in, bumped into something with metal legs, cursed, walked in deeper. When their eyes got accustomed to the dark they saw some square and rectangular shapes and perhaps high shelves. The light from the street lit up the end of the space, a parallelogram catching the edge of a desk crowded with paper and files, and a corner of industrial shelving. Nothing more.

They tried the door across the landing. It opened up with barely more difficulty. It was a printing loft. The two doors on the third floor were metal and turned out to be impenetrable. They knocked on the first door on the fourth floor and got no response and Johnny was about to wedge his crowbar in when the floor creaked and a man's voice asked, what is it, with an edge of hostility. Sorry, Eva said, we knocked on the wrong door. Nobody lives in this building, the voice answered. Okay, they said and tiptoed up to the top floor.

As soon as they got the last door open, they could tell, from the smell, that the place was being lived in. It was a big L-shaped loft, with two old velveteen couches facing each other, a narrow foam mattress with a sleeping bag rolled back on it, a little kitchenette behind a half-built partition of exposed drywall, a couple of computers, a couple of electronic pianos, some music sheets, and in a corner of the L a huge circle made of rocks, laid out as if for an Indian ritual.

This is it, Eva said, this is the place.

How do you know? Could be anybody's place.

I know.

There were some dirty pots on the stove and used silverware and plates in the sink.

Somebody's living here.

Yeah, somebody, but who?

They looked for closets, personal items, toiletries, cigarettes, anything signaling Frank and Mimi's presence. There was canned food in the kitchen cabinets. There were cigarette butts in an ashtray in front of one of the couches. Eva sniffed at them. Johnny found a pair of old rubber boots and a mackintosh in a closet. There was a used-up bottle of after-shave and a pink one of Pepto-Bismol and an opened tube of toothpaste on the shelf above the sink, a dirty towel on a rack in the bathroom. Eva leafed through the sheet music. I just know it's the place, she said. She looked out the window into the street. You could see the edge of the stoop from there, lit up by the streetlamp. The window was slightly to the right if you looked at it from the street. It could have been one of those that was lit up two nights before. Frank might have seen her, Mimi might have heard her scream her name and cried. Eva pulled out the pillows on the couches, zipped the sleeping bag and shook it. She crawled behind the computers and moved the boxes piled against the wall.

If Mimi was here or had been here, Johnny said, wouldn't we find something of hers?

Eva went on her hands and knees and turned the corner of the L. The floor sculpture was lying at her feet, a huge primitive circle looking vaguely religious, ritualistic. She picked up a few of the bolts and felt them with her palms. They were smooth and of various shades of gray and anthracite. Together they formed an interesting and mysterious pattern. A string of silver-colored nuts caught her attention. She stretched her hand over the wide expanse of the circle to touch them. But she felt something soft. Caught under one of the nuts was a piece of silver-gray fabric. Eva pulled it out and looked at it under the light. She recognized it right away. It was a tiny, silver-gray pair of Barbie pants.

Eva wanted to stay and wait for Mimi and Frank to return. Johnny thought it would be useless, because none of their clothes were there. But Eva reasoned that Mimi only had the clothes she had left with and maybe Frank kept all his personal stuff in another apartment. They had to take the chance. Johnny made them some instant coffee in the kitchenette. They turned off all the lights and settled on the mattress in the far end of the loft, the two mugs at their feet.

There was a dark silence, no sound from the street, no traffic. They sat, their backs against the wall, legs stretched out in front of them. It was cold. They kept their jackets on. Johnny put his hand on Eva's knee. The smell of his sweat and his breath came to her mixed with the smell of leather. She leaned sideways against him. They got used to the creaking of the building in the night. The sounds of its joints. But there was no heart pumping, no pipes cracking, bringing heat in the radiators. Their breath hung in front of them. A dog barked. Almost simultaneously they thought they heard a door slam. They sat up, ready to spring to action. The sounds died away. Johnny got up and made some more coffee. He told Eva, what is important is that you do not panic. Fear is what trips us up. Keep the faith, believe that you will see her, maybe tonight, maybe another day, maybe not before a long time. Convince yourself that you will. See her coming to you with her arms open. See yourself hugging her. Eva closed her eyes and saw Mimi climbing up the stairs, opening the door, speaking loud as they entered the loft. They stayed awake for a long time, then dozed off. At four A.M. Eva woke up and admitted they wouldn't come back tonight. Frank wouldn't stay out so late with Mimi. They're spending the night somewhere else. They waited until eight in the morning. It was a pure blue morning with a brilliant sun. You could tell even through the grime on the windows. Johnny got up abruptly and said he had had it with Frank Jackson. I can't stand it, he's dominating your life, he's disrupting my life. This guy only spells trouble.

Eva watched him zip his jacket, slap his hat on his head, wrap his scarf around his neck.

Thanks, she said. Thank you for your support.

He turned angrily toward her.

I helped you, didn't I?

Eva stayed behind, now in daylight, crawling through every square inch of the loft in search of clues. In the bathroom, behind the toilet, she found a green glittering stick-on earring of Mimi's. She held it tight in her hand and smashed her fist against the cabinet over the sink, breaking the mirror in a star of shards. She had blood over her knuckles and had to pick pieces of glass from her skin.

Back in Manhattan, a cloak of depression fell upon Eva. Anxiety was poking its monstrous three-pronged fork in her ribs and she kept going in dull stupor. She found herself drifting in the direction of Madame Rosalita's storefront and soon staring at the pair of neon hands and the empty wicker chairs and she knew that if there was one person on earth who could help her it was Madame Rosalita.

Nobody answered her knock and she walked in. The door to the apartment at the back was open. She took a peek and there was Olga serenading her baby.

Sorry to barge in so late, Eva said. But the door was open.

Is okay. The baby is up. Señora Rosalita not here, she said.

No? When are you expecting her?

Olga kept rocking the child in her arms, but he was fast asleep, eyelids tight, fists tight.

No coming back.

Not coming back? Eva leaned against the door frame. Her last hope dissolving before she had a chance to indulge it. She felt panic, as though it was a bad omen.

Madame Rosalita not in New York. She went home.

Where is home? Eva asked hopelessly.

Puerto Rico.

When is she coming back? Eva felt so weak the words came out as a sigh.

Olga shook her head again. Don't know. She didn't say. Family business.

Family! This could mean months.

Is anyone else here? I mean, is anybody running this place while she's away? Are you replacing her?

A sweet smile spread across Olga's face. She stopped rocking the baby. The idea seemed wild to her. She shook her head again.

Me? No. She has the power. Olga said that with a certain awe. I don't. I read palms, if you want. I do tarot cards for you.

Olga turned around and carefully laid the baby in his crib.

I can do now, if you want. What you want: palms or tarot?

It all seemed so domestic. Eva wasn't sure she trusted the girl to have any insight. Olga was wiping her hands on her skirt and swiveling on her high-heeled shoes and marching toward the storefront where they did straight palm and tarot reading, her face bearing an obvious bored look. Eva followed her. Olga locked the front door, picked up a deck of well-thumbed tarot cards from the side table and went back inside. Too late, she said, dangerous to be in front at this hour.

No, Eva said. Not the tarot. She was scared of the tarot cards. She thought they brought news of death, or at least fatal diseases, ruin and bad luck. Things were bad enough as they were without fooling around with fate and landing a terminal case of doom.

Olga took her right hand, turned it palm up. Eva pulled back.

Don't be scared, Olga said. Is always hope. The well-manicured hand was warm and reassuring somehow, and Eva let her proceed. Olga ran her red nail along the lines without saying a word, her face blank.

(Don't tell me. I don't want to know. Don't tell me.)

I see a dark young man. Very handsome.

(Please.)

I see . . . what a long love line you got.

(What long teeth you have, Grandma.)

I see a lot of men in your life. Right now I see two. I see one a little older than the other, the dark one, the one I was talking about. I think he wants to marry you. You're going to have children with him.

(Please.)

You have traveled a lot in your life. I see traveling again in your future in a few years. You will finish your life abroad.

(I'm already living abroad.)

You work in the arts. You are very artistic.

(What about Mimi?)

The nail hit the intersection of two lines and ran back and forth over her palm.

(You're tickling me.)

You are very worried right now. A close relative, your mother? is having trouble, is sick? You're very worried about her. The nail ran down one of the lines. But is going to be fine.

Eva pulled her hand away.

I not finished, Olga said.

That's okay. You've told me enough.

Eva walks out in the night. Damp night, crisscrossing lights. The homeless are sleeping two to a doorway sausaged in sleeping bags or layers of blankets. Every doorway a bundle of clothes and newspapers, the luckiest ones have a mattress or an old couch squeezed between buildings. The sidewalks bustling with bodies stretched out or curled up fetus-like. It's like another city lying down at the other's feet, the rich locked in their citadels guarded by their watchmen at the door, soon they'll leave their buildings in helicopters to avoid making eye contact with the down-and-out at street level.

You turn your head away. You float a few feet above the ground where the stench of human misery doesn't reach you. You step over bodies, heads stretched back, sleeping, drunk or high, you are afraid to know. From up above, the city seems littered with corpses, casualties of a capitalist economy. Forcing the poor out of jobs and out of homes to finish them off with crack and AIDS. Eva wonders when someone will get the brilliant idea to gather them in Yankee Stadium with drugs and infected needles dropped from planes in order to speed their demise and clean up the streets of their slow decay.

She went to the Port Authority and scanned the bodies lying on benches or clustered along the walls. Would Frank and Mimi be waiting for a bus in the middle of the night? There were families with little kids Mimi's age and babies, children wandering alone running errands for the adults sprawled on the ground. It was an exodus, a crowd of refugees bound for nowhere. She got tired of searching the faces, it was absurd, there was not a chance in a million that they would be here. She slowly walked back along Forty-second Street, back to her place and returned Lola's calls. There was a valentine from Max, something about the shape of her breasts and her ass, nothing special.

His eyes shine like rocks under water

Felix is dead. Just two weeks ago he was sitting on his hospital bed shivering with fever, blood flowing into his arm from the clear blood bag hanging from the trolley, the body racked with chills, blood pumped up into the arm and just as fast leaking out the ass, and then all of a sudden

he is dead and there is the chant, bleating in her ears, a swell of voices marching to the beat of the gong in the overlit Buddhist temple way out in Queens, and his picture, blown up and propped on a lectern, a barely recognizable Christ-like face with dreadlocks. His body never got a chance to really shrink, thin out, fade away in the long deadly disease, it just imploded from inside, and here it is, burned to ashes. What do the ashes look like? Mimi once asked, they were talking about cremation with Albertine. Can you see them? How do they know it's this person's ashes, not somebody else's ashes? What color are they?

The fever had been terrible, 105, 106, 107, shooting up and down, they had to alternate the cooling and the warming blanket, it was getting confusing, interpreting the chills, the fever, riding the degrees, getting the temperature down to 99, a little breathing space, a little peace, which is the moment a nurse usually chose to appear with a wheelchair to take him down for a CAT scan, to some obscure test of the bone marrow, plunge a tube down his nose, down the whole complex, tight digestive system all the way to his rectum, imagine the pain, the unbelievable discomfort, the violation of the body forced to open its secret passages to probes roaming its insides, its bowels, all in the name of medical help, of course, trying to spot the actual source of the bleeding, where did it come from, all the consciousness of that pain now gone with him, gone with his essence that lingers with them yet like a fading scent, and then just the memory of it.

And all this time she sees his body, tight, strong muscles well defined by the workouts but not bulging, good round thighs, short torso, long legs. Smooth, brown skin, the dazzling smile under the straight mustache. The long tapered fingers on the ivory keys. That body . . . is just not here anymore. Took a temporary leave of absence from the material world, but not from her memory.

It took a little while for Felix's father to fill the glass, he was extremely careful, didn't want to spill a drop. He went at it with the bottle neck pressed hard against the brim of the glass, knocking against it in his effort, a tiny click-click of glass and his hand trembling. He was concentrating so hard tears swelled in his eyes. Eyes so dark, charcoal with that glow, the pupils filled the eyes with that shiny black like polished rocks at the bottom of a creek, that's what his eyes looked like. He had drunk so much his eyes were bulging and brimming with tears, he was ready to spill out his heart. But his son had just died and he still didn't get it, still didn't quite. . . . So he'd been cooking the whole afternoon. His son is dead and he is taking his place, as it were. His son used to cook. He used to be a really good cook, he would throw a party for thirty people and roast the chicken the whole afternoon, get the black beans, the pinto beans going the day before, throw in the spices, boy, these spices he put in there, remember, he had the whole alchemy of cooking down, he was the master of the jalapeño pepper, the grandmaster, and his potent daiquiris and bloody marys, shit, but he made some mean dip with horseradish and a kick like a son-of-a-bitch, yeah, I know, a dip, right, what's a dip, but his dips were powerful, man, they were manly, they lit God's fire under your ass. So now the old man's cooking. He's cooking the shit out of himself, capon stuffing and pumpkin puree up to his elbows, but that was much earlier, before he got drunk and his eyes started to shine like rocks under water. Felix's eyes, they shone like that too. He had his old man's eyes. Almond-shaped polished stones, especially when he'd smoked pot or when he had downed a few of his vodka-orange, then his eyes were brimming, they became live animals. Well, anyway, all that is gone now, the smile, the fucking great smile, the irony on the lips undercutting the eyes brimming with feelings, all that trapped into a little rectangular black box seemingly made of cardboard with a white label neatly typed taped to it, with his name spelled correctly and a cremation number and that extraordinary black-and-white photo of him at twenty with ringlets all around his head and a full black beard and these high flat cheekbones that claimed his Indian blood over his Latino inheritance, both, the box and the print, now displayed on the fireplace mantel, surrounded by tall votive candles replaced as they went down. The photo, propped against the wall and framed by the candles, takes on an iconic power. Look at the eyes, not so much brimming there but a steady gaze, peaceful, the direct gaze, unsmiling and the steady confidence of the mouth and the jaw, the beard, the ringlets, yes, plus the chanting and the smell of incense and the flickering and the dim glow, this is an icon. He has died at thirty-three, he has been nailed to the cross of AIDS. With the chanting swelling, his peaceful gaze bathed in the glow of the candles, his face has become that of a hero. He has been sacrificed in the war, to the God of Destruction. Capital letters rising in front of every word.

The chanting, rising and falling, the smoke of incense clouding the light, the regular rubbing of the string of beads between the palms. Here, somewhere whispers to her, handing her a string of white beads, it was his. She glances left and right to see if anybody is paying attention to her and pretends to rub once in a while. But the chant doesn't seem to want to come out of her throat. She mouths the words at times but mainly keeps her hands folded over each other and stares at the photo. From a certain distance his face has the smile of an angel.

Meanwhile the father is cooking downstairs in the narrow kitchen. He bastes the capon with thick juices. He has a pot of rice mixed with diced vegetables, carrots and peas, and a pot of beans going on the stove and a stack of six pumpkin pies ready to go in the oven, once the bird has been removed. He's got a row of dips and bags of blue corn chips lined up on the table. But his dips don't have the same kick as those of his son and his guacamole is smooth and sweet as butter instead of chunky and hearty and cut with bits of tomatoes as his son used to serve.

So he's talking with people drifting into the kitchen because they're uncomfortable with the chanting business. He is talking and flourishing the wooden spoon, while a tape of Felix at the piano plays in the background. The pain flows out in his words.

The blood. He bled to death. He emptied himself out worse than when Eva lost the fetus. The flow of life ran through him and into the ground. Poisoned blood. Panic blood. The sterile cold hospital ground. It didn't go any further than that. It was wiped up with a mop, handled by an orderly with protective gloves. The mop was then thrown out. It joined a heap of garbage sprinkled with dirty syringes and rags stained with pus.

He looked like himself till the end. Of course the face had become strained, its dark glow turned to a dull gray, his whole body had taken an ashen color, down to the soles of his feet. But his body that was shaking so bad, his body was still beautiful. He died beautiful, fell to the ground, in his blood and shit.

Letter from France

L***etter from Eva's mother: When you start looking at the shit without flinching, you've gone a step further, you've passed a stage. She doesn't control her body functions anymore, and I clean her. With my own hands. I carry her. Old people's bodies are stiff and soft at the same time. Light, but***

resisting. You pick them up from their bed, you bend forward. You can really kill your back. It's a technique. You have to learn how to do it. The nurse taught me. I'm doing it every day, now. When I got here, I couldn't bring myself to clean her. Now I want to do it. I wouldn't say I enjoy it, but I get a certain pleasure from it, that of mastering a difficult job. I am amazed at the fact that I don't feel any repulsion anymore. The first time I thought I was going to throw up. We are taught repulsion to body matters as soon as we are born. One time when you were little I found you eating your poo-poo from the potty. You had it all over your face, and your hands and arms were covered with it. We punished you and told you never to do that again. I was very proud that you were toilet-trained at thirteen months old. We taught you disgust of your shit, like I was taught. And now I am learning how to accept it. Accept decrepitude. Decay has set in. Her teeth have almost all fallen out. She's losing her hair. She has no more control of her body functions. The nurse pinches her nose when she carries the soiled sheets to the laundry room. They make these diapers for old people nowadays so she never smells bad. She smells of that powder they put on babies' fannies. Like talcum powder. The whole process of aging is like returning to baby stage. You come full circle. That's something I am learning.

Going west

Where are we going? Mimi asks.

None of your business.

From the back of the car she throws her fists at Frank's shoulders. He cranes his neck and jerks his right forearm back to stop the blows.

Now you sit down and buckle your seat belt and behave.

She sits up on her haunches and screws her tight fists on her hips.

Oh, no I won't, not until you tell me where we're going.

We're going out in the country.

Well, I can see that. But where are we going, mister?

What did you call me, buster?

I said, where are we going, *mister?*

Frank veers the car to the side of the road, gets out, slams his door shut, opens the back door and tries to buckle Mimi into the seat belt.

Don't want to have an accident on top of everything else.

Mimi worms her way out of his hands.

I'm hungry, she whines.

We're going to stop at a restaurant and eat and go to the bathroom.

Frank turns on the ignition.

I want salmon, Mimi says.

What?

I want to eat bagel and cream cheese and salmon.

We're having dinner. You eat soup or meat at dinner, not bagels.

I want a bagel with salmon. I am not going to eat anything else.

It's pitch-black, just past the Pennsylvania-Ohio border, one-eighth of the road to California. To Mimi it's a long snake, a dark road with taillights in her eyes and no end in sight. By the time Frank finds an adequate place to stop, she's fast asleep under an old blanket, far from any bagel desire. He leaves her lying on the backseat to grab a hamburger and a coffee. The road is long. He drives all night. He drives like a man who doesn't look over his shoulder or even to the side. He looks straight ahead of him, his eyes on the imaginary line of the Pacific Ocean, at times flipping a cassette over in the tape deck. He listens to rock 'n' roll but he keeps the sound down not to disturb Mimi, even though she doesn't give signs of life. He barely hears her even breathing. Then he switches to the radio.

He starts picking up country and western stations. He listens to pop psychology shows in which lonely souls bare their heart to the shrink on duty between two Willie Nelson songs. Turnpikes branch out into interstates, exit into highways, narrow down into country roads. Exit ramps circle back into freeways. Frank chain-smokes and keeps the window half open to let some fresh air in, but not so open that Mimi would feel the cold on her head. He stops to stretch his legs, rotate his shoulder blades, massage his forearms. He sits on the embankment smoking a cigarette, Mimi doesn't even stir. The air is getting raw. He zips up his jacket, gets back into the car to put his fur hat on, sits some more outside. Before setting back on the road he watches her sleep. Sensing a presence over her, maybe, she moans and sighs as she changes position. But she doesn't wake up until dawn breaks, pink in a pure sky, at their back. So now is the time for your bagel and cream cheese, he tells her. You missed it last night. And lox, she says. I want cream cheese and lox. He lets her climb up in front on the condition that she buckles the seat belt and she sits straight up to see as much as she can from her low vantage point.

Do you know why Cinderella wasn't a good ballplayer?

I didn't even know she was a ballplayer. What did she play, football?

Frank!

Okay, so why wasn't Cinderella a good ballplayer?

Because she had a pumpkin for a coach.

He sighs. He asks her, how would you like to go to California?

You didn't even laugh at my joke.

So, what about California?

Is that where you're taking me?

I didn't say that. I asked you what you thought about it.

I don't think anything about it. I've never been there. She bursts into a horse-like laugh. I want cream cheese and lox first. Then you have to let me call my mom.

Just then he catches a glimpse of a Howard Johnson. He gets off the road and parks the car.

Vamos for lox.

You got funny hair, Mimi says, when the bagel is finally brought by the waitress and placed in front of her.

What's funny about my hair?

She reaches over to him—they're sitting side by side on the banquette—and runs her fingers through his matted crew cut.

You're growing it?

Yes. No. I don't know.

She rubs her hand lightly on top of the hair. He takes her hand away, and pats her own head.

Your hair feels a little like mine.

She shakes her curls that are turning into dreadlocks now that Frank has given up brushing them. They just hang, at odd angles from her head.

No, it doesn't.

I'm going to grow my hair as long as yours and then you'll see. It'll look just the same.

No way, José.

You want to see something?

What kind of thing?

Frank pulls his wallet out of his pants pocket, and out of his wallet an old photo that he holds in the palm of his hand.

See this?

She doesn't need more than a glance. She already knows what he's driving at.

She crosses her arms on her chest.

I don't think you look like me at all.

No?

First of all, you're black.

Oh, yeah, and what about you?

She puts her hand next to his, making sure she doesn't touch it, but close enough.

Look, she says, look. You're dark, I'm light.

Yeah, so?

He pulls up his sleeve, lays his forearm flat against hers, pulls a hair with two pinched fingers.

Look, even our body hair looks the same.
How old were you in that photo?
Don't know. Six, seven? About your age.
Let me see. He drops the photo next to her plate.
You look so serious, she says. Did you have any brothers and sisters?
Three. I still have them. Two brothers, one sister.
Where do they live?
One's in New York, one in Detroit, one in South America.
What do they do?
One's a musician, one works in a car factory, my sister married a Brazilian, she used to be an actress, she might be a singer now, I haven't heard from her in a long time. She didn't keep contact. You're not going to finish your bagel? After you bugged me about it all night?
She studies the photo for a minute, hands it back to Frank.
I'm not hungry anymore. You can have it.
She pushes the plate toward him.
I look like my mom, she says. Everybody says I look like her.

After ten more hours of driving through the flat plains, Frank thought his arms were going to fall off his shoulders, there was an exit ramp coming right up, he made a sharp right, veering on his hubcaps. There was a sound of something collapsing coming from the backseat, like dominoes. Hey, watch out! Mimi screamed from the back. Look what you made me do! Watch out what you're doing. All my crayons are on the floor. What am I going to do now? He mumbled an apology. He drove straight out into town, a glittering strip of motels and Pizza Huts and International Houses of Pancakes and Chrysler dealerships on a background of green dusk, trying to blank out her screams and the kicks she rhythmically planted on the back of his seat, he was driving like a madman, hitting the gas pedal and the brakes alternately, looking for a place to stop. He found it on the right-hand side, a little way off the road, there was an elongated sign underlined in pink and mauve neon saying "The Blue Lagoon" in fancy blue script. He parked in front of the office, leaving Mimi kicking and screaming in the car, got a key and parked the car in front of a room at the back. He shook the keys under Mimi's nose, who stopped dead in her tracks, rushed out of the car and inspected the motel room while Frank brought their bags in. There were two twin beds and a TV and a phone without a dial. Mimi picked up the receiver to check it out. There was no dial tone. She turned the TV on instead and settled cross-legged in front of "Wheel of Fortune." There was a Bob's Big Boy on the same side of the road and Frank took Mimi there for a steak dinner, no gravy, mashed potatoes, no string beans and a glass of cherry Coke. That last touch brightened Mimi up and she stayed quietly nailed to her bench until he sipped the last of his coffee. He felt a dull pain around his collarbone from tension and he decided to skip trying to look for a newspaper and go straight to bed. They got undressed and lay down on their respective beds. Mimi took a book from her bag and read. Frank Jackson turned off his light and went straight to sleep. In about five minutes she heard regular snoring sounds coming out of his open mouth. She thought it was pretty yukky and turned her back to him. She read a few more pages and got up to go to the bathroom. She flushed the toilet, came back into the room. He hadn't moved. She was wearing pajamas made of a pair of long johns and a T-shirt. She put on her sweatshirt on top and her sneakers without tying the laces. Then she tiptoed to the chair where his clothes were lying in a messy heap, a jean leg hanging on the carpet. She picked it up carefully and felt around for a pocket. Frank made a sound as if he was choking to death, moaned and turned on his side. Mimi stayed paralyzed stupidly holding the jeans in her hands. His breathing calmed down. She found a front pocket and stuck her fingers in it. It was what she was looking for, the pocket with the loose change. She went through it with light fingers, pulled out a handful of coins in total silence, then tiptoed back to her lamp to count the money. There were six quarters, five nickels, two dimes, seven pennies. She didn't know what she would need. She kept everything in her hand, just in case. She ran to the front door, confident that Frank wouldn't stir. It was easy to unlock the door, all it was was a knob to turn to the right, which she managed to do at the first try.

It was gut-freezing cold but no way was she going back to the room, risk waking up Frank with a crack of the door or the floor. She clamped her arms against her chest and ran alongside the rows of motel room doors, toward a light at the end of the building, a round lamp, which she thought might be over the office door. But it turned out to be the ladies' room. She pulled herself together, passed the corner, and ran some more. There was another row of motel rooms, all dark, except one that had a line of light around the door and the window. She could see the edge of an alley of gravel and the corner of a lawn, or a field. Beyond that, everything was pitch-black. There was no car, no sign of life. She heard some steps on the gravel and panicked, started to run in the direction she was coming from. She passed by the ladies' room and locked herself in. She realized she was shivering. She used the toilet to pass the time, but didn't dare flush it. When she was sure she couldn't hear the steps anymore, she silently got out. She found the office on the other side of the compound, had to cross a parking lot with neat rows of cars softly gleaming in the night. The office door said OFFICE in red neon letters. The door was locked but there was a pay phone right outside. She made a beeline for it and collapsed against the cold metal. From where she stood the parking lot was a sea of dark roofs and dark shadows, every one of them might have served as a hidey-hole for a witch or a goblin. The pay phone was just hanging against the wall. There was no door to close behind her. She pressed herself sideways against it, to see the enemy coming, and dropped a quarter in the slot. She heard the taped message telling her how much money to put in, but she didn't remember how much quarters and dimes and pennies were worth, even though Albertine had once spent a whole afternoon with her and a pile of shiny coins to help her figure them out. She tried to feed the machine a couple of times, but kept getting the same message, and finally pushed every one of her coins into the slots. The phone rang three times followed by a click and Mimi's heart was dancing the mambo with excitement, her knees were going weak. It was Eva's canned voice. Still, it was better than nothing. Mimi left a breathless message, realizing midstream that she had no idea where she was. We went through Pennsylvania and Ohio, she finally managed to remember. Maybe we're still in Ohio. I heard Frank say something about California. Maybe we are in California. It's very cold, I think it's going to snow. I have to go, now, Mummy. I love you.

Frank hadn't moved. He was breathing in a one-two tempo, a little more noisily than when she had left. He was lying flat on his back, his mouth slightly opened. The outside light shone right through the blind, parallel rays of light across the beds and the carpet. She moved like a ghost and got into bed. She pretended to sleep in case he would wake up and couldn't. She thought the night was the longest she ever had to live. But he had to shake her up in the morning and she groaned, not understanding where she was. He wanted to have an early start. They still had a long way to go. How long? Mimi asked. Where are we going? I already told you, California. She wanted to know where they were now. Ohio, he said. Yes, but what city? He said, what does it matter, what city? It's just some hellhole motel in nowheresville. She insisted that the city must have a name. He said he would check it out on the map when they had their breakfast.

Later that morning she demanded that they stop at a circus she saw setting up on the outskirts of a town. It was called the Fab Four Flying Trapezists, at least it said so on a banner, in golden letters on red plastic flapping in the wind. In lieu of trapeze artists, though, there were a dozen elephants grazing on a few clumps of sodden grass in the middle of a defrosting field. A long brown canopy jutted to one side of the circus tent, protecting the animals from the weather. Some of the elephants had seats fastened to their backs with golden flaps hanging down their sides and little kids were lining up to have an elephant ride. The tour was going up and down the canopy at a nerve-killing (at least to Frank) slow pace. They saw all that at a red light which was conveniently located at the entrance to the circus. Mimi immediately set to work jumping up and down and kicking the dashboard with her heels. When Frank started the car as the light turned green she threatened to throw herself out the door, she was already pulling the handle. He slammed on the brakes and made a sharp turn into the field where the circus was setting up. For a buck a kid could get on top of the animal and travel the length of the canopy four times. They waited in line for a half hour and Mimi almost flipped out when she was finally hoisted on the elephant's back. She screamed it was too high, that she was sure she was going to fall off. Frank had to walk alongside the beast holding her hand until she cried uncle and begged the attendant to help her get down before her tour was over. After that she kept quiet and basically let Frank have his way the rest of the day.

That night, Frank, for some reason, didn't feel sleepy, or maybe it was the football game, he settled down on his bed with two pillows wedged behind his back and the TV on, the Browns vs. the Bengals. Mimi tried hard to concentrate on it, then she read to herself two books that Frank had bought her at a gas station variety store, but still he wasn't giving any sign of weakening and she gave up first, her light on, the book in her hands. When she woke up, Frank was still asleep but it was already daylight and she knew it was too risky to take a chance. At breakfast she asked Frank to look at the map and obligingly he opened up the road atlas in front of them after the table was cleared off and pointed to the next city they were heading to. We might even be there tonight, he said, pointing to a town the name of which Mimi couldn't read. What state is that in, Mimi wanted to know, and how far from New York are we, and when are we gonna get there? Where? Frank asked. Wherever we're going, where you're taking me, Mimi answered, California, exasperated that he was playing dumb like grown-ups do when they don't want to answer a question.

Why are you doing that to me? Mimi asked.

What?

You know, taking me away like that.

I wanted to spend time with you.

You didn't have to do that. You could have taken me out to the movies again, or we could've gone to the park. What's so important that you have to drive me so far? You want to hide me somewhere?

Frank motioned to the waiter. Scribbling in the air with his thumb and forefinger, asking for a check.

Mimi's eyes turned vague. Her hand mimicked Frank's hand, a stylized replica of his movement. Then she got up and followed him to the cash register.

I got to go to the bathroom, she said, when the cashier handed him the money. He nodded and told her he was going to get gas in the meantime, he showed her the pumps through the glass doors. She said she'd find her way no problem. The ladies' room was down a short hallway. At the end of it was an alcove with a public phone. Mimi had a new pocketful of coins she had taken from Frank's dungarees. She unloaded them in the slot and dialed Eva's number. A bunch of coins fell noisily in the return hole when the machine picked up. Mimi told the machine where she was. Then she called Albertine.

Albertine was basting an organza skirt for an Easter wedding. She cursed under her breath, a *merde* bitten through her lips. She let the phone ring at least three or four times, she didn't want to lose her rhythm with the needle, She always caught five or six stitches at the same time with the tip of the needle and pulled it all together. It went faster and the basting was more even. Then she put down her work and stretched her hand to the phone. She couldn't believe it was Mimi. All she could say was Mimi, repeating, where are you, Mimi, where are you, Mimi where are you? Mimi tried not to break down. She had about two minutes until Frank might wonder what she was doing. I am near the bathroom, she said, it's a restaurant, near the gas station. But where, Albertine asked, WHERE, FOR GOD'S SAKE? WHAT CITY, WHERE ARE YOU GOING? Mimi said they were going to California and Albertine told her to go and talk to someone in the restaurant, like the manager and ask for help, tell them to call the police.

Just then Mimi saw Frank walking through the glass doors, looking for her.

I got to go now, Albertine, she said. 'Bye.

They stopped at the Cozee Cove Motel, then the next night at the Sunset Motel. But there was no cove or sunset, only strips of highway in the night illuminated by neon signs when they got off the freeway. Mimi wondered why it took so long to get to California. You don't even speak to me, she said. You don't even like me. Why are you doing that?

Frank's hand went to touch Mimi's curls. Tentatively. He crushed some hair in the flat of his palm. She pulled her head back. You're my daughter, he said. I like you.

She moved her shoulders as if to shake him off of her and scooted all the way to the door. She crouched in the corner, playing the fearful animal, and flashed him a murderous look.

No, I'm not.

You're not?

I have no father. I am a bastard.

That's what Eva tells you, right? Man, I can't believe what people tell kids. Girl, I'm your daddy, and that's a fact. I don't care what your mother says about me. She can't deny that.

Don't say daddy. I don't want you to say daddy. You're not my daddy, I don't care what you say. And even if you are, I don't want you.

Frank's hands were on the wheel again, tight at the knuckles.

He pushed the blinker and exited on a ramp leading to a rest area. He asked Mimi if she was interested in some ice cream or hot chocolate.

You only say that because you want me to like you.

Frank smiled, caught red-handed in his corruption attempt.

That, and because I want to stop for coffee. The offer stands, I don't care what you think.

They got out of the car and sat down at the restaurant counter.

So? Frank asked when the waitress came to take their orders. Make up your mind.

Chocolate ice cream in a cup, Mimi said to the waitress.

She turned to Frank: and don't think it's going to make me be nice to you.

I have no illusion, Frank said.

On Mimi's trail

At six o'clock one morning, Eva got a phone call from Mimi, whispering that she was in a house in Venice, near the ocean. She said the house had a garden, that it belonged to a woman who had a dog. She abruptly hung up, because someone was walking in the hallway. Eva flew straight to

Los Angeles. She rented a car at the airport and drove down Lincoln Boulevard to Venice Boulevard to Ocean Avenue and parked on a side street off the boardwalk. She got to the beach just as the sun was going down. She dug her heels in the sand and stopped at the edge of the ocean, eyes tearing from fatigue and the red light. She took off her leather jacket and sat on it, rubbing grains of sand off her nylon hose. She was dressed in New York black, coming out of the winter night. Looking, in the southern California sunset, as if she came from a funeral. She stopped shielding her eyes. The sun was being sucked in by the ocean. The air was so balmy she stretched her whole body and let the warm breeze blow over her face and her legs.

Eva found a room in a motel that had a couple of banana trees swaying in the dirt courtyard and fell asleep listening to the dogs bark at the cars coming up the driveway.

The next day, she took a position at a café on the boardwalk, with a pile of books and magazines and her notebook. She put on a big straw hat and a pair of sunglasses and waited.

Kids flashed by on roller skates, aging hippies hung out in clusters. Some had clearly fallen over the edge, homelessness had thrown its tentacles all the way to the Pacific Ocean. But at least the weather was soft to them. The nights were gentle, nature hospitable. Eva thought if she was a bum she would try to make her way to the West Coast rather than freeze in the northeastern urban centers. But maybe it's not possible to live as a hobo anymore. Hop on a train and make your way across the continent. You need hope to do that, some vision, enough sense of freedom to be able to imagine another life. Eva wrote in the little notebook in front of her. In it she had been recording her daily moods since Mimi had disappeared. It was like a weather map, with the precipitations, the clouds, the storms, the sun. Today was sunny. The pain had turned into hope. Wild hope to see Mimi jumping rope along the boardwalk, playing tag with a bunch of kids, strolling hand in hand with Frank Jackson.

Mimi called Albertine, told her she had read the street name on a signpost and the house number was outside the front door. Eva slowly drove down the sleepy block, in a down-and-out section of Venice, right past the railroad tracks. It was early in the morning. Two wrought-iron numbers were hanging from two nails in front of a yellow stucco house with a little wooden porch. The porch was run down with the wood showing gray and chipped under the peeling paint. An old rusty bicycle was leaning against the wall under the right front window, and some plastic crates were piled up on the other side. There was a white magnolia in bloom along the fence. She parked the car across the street, turned the radio on low and waited. She couldn't believe Frank had been so careless as to let Mimi come near a phone. Mimi was a master of the quickie call, sneaking out of her classroom to steal a thirty-second phone message to Albertine telling her she wanted to come home, then abruptly hanging up and running back to her classroom before the teacher even realized she had been missing.

At five past eight, a woman opened the front door, let a mangy white-and-black dog leap out and tumble down the front steps, and stood for a moment in the cool morning air. She was an ex-blonde whose hair was turning salt, wearing a pair of dungarees and an oversize Hawaiian shirt. She watched the dog dig a hole by the magnolia tree, sniff around, and lift its hind leg beside the trunk. She whistled to call him back. Biding his time, the dog cavorted for half a minute, then pushed past her inside the house. The woman walked in and closed the door behind her. Eva lit a cigarette, fiddled with the radio, looking for another station.

After a long time, the front door opened and Frank came out.

Eva was holding a pocketbook shaped like a small hatbox on her lap and when she saw Frank, she started fingering the clasp. It went click, click, click all the time Frank walked down the steps of the porch, gave a big yawn, adjusted his sunglasses and headed for the center of town.

Eva turned the radio off. The house settled into silence.

Maybe they were keeping Mimi locked in, maybe she wasn't even allowed to play in the little dusty front yard.

When Frank came back about forty minutes later carrying a paper bag of groceries and the *L.A. Times* tucked under his elbow, the yellow stucco house hadn't given a peep. Eva had rolled down the window and strained her ear to try to catch the sound of Mimi's bubbly voice, but there was only silence.

Shit, Eva said.

Frank knocked on the front door, but there was no telling if Mimi was waiting for him behind that door.

It started to get warmer. Eva rolled down both front windows of the car and watched a couple of teenage boys careen down the street on skateboards. A young black man came out with a pail and started washing his car next door to the yellow stucco house.

Suddenly, the door swung open and Mimi burst out carrying a jump rope. She looked healthy, if unkempt. She was wearing a pair of jeans, and her hair was a mess of dreadlocks. She skipped the length of the porch with the jump rope.

Eva got out of the car.

MIMI!

Frank came out right behind Mimi.

Eva had already run across the street. Mimi saw her, dropped her rope and stumbled down the stairs.

Mummy, Mummy, she said. Oh, Mummy!

Eva felt her tight little body, these frail shoulders under her hands, this narrow back that she always feared she might break by accident, squeezing her too hard. But there was so much emotional power packed between these arms that she felt herself getting squeezed out of breath. She squatted and picked up Mimi on her hip, stood up and twirled her around, chanting Mimi, Mimi, Mimi, Mimi, while Mimi giggled and chanted in unison, Mummy, Mummy, Mummy, Mummy!

Frank froze at the door, the woman with the salt-colored hair appeared behind him and the dog rushed out between her legs, running to his favorite hole near the magnolia tree.

Mummy, Mummy, you found me, Mimi said, showering Eva's cheeks with tiny kisses. You found me, you found me!

Frank still wasn't moving.

Eva put Mimi down, holding her firmly by the hand, and turned to face Frank.

What the fuck did you think you were doing, Frank Jackson? Are you out of your fucking mind? How dare you? I've been in agony for days. I thought I would never see Mimi again.

How did you get here? he just said.

I have my spies. Frank, just what the hell did you think you were doing?

Frank looked at her in mock appraisal.

You're beautiful when you get angry.

Cut it out.

I wanted to spend time with Mimi. I didn't force her if that's what you think.

Terrific! Want a medal?

Mom, don't yell at him.

Don't yell at him! Why, he takes you across the country without saying a word, and I'm supposed to keep my mouth shut?

Mom, don't yell at me. I didn't do anything wrong!

Eva put her arms around Mimi's little chest.

Of course you didn't. Tell me something, Frank, if Mimi was so willing to go with you, how come she sneaked out to call me or Albertine every time she got a chance?

So, that's how you made it here. You little traitor!

Mimi pulled out of Eva's embrace and placed one angry foot on the front steps. She stomped it irritably.

I'm not a trait . . . trai-tor, whatever it means.

Frank, there's no justification for what you did. It's totally irresponsible. It's cruel, it's . . . it's insane.

Frank shrugged and dug his fists into his pants pockets.

Mimi burst into tears and sat on the steps.

All right. All right! So I fucked up. So it wasn't the thing to do. But I tell you one thing, I gave her something she'll never forget. And it wouldn't have happened if you hadn't been so uptight about my seeing her. What's bothering you about me? Huh?

Eva stares at him. You really want to know?

Mimi puts her hands on her ears, squeezing hard any sound that would be threatening to pass that barrier, rocking back and forth on her hips.

Stop it, she screams, stop it, don't fight!

Frank flashes one of his big, provocative smiles.

So I don't play by your rules. Sorry. But guess what, without me you wouldn't have a child. Yeah, you'd have her believe she was an immaculate conception. You believe in that Catholic shit, right? You wish you could have made a child without a man, right?

Back off, Frank. Don't put words in my mouth. Honey, you cut yourself off from the deal. To you, nothing happened. What happened anyway? A little sperm swam the wrong way by accident. What's that? You told me, you said you wished it hadn't happened, remember?

STOP IT, PLEASE! screams Mimi, getting up, stomping the steps with both her feet. STOP IT!

The ex-blonde calls Mimi from the door.

Want to come and play inside?

Mimi doesn't answer. She grabs Eva around her waist.

STOP FIGHTING! she pleads.

I was fucked up, Frank says. I had problems then.

Eva strokes Mimi's hair.

Nothing's changed. You're still fucked up. Look what you've done!

Mimi slips away from Eva and goes to the magnolia tree, picks one of the wide overripe white flowers and buries her face into it. The dog, meanwhile, is digging up a storm and makes a huge turd while nobody is paying attention.

All right. All right. I made a mistake. All right?

I don't care what you have to say.

Come on, doggy-dog, Mimi says, trying to grab him around the neck. The dog furiously swings its tail and slips out of her grasp.

You're pathetic, Frank. I wanted to kill you when you took Mimi away. But now, I feel sorry for you.

So do it. Here. Take my knife.

Eva grabs Frank by the shoulders, she shakes him violently. He grabs her wrists. They look at each other. She lets go of him.

You took my child away from me. You took Mimi! You kidnapped her. Frank, you're going to have the police on your ass, man. Do you realize what you've done? It's a criminal offense, punishable by fifteen to twenty-five years in the can. You scared the shit out of this child.

The ex-blonde walks back into the house, lets the front door close softly on its hinges.

I did not.

What?

Scare the shit . . . did I scare you, Mimi?

Mimi doesn't turn around. She's playing with the dog. Then she utters a small no.

Admit it, the person I scared the shit out of was you.

He pushes her away from him, she collapses on the old plastic crates. Frank leans against the outside wall of the house.

And, between the two of us, you deserved it.

She stands up and holds her pocketbook with both her hands, firmly, as if she was going to throw it in his face, then lowers it, lets it dangle from her hand.

Eva . . .

What?

Say we forget all this and we start again?

What? You are out of your mind! No way, man. No way.

Mimi cuts another magnolia flower, with a longer stem, and sticks it in her locks above one ear. She puts her hands on her hips and starts shaking her bottom.

Seeing Mimi dance, the dog stands on its hind legs and offers its front paws. Mimi takes them and tries a two-step that fails when the dog licks her mouth.

Hey, yuck! Go away, go away!

Mimi, are you ready, we're going now, Eva says.

Where are we going?

Back to New York.

Back to New York? But it's so far!

Yeah, it's far, thank God.

Not far enough, right, Eva, Frank can't help saying. Wanna kiss me good-bye, Mimi?

Eva walks down the steps and waits near the open gate.

Mimi runs up the steps and hugs him.

You like the magnolia in my hair?

Yeah, I do. You're very pretty, Mimi. He winks at her. Take after your old dad.

She lands him a light uppercut on the jaw.

I don't, mister. Don't look like you a-tall.

Will you come back and see me?

Where? Here?

No. I'll come back East too in a little while.

He glances at Eva, who's turned her back to him, who's ready to cross the street and hop into the car and fly straight back to New York City.

Come on, Mimi, she says. Let's go.

Will you take me to Coney Island again when you come back?

You better go, Mimi. Your mom's waiting for you.

Will you let him, Mom?

Maybe, Eva says, her back still turned to them.

Mimi gets in the car, buckles herself into the front seat and waves at Frank from the back window. He can see the white shape of the magnolia until they turn the corner.

A date

I *Ching, Book of Changes,* hexagram number five, *Hsu,* Waiting.

Six in the fourth place. "The fourth line, divided, shows its subject waiting (in the place of) blood. But he will get out of the cavern. [He has entered on the scene of danger and strife. He retreats

and escapes from the cavern, where he was engaged with his enemy.]"

Albertine had a roast ready for them in the oven, with mashed potatoes and steamed broccoli, Mimi's favorite vegetables, and chocolate ice cream for dessert. The table was cleared of all sewing equipment and Albertine had taken off her apron and was wearing her Sunday-best dress, black with a rhinestone pin above her chest. She kept nodding in wonderment and looking at Mimi, who couldn't keep still, and heaving deep sighs of relief. I felt so guilty, she said over and over to Eva, so guilty to let her go with him. Which didn't stop her from popping open a bottle of Beaujolais and they both went at it with gusto, Albertine with a little more gusto than Eva, while Mimi kept running to her room and bringing armfuls of toys to play with until Albertine snapped at her and told her to clean up if she wanted dessert. Mimi burst into tears and Eva said it was time to go home. She wanted Mimi to sleep at her place for her first night back.

The lobby is funereal, with Morris at the desk fingering the *Post* with a pained look in his eyes as if his lottery ticket had been one beat away from the winning number. The front page clamors TIMES SQUARE RAPIST ARRESTED over the shot of a bespectacled white man, his hair thinning in a tonsure, his left hand attempting to cover his face with the upturned lapel of his trench coat.

Eva walks across the lobby, Mimi in tow. They go straight to the desk. Eva leans over the desk, she says, do you mind, Morris?

Morris is startled. He looks into their tired faces, they have moon faces, white, bags under their eyes.

Oh, you found Miss Mimi, Miss Marquand, he says. I'm so glad!

But Eva is turning the newspaper around.

Isn't that something? he says. I'm glad they finally got him. I'd go home at night and feel nervous for women like you, all alone, in this neighborhood. How you doing, Miss Mimi?

Good.

Morris lifts Mimi up and sits her up on the desk.

Wait, Morris. It's Max. Take a good look at this guy. Doesn't he look familiar?

Gee, Miss Marquand, you don't say . . .

Are you thinking what I'm thinking, Morris?

Gee, I don't know. Let me see.

Who's this guy, Mom, Mimi asks, screwing up her face.

Morris! It is him. Look at this: the trench coat. The glasses. The thinning hair . . .

D'you think so, Miss Marquand? You know, you may be right. My God, to think . . .

Have you seen him lately?

No . . . oh, gee, as a matter of fact I didn't. Not for a few days. You might be right, Miss Marquand.

It's past the middle of the night, dead-of-night sliding into predawn, sulphurous light tainted with red filtering between the slats of the shades. Mimi's asleep next to Eva, flat on her back, head tilted back on the pillow, her mouth slightly opened on the gap of one missing tooth and one halfway grown. She breathes a little heavily through her mouth. She was in Eva's dream, too, but with all her teeth. Eva had just had a baby, it looked like Johnny. It was crawling around in diapers. She was wearing a dress with a wide skirt, flaring around her calves. There were all these stains on the dress. Large, rusty-colored stains of dried-up blood looking like brown flowers twirling with the skirt. Her period had caught her by surprise—my first period since the birth, a voice had announced triumphantly—and splashed all over the dress. Eva walked around a room full of guests with the bloody dress on, serving tea and cookies.

The image of the dream keeps her awake. Mimi groans in her sleep, wildly throws one arm behind her head, turns over. Eva sniffs in her neck. There's a smell of wild flesh hidden behind that of flowered soap. She has soaked her in the bathtub in the evening but has not been able to make a dent in the bushy forest of her hair.

Eva lies wide awake, watching the night turn into gray shadows, every object with its trail of shade getting imperceptibly more defined. Fear is like that too, the shade of death you carry around behind you. Eva wonders what life would be like if one went about it in the clear noon sunlight of total confidence. There was a long message from Max, left days earlier, on Lola's answering machine when she got back. She listened to it after Mimi went to sleep. His lurid descriptions of sex were like homecoming, like saluting the man with the helmet and the twenty shopping bags who was sleeping in the hotel doorway under a blanket of cardboard boxes.

Hi, *baby*, the message said. *Long time no hear. Been missing you, baby. My cock is big, you wouldn't believe it. I think it's grown a full inch since last time I looked. I'm touching it right now. I've just pulled it out of my pants. I got the biggest balls you've ever seen. Baby, I want to push it in your ass. How much you gonna gimme for that? I want to fish for your shit, flush it out of your ass, make room for my dick. You won't talk to me, baby. You're not returning my calls, so I'll talk to you. Or maybe I'll pay you a little visit sometime. And I won't even charge you. You'll get my calls free and my dick free. If you saw it you'd never want another man again. It's purple and straight and fat all the way through, not like those kinky ones that curl up like a banana or taper off to a pinhead. No, baby. And I can stay hard for hours. I walk down the streets with a big hard-on in my pants. I have to hide it with my raincoat, otherwise women wouldn't leave me alone. When I sit down I fold my raincoat up and spread it on my lap, but you know that, you've seen me, and I slip my hand underneath while you sing and I jerk off. My pants are stained all the time, you should see my cleaners' bill. 'Bye, baby. Talk to you soon. Keep it wet for me.*

At twelve-thirty a phone call announces Johnny in the lobby. He comes up to Eva's apartment and waits on the couch while Eva and Mimi get ready. To celebrate Mimi's return he's taking them to the restaurant. Eva is wearing a little twill suit with a skirt cut well above the knees and a pair of high-heeled pumps and she totters around, making the female sound of clapping heels each time she walks the short stretch of hardwood floor separating the bathroom from the bedroom and Mimi hates her for it because all she is wearing is a pair of flat patent-leather shoes that don't even begin to sound as grown-up and as loud as Eva's and she's sulking on the bed while Eva plays with her jars of makeup, dabs some silver gray on the crease of the eyelids, rubs some charcoal on her eyebrows, making them stand out, thick and dramatic against the pallor of her skin. I hate you, Mom, Mimi says in a flat tone, all emotion concentrated in the rhythmical pounding of the wooden frame of the bedspring with both her heels alternately. Bang, bung. Bang, bung. Bang, bung. Bang, bung. BANG. BUNG. BANG. BUNG.

STOP IT! hollers Eva, her voice, naturally low, sliding dangerously high up her vocal cords, threatening to break. STOP IT! You're driving me nuts.

In the living room, Johnny is waiting, his legs sprawled in front of him, taking a swig from the flask of bourbon he's pulled out of his pocket.

Can I put on some of your lipstick? Mimi asks, slowing down the pounding but keeping a low, steady, unnerving rumble as background to the conversation.

No. Not to go to the restaurant.

MUM! Sound of a body hitting the side of the bed simultaneously with the carpeted floor. A scream exploding followed by a cascade of sobs.

I fell off the bed. You pushed me!

Kicking resumes against the bed frame.

Okay. You can have some lip gloss. That one over here.

No, I want the lipstick. The red lipstick you have on. And it's final.

NO! The lip gloss or nothing.

All right. Gimme it.

Johnny lights a cigarette and walks to the window, surveying the traffic on Broadway from the thirty-seventh floor.

Eva looks at Mimi in the mirror, at her lush lips glossy like water, a smaller version of hers, except hers are bright red and they both make a pout and burst into laughter. Mimi jumps into Eva's arms, straddling her with her thighs hooked around her hips, her arms slung behind her neck. She wildly swings from side to side. Little Mommy, she says, little Mommy. I can't even kiss you 'cause of the lipstick. Eva's two hands are crossed under Mimi's tight buns, she bounces her up and down. They walk out of the bathroom.

Pretty soon I won't be able to carry you anymore, do you realize that?

Johnny wheels at the window, leans against the sill, watching them.

Ready, girls?

I want you to always carry me, Mimi says to Eva, even when you're ninety years old! I don't want to be grown-up. I want to always be a little baby.